"NO!" ANDREA SCREAMED. "IT CAN'T BE HAPPENING AGAIN. I WON'T LET IT!"

She collapsed onto the bed, weak with fear. There could only be one explanation—she had had a blackout.

Suddenly her mind reeled sickeningly. A scene flashed before her eyes: a graveyard at night, a young girl dressed like her twin brother, kneeling on his grave . . .

Frantic, Andrea got up and began to dress. Opening the drawer, she grabbed for a sweater. Her hand touched something metallic, cold. Moving the clothes, she saw the small handgun—a revolver, its dull black surface nicked and scratched.

Where had it come from? Why was it loaded? As Andrea gaped at it, horrified, she tried to tell herself that it had to be a toy . . .

BAD BLOOD

Barbara Petty

A DELL BOOK

Published by
Dell Publishing Co., Inc.
1 Dag Hammarskjold Plaza
New York, New York 10017

Dell ® TM 681510, Dell Publishing Co., Inc.

ISBN: 0-440-10438-6

Printed in the United States of America

First printing—August 1979

For my husband, Steve

BAD
BLOOD

PROLOGUE

Mapleton, Wisconsin—1968

Hold your breath and squeeze the trigger. Gently, gently. Not too fast. Don't jerk it. Andrea Donahue kept repeating to herself her brother's instructions while she concentrated and sighted down the barrel of the gun at the beer can nestling in the crabapple tree at the far end of the field.

She had goaded him into letting her practice with this particular gun, his favorite in their father's collection. It was an automatic, a Walther PPK, brought back from Germany by Art Donahue as a war souvenir, and, as Andy liked to point out to his friends, the same gun used by his hero, James Bond. At fourteen, Andy was already a deadly shot. But Andrea had never shown the slightest interest in guns before today.

Crack! The gun suddenly barked and Andrea's arms jumped in recoil. But the beer can remained where it was, placidly glinting in the August afternoon sunlight. Andrea's face fell as she squinted at it.

Andy was sitting on a large rock behind her and slightly to the left. He chuckled at her woebegone expression and shook his head, a crooked grin on his face. "Try it again, Andy," he said, calling her by the name he only used when they were alone together. "And this time don't jerk it."

Andrea fumed at the patronizing tone in his voice. "I didn't jerk it!" she protested sharply, whirling around. "And don't you laugh at me!" She started to shake her fist at him for emphasis.

Her twin's face went pale beneath his freckles and ruddy tan. "Andy! No!" he cried and made a sharp, lurching movement.

Andrea wondered why he looked so strange. The rest was a blur—something she would try to recapture forever in her memory but could never make sense of. She didn't remember the gun going off, never even heard the sound. No, it was more as though she felt it inside her—an explosion. Suddenly there was a hole in Andy's chest, but there must have been one in her own, too, to cause the searing pain she felt there.

When the world came back into focus, she could see her brother lying splayed across the rock, and she could hear choking sounds coming from his throat as he gasped for air. His arms and legs strained and quivered with every effort he made to breathe, while the splotch of red on his chest grew larger.

Andrea stared mindlessly at him. Then, feeling

as though her own insides were slipping away, she staggered toward him.

"Andy?"

There was no response, no movement—except for the blood bubbling out of his chest, staining his white T-shirt.

"Andy!" she wailed, her eyes pleading with him to get up, to stop this silly game. Ever so slowly she reached out her left hand to touch his shoulder, but hesitated, her fingers inches away from him. Her eyes dropped to the gun, still clutched in her other hand. With a convulsive motion, she flung it away from her. It thudded into a patch of weeds several yards away.

"I didn't mean it, Andy," she cried, bending over him and lowering her face to his. But a veil seemed to have descended over Andy's blue eyes. The gasping sounds had stopped. She pressed her mouth against his, hoping to feel some reaction, some breath. When none came, she frantically tried to remember the procedure for mouth-to-mouth recuscitation.

Again and again she brought her mouth to his, forcing her breath down his throat—until she could feel herself growing dizzy with the effort. She stopped briefly, then began again, panicked now. For the thought that Andy might be dead had begun to seep into her consciousness. She had to push it away.

So she kept on, gulping at the air, and then exhaling it into Andy's mouth. Each time she bent her head over his, strands of her long, reddish-gold hair fell over his face, across the glazed eyes, and mingled with his own hair, which matched hers so perfectly they blended into one.

Only when her lips grew numb and she could no longer feel Andy's did she stop. Rocking back on her heels, she picked up her brother's limp right arm and slowly brushed her tear-stained cheek along the length of his forearm. When she reached the wristbone, she kissed the brown oval of his birthmark, remembering how, as a child, she had once tried to paint a similar shape on the tip of her own wrist so that she would no longer be different from her brother. "Oh, Andy, I'm sorry," she sobbed. "I'll try to make it up to you."

Tenderly she placed his arm back on the rock. Then she stood up, wiping the tears from her eyes. "I'll find the gun, Andy," she said, her voice gasping, her mouth barely able to form the words. "I'll find it and you can use it on me. It's only fair. It's what I deserve."

Her eyes darting back and forth, she searched the tall grass for the glint of black metal, then, eyes still darting feverishly, she dropped to her knees and began to crawl through the weeds, stopping every few feet to push the green stalks apart, hands working wildly, pulling clumps of grass angrily out by their roots.

The sun beat down mercilessly, but Andrea barely felt the stifling heat as she continued her frenzied search for the gun. She was blinded by tears, and her vainly grasping fingers led her farther and farther away from the spot where her brother lay, the blood on his chest already drying into a thick brown crust.

She was nearly down to the crabapple trees when her father came rattling across the field in his pickup truck. Art Donahue was all set to scold his kids for taking the Walther without his permission and for going off without telling their mother where they'd be.

He spotted Andy lying motionless on the rock. So that's why that darn kid had sneaked off! Well, if he liked snoozing in the sun so much he could spend the whole day tomorrow out in it—working in the fields.

Art honked his horn a couple of times before he brought the truck to a stop, and he was surprised when Andy didn't jump up off the rock. He got down from the cab and slammed the door shut. "Andy!" he shouted. "Better get your ass in gear or there's going to be hell to pay!"

What was wrong with that kid? He still hadn't moved a muscle—did he think he was being cute playing possum like that? "Andy!" Art shouted once again and started walking toward the boy.

The ground was uneven and he had to watch his step. It wasn't until he was about twenty feet away that Art looked at his son again. He saw the brown, abstract design on the front of his T-shirt and wondered why all the flies were buzzing around it. Then he noticed the odd, stiff angles at which Andy's arms and legs lay. *Just like the corpses he had seen littering the battlefields of World War II . . .*

"No!" He started running, his arms flailing wildly to shoo the flies. "Get away from him!" He reached the rock and bent over his son. A few flies had been intimidated by his presence, but the rest kept crawling around the ugly, gaping hole in Andy's chest. "Leave him alone!" Art cried. But he knew it was no use.

Death had turned his boy's face pale and waxen. His blue eyes were open and fixed on the sky above. Art stared into them for a moment, and then with his rough, calloused fingertips touched the delicate skin of Andy's eyelids and pressed them shut. He ran his fingers down the still-warm cheeks and felt the peachfuzz that had only just begun growing there. *Not even a man yet.*

Art drew his hand away, his fingers tightening into a fist. It was *his* fault—he should have listened to Bernice and not let Andy handle his guns until he was older. Then this never would have happened. "But I didn't know," he gasped, pounding furiously on the rock. "I didn't know!" He brought his fist down again and again.

When he had scraped the side of his hand nearly raw, he realized what he was doing and forced himself to stop. He must try to calm down. Nothing he could do would bring his son back to life, so now he must think of the living—Bernice, Andrea— and how this would affect them. What about Andrea? Where was she? Bernice had told him that she'd seen the two of them whispering together and the next thing she knew both they and the gun were gone.

Art lifted his eyes and scanned the pasture. Something was moving through the tall grass down by the crabapple trees. "Andrea?" His voice sounded like a stranger's to him.

She didn't answer, but now he could clearly see that it was his daughter. She was down on her knees—my God, had she been shot, too? Art started running across the field, his vision going watery. Please, God, he prayed, let my little girl be all right. I couldn't bear to lose them both.

But she wasn't all right. He could see that the second he drew near to her. Although she turned her face toward him, her eyes looked past him with a vacant, glassy stare. The skin around them was still puffy and red from crying, and her cheeks were streaked with the paths of dried tears. Her hands and forearms were covered with dirt, and even as Art stood there watching her she continued to burrow in the earth—like a dog digging for a bone. "Didn't mean to do it," she kept muttering. "Got to find gun. Didn't mean to do it."

She shot Andy! A cry of rage rose in Art's throat, but he tamped it down. What good would it do to rail at his daughter? She was obviously beside herself with guilt and grief already.

"Andrea, stop that," Art said as gently as he could. She shook her head, but he grabbed her arms and pulled her to her feet. "Let's go home now." She tried to break away, but he put his arm around her. "Let Daddy take you home." Suddenly she let out a harsh sigh and leaned heavily against him.

He held her there for a moment, and then began to lead her across the pasture to the pickup. As they approached the rock Andrea looked over at her twin and then up at her father. "Can Andy come too, Daddy?" she asked in a small, quavery voice.

Art stared into her guileless blue eyes. "No, honey," he said. "Andy's d— Andy's got to stay here."

She started to protest, but Art opened the door to the pickup, pushed her up into the cab and climbed in after her. He took one last look at his son's body, and then turned on the ignition.

But even as the pickup bounced across the dirt road which led to the farmhouse, he knew that the worst was yet to come. *Bernice.* How was he going to tell her that Andy was dead? It would break her heart. And it would break *his* to tell her that Andrea had done it.

Andrea was quiet all during the ride, but when they pulled up in the farm yard a look of terror crossed her face. "No," she said when Art tried to help her out of the truck. He started to plead with her, but then Bernice appeared at the back door. "Well? Where were they?" she called out.

Art glanced at Andrea and then walked over to his wife, avoiding her eyes. "Let's go inside, Bernice," he said. "I've got something to tell you." He put a hand across her shoulders and tenderly propelled her toward the door.

Bernice opened her mouth to speak, then closed it, frowning. She let Art open the screen door for her and guide her into the kitchen. But when they were inside she whirled around, her eyes full of questions. "Something's happened to the kids," she said shrilly, her face suddenly haggard with fear. "I knew it. I could hear it in your voice."

Art collapsed onto a chair. He drew in his breath. The kitchen smelled of potatoes—a pot of them were simmering on the stove. "Sit down," he said. But Bernice remained standing, one hand curled tightly around the edge of the sink.

Art looked up at her and wished that it was he who was lying dead on that rock out in the meadow. He shifted his eyes away from hers. "There's been an accident," he said softly. "Andy's dead."

"What! What are you saying?" Bernice's voice said that she didn't believe it.

"I—" Art gritted his teeth. "God, Bernice. Don't make this any harder for me than it is already. He's dead. Andy's dead. I found him myself—out on that big rock in the north pasture."

Without saying a word or making a sound, Bernice pushed herself away from the sink, pulled out a chair from the table, and dropped onto it. Art followed her movements with his eyes, feeling more helpless than he had ever felt in his life.

Bernice's eyes remained dry but her mouth twisted with agony as she spoke. "How did it happen?"

"I don't know for sure," Art said, getting up from his chair. He went over to the window and looked out. Andrea was slumped over the pickup's steering wheel. He hoped she would be all right—just until he could explain things to Bernice.

He turned away from the window and went to stand behind his wife. "I guess they were playing around with my Walther," he said weakly. "It must have gone off."

Bernice spun around in her chair. "No!" she cried. "Not Andy! He knew better than to play with loaded guns. He wouldn't do that!"

Art backed away from her fury. "No," he sighed. "It was Andrea."

"Andrea!" Bernice jumped to her feet. "Where is she? I want her to tell me—"

"No," Art said quickly, moving between Bernice and the door. "She's not in any shape to talk about it. She's—well, she's not herself. I think we'd better let Ken Anderson take a look at her."

"For what she's done she doesn't need a doctor. She needs a priest!" Bernice said harshly.

Art winced. "Don't talk like that," he said.

Bernice's eyes narrowed. "I should have known you'd defend her. You've spoiled and pampered her all her life—you and Andy both—you always let her have her own way. And now she's killed him, and you expect me to feel sorry for her!"

"But it was an accident!" Art burst out. "You sound like she meant to do it!"

"I—I don't know what to think," Bernice responded dully. "I don't want to talk about her anymore. Bring her in the house, call Ken, call the sheriff—do what you have to do. I just don't want to see her." She turned and walked out of the kitchen.

Art stood there, listening to Bernice's heavy footsteps on the stairs. When he heard the door to their bedroom close he drew himself up and went out to the truck to bring Andrea inside.

Andy's funeral was several days later. Nearly all

of Mapleton turned out for it, crowding into the church. The day was sweltering and the service was mercifully brief, with two of Andy's friends and one of his teachers delivering terse, manful eulogies.

Art and Bernice sat in the first pew, their heads held high and their hands clinging to each other. Andrea sat on the other side of her father, slouched against the back of the pew. Her eyes never once left the bier where her brother's body lay.

At the end of the service the townspeople gathered in front of the church, waiting to make the short ride to the cemetery for the interment. "I was surprised to see Andrea here today," one woman said to another standing next to her. "I heard she was in a real bad way. She must be getting better."

"No, she's not," the second woman said. "But Ken Anderson told me she insisted on coming. He's got her on sedatives."

"Do you know if she's told them how it happened yet?" the first woman asked.

"Well, I don't know for sure," the other woman responded, lowering her voice conspiratorially, "but *I* heard that she can't even talk about it without going into fits. She got so wild once that Art and the sheriff had to hold her down on the bed so Ken could give her a shot to calm her nerves."

The first woman's husband joined them, and the two women fell silent. The man studied his wife's face and then said sharply, "You were talking about Andrea, weren't you? Why can't you leave that poor girl alone? Can't you see she's going through enough hell without everybody dragging her over the coals?"

His wife gave him an exasperated look. "Isn't that just like a man?" she said to her friend. "Just because she's young and pretty he's got to feel sorry for *her*." She turned to her husband. "What about her folks?" she asked him. "What about all the grief she's caused them—not to mention what she did to her very own brother."

The man shook his head. "I'm not saying what she did was right—Lord knows she's going to pay for it for the rest of her life. I just think she could use a little Christian charity from the rest of us right now."

"From what *I* hear she can use a lot more than that," his wife harumphed.

"What are you talking about now?" the man asked.

His wife turned to the other woman. "Tell him what you told me before—tell him how crazy she is."

"Well, I really don't want to go spreading tales," the second woman said reluctantly. "But Madge Burton works in Ken Anderson's office and *she* told me that Ken thinks they might have to send her someplace where they can watch over her all the time—you know, a rest home, or something like that. The only problem is Art won't hear of it. He keeps saying she'll get over it."

"Shhh," the man said. "They're bringing the coffin out. We'd better get ready to go to the cemetery."

The crowd in front of the church moved back as the pallbearers carried the coffin down the steps to the waiting hearse. Art and Bernice walked woodenly behind the coffin, their eyes sweeping blindly over the familiar faces surrounding them.

Andrea walked alone, several paces behind her parents. She wore dark glasses and a black dress that only served to emphasize her youth and her gaunt height. Her long red hair was pulled straight up into a black pillbox that sat starkly on top of her head.

"My God," the first woman whispered to the second. "With her hair up like that, she looks more like her brother than ever." She gave her husband a nasty look as he nudged her in the ribs to be quiet.

The coffin was placed in the hearse and the Donahues got into a black Cadillac behind it. Then the mourners went to their own cars to join the procession to the cemetery on the edge of town.

The gravesite was sheltered by shady trees and a gentle breeze gave some relief from the heat of the day. Bernice, Art, Andrea, and their closest relatives sat on a row of folding chairs while the priest recited a final prayer.

When the ceremony was over, the priest approached the family, and Art stood up to speak to him. Bernice did not even glance at the clergyman. Instead, she turned toward her daughter, her eyes glinting with hatred.

Andrea was staring dully at the coffin. Her mind was filled with images of Andy: the way only one side of his mouth turned up when he smiled, giving him that funny, crooked grin; how he always had so much energy he could never be completely still, some part of his body was constantly in motion—his feet would be tapping or his fingers beating in time to some inner rhythm. . . .

It was several seconds before she became aware of her mother's gaze. She swiveled her head slowly, as if she were doing it against her will, and looked straight into her mother's eyes. Her face went ashen as the force of hate and accusation from those cold blue eyes held her for a long moment.

Then suddenly Andrea was on her feet, stumbling through the press of mourners. Before anyone realized what she was doing, she had jumped behind the wheel of the black Cadillac and gunned it down the cemetery road, gravel flying under its tires.

Art stared after her, his eyes growing wide with horror. Then with a glance over his shoulder at Bernice, he grabbed Ken Anderson by the arm. "Let me take your car," he cried. "I've got to catch her!"

"Sure," Ken said. "The keys are in it. Do you want me to come with you?"

Art shook his head as he raced across the grass toward Ken's Lincoln. The engine screeched as he started it up and pressed the accelerator. By the time he got out of the cemetery the black Cadillac was nowhere to be seen, but instinctively he headed out of town on the road to their farm. He had driven nearly a mile before he saw the rear end of the Caddy disappearing over the rise of a hill up ahead.

Art looked down at the speedometer and panicked. He was doing well over eighty and he wasn't anywhere close to catching up with Andrea—she must be doing nearly a hundred miles an hour! Frantic, he pressed the gas pedal to the floor and the powerful engine of the Lincoln responded, yet he was still barely able to keep the black Caddy in sight.

The road was narrow and unevenly paved, and for all his skill as a driver Art was having a difficult time just keeping the Lincoln on the road. Andrea had only learned to drive this past year— she wasn't even old enough to have her license yet—and she and Andy had never driven anywhere but on the farm. Dear God, Art kept praying, please don't let her lose control of that car.

Then, without warning, Andrea turned off on to a side road, a rutted dirt track. Art was forced to keep well back of her, to avoid the roiling cloud of dust she had raised. But it didn't matter, now that he knew where she was headed.

When he finally broke through the dust he could see the Cadillac parked in the field, its gleaming black finish dulled by a thin coat of Wisconsin farmland. The door on the driver's side was ajar. Andrea was nowhere to be seen.

As he got out of the Lincoln, Art saw that the front end of the Cadillac was smashed against the rock where Andy had died. It was pretty easy to figure out what Andrea had done: she had tried to run the car into the rock, but the rough terrain of the field had slowed her down and when she hit the boulder she hadn't done much more than crumple the front bumper and the radiator grill.

She was lying face down on the rock, beating on it with her fists and the shattered sunglasses. Art bent down and slowly began to stroke her back. "Oh, Andrea honey," he said gently, "killing yourself isn't going to bring Andy back."

Andrea's head jerked up. "Oh, yes, it will," she whimpered. "Andy wants me to do it. Then we'll be together again." Her eyes were filled with tears and defiance. Art was reaching into his pocket for his handkerchief when suddenly Andrea's eyes bulged outward and her hands clutched at her chest. "Oh, Daddy, it hurts," she gasped. He felt her body go rigid against him, before she collapsed, unconscious.

"Andrea?" Art cried, his arms cradling her limp form. Her head lolled on his shoulder and Art could feel her breath warming his neck. He picked her up as if she were a baby and carried her to the front seat of the Lincoln. All the way back to the farmhouse he drove with one arm around her, holding her close to him, afraid to let go.

Bernice had not yet returned by the time they got home, and Art was relieved. He didn't want his wife to see Andrea like this, so he got her out of the car and upstairs and into her own bed as quickly as he could. Then he tried to get Ken Anderson on the phone. There was no answer. Evidently Ken hadn't gotten home from the cemetery yet.

Art went back to sit at Andrea's bedside. Her

eyes were still closed, but she was moving restlessly around in the bed, her arms pushing against the air. Art watched her and wondered what unseen foe she was struggling against. When he heard the sound of a car in the driveway he went to the window. Bernice was just getting out of one of their neighbors' cars, and Ken Anderson was with her.

"Ken!" Art shouted out the window. "Come up to Andrea's room right away!"

Both Ken and Bernice looked up at the sound of his voice, and then Ken made a beeline for the back door. Bernice just stood there, staring up at Art, her jaw set in a determined line.

Art turned away from the window. When Ken Anderson came into Andrea's room he told him briefly what had happened in the field. Then he went downstairs to face Bernice.

She was sitting at the kitchen table. As Art walked into the room she took off the black hat she had worn to the funeral and set it on the table in front of her. Like she's getting ready to get down to business, Art thought to himself.

"All right. What happened?" Bernice said. It was more a command than a question.

Art sighed and sat down at the table opposite her. "Nothing happened," he said. "She banged up the front of the funeral home's Cadillac a little, that's all."

Bernice glared at him. "Don't give me that. I saw the way she drove out of the cemetery. Everybody else in town saw it, too. Now *they* know she's crazy—"

"Stop it!" Art cried, slamming his fist down on

the table. "She's not crazy!" He opened his hand slowly, his fingers stretching across the waxed tablecloth. "She's taking this a lot harder than anyone else, is all. She'll be all right—it's just going to take time."

Bernice put her hand on top of her husband's. "I wish to God that were true," she said, "but you've got to face the facts, Art. She's dangerous, and we can't handle her any longer. There's no telling what she'll do next."

Art wrenched his hand away from hers. "Don't put on that pious act with me," he sneered. "I know how you feel about her. You'd like to see her put away, shut up in some institution where she'd never see the light of day again!" He jerked to his feet and strode to the back door. "But I won't let you do it—over my dead body!" He shoved the door open angrily and let it slam behind him.

He was halfway to the barn when Bernice caught up with him. "If you won't listen to me, will you listen to Ken?" she begged as she trotted along beside him. "He says he knows of a place, a private clinic where they'd take good care of her. It's not cheap, but he says it'd be the best place for her. Why don't you at least talk to him about it?"

Art whirled around to face her. "My God! What kind of mother are you?" he bellowed. "She's your own flesh and blood—just as much as Andy was! How can you hate her so much?"

Bernice's eyes blazed. "What about you?" she shouted back at him. "How can you forget what she did to Andy? And let me tell you something—*she* hasn't forgotten either! That's what's driving her crazy—it's her guilt! And she's never going to get over that!" She lowered her voice to an ominous tone. "And neither will I."

Art fought back a sudden impulse to strike Bernice. He had never laid a hand on either her or the kids, had never even come close to it—until now. Instead, he turned his back on her and walked into the depths of the barn.

That night, as the Donahues lay in bed in stony silence, neither of them able to sleep, the phone rang. Art picked it up after the first ring, to hear a gruff, hesitant voice. "Uh, Mr. Donahue, this is Charley, the caretaker at the graveyard?"

"What?" Art thought it might be some kids playing a cruel joke.

"Mr. Donahue, there, uh—well, I think you better get on in here. There's somethin' funny goin' on at your boy's grave."

A pause, then calmly, "I'll be right there."

As Art hung up the phone, his wife's voice came out of the dark. "What is it? Where are you going?"

"Now, Bernice," Art stalled, "it's nothing for you to worry about. Just some kids pulling a prank—"

"Some kids—where?" she interrupted. "What are you talking about?"

He was already pulling his clothes on over his pajamas. "At Andy's grave," he said, trying to make himself sound more controlled than he felt.

"The little bastards!" Bernice was sitting up in bed and turning on the light. "You just wait for me. I'm coming with you!"

"I wish you wouldn't—" Art began halfheartedly. But he knew it was no use. He didn't have the stomach to start up another fight with her now.

It was a fifteen-minute drive to the cemetery on the edge of town. It took them only ten minutes, although it seemed more like ten years. And yet Art had held back, not quite letting himself put his foot to the floor. He was just a little afraid to see what might be waiting for them at Andy's grave. He was not a superstitious man, but there was a prickly tingle at the base of his spine and he had broken out in a cold sweat.

As they pulled up at the cemetery gates a flashlight waved at them from out of the dark, signaling them to the side of one of the entry pillars.

Art turned off the engine of his big Buick. "Charley! Charley Burritt! Is that you?"

"Yeah, it's me." Charley's gaunt face appeared at the open window on the driver's side. "Mr. Donahue—oh, hello, Mrs. Donahue . . ." Charley began, then stopped, caught off guard by Bernice's sharp, "What's going on here?"

The caretaker took a step back. "I think maybe you better come see for yourself." He added pointedly, "Mr. Donahue, you better come alone."

Bernice started to protest, but Art was already opening his car door. "Should I bring my shotgun?" he asked Charley in a low voice.

Charley shook his head. "Dunno. Guess you might as well. It can't hurt none."

As Art went back to open the trunk, Bernice scrambled out of the car. "I'm coming with you,

Art," she said. "And you'd better not try and stop me!"

Art was bending over, groping in the corner of the trunk for the butt of his shotgun. He picked it up and slammed down the trunk lid with his other hand. "No, Bernice," he said, biting off his words. "You're not coming until I see what's out there. And that's final."

"But, Art—"

"Don't argue with me. I'll come back and get you. For now, you stay put."

Bernice hissed something at him under her breath. But she got back into the car.

Art walked over to Charley, who had discreetly stepped into the shadows.

"Okay, Charley," Art said as they walked under the iron sign above the gate, picking their way carefully. This piece of earth with its erratically marked-out plots, spreading trees, and narrow gravel road had been explored by them as children, in the same daring way that they had climbed the Civil War monument in the center of town. Years ago, Art was the one who had gotten Charley the job as caretaker here.

The blackness surrounding them was broken only by the gray, looming shapes of tombstones as they passed them, walking in silence, the only sound, the crunch of gravel under their feet. Suddenly Art felt Charley's bony hand pulling him over to the side, onto the grass.

"Mr. Donahue," he whispered, "he'll hear us coming."

"You mean there's only one?"

"Yep—though it sounds like more 'n one."

" 'Sounds'? What do you mean *'sounds'*?" Art was straining to keep his voice down to a whisper.

"He's makin' noises," Charley explained. "That's what caught my attention. I was in my house—on the other side of the wall—and I just turned off the TV and was gettin' ready for bed when I heard this funny sound. At first I thought it was some dog sniffin' around, but then it seemed I could hear *words*. I couldn't make out what they was, but I could tell it wasn't no animal."

"But how do you know it's Andy's—Andy's grave he's at?" Art asked. *Dear God, let this all be a mistake.*

"Well, I snuck outside with my flashlight and I went 'round the wall until I was right in back of where the sounds was comin' from. The very spot we buried your boy in."

"So what did you do?" Art snapped. "Didn't you try to stop him?"

Charley stopped in his tracks. "Yes, but—"

"But what?" Art halted too. He couldn't see Charley's face in the darkness, but he could hear the hesitation in his voice.

"Well, I shone the light on him—"

"And? Who was it?"

"Mr. Donahue, I ain't crazy. I lived next door to this graveyard nigh on eighteen years and I ain't never seen nothin' weird here 'cept for when the kids get in on Halloween . . . but tonight I swear—I *swear*—I seen your boy Andy. Heard 'im, too."

Silent minutes passed between them until Art said softly, "That's not possible, Charley. That's just not possible. Andy's dead. You put him in the ground yourself."

"That's what I keep tellin' myself," Charley said. "So it's got to be somethin' else."

"Right," Art said. "And we're going to find out what it is." He started forward again with a newly determined step.

Charley fell in behind him and they moved noiselessly through the grass. The only sounds they heard were the whirrings of crickets and the flutter of leaves in the trees above them, dancing to the rhythm of an occasional puff of breeze.

But when they were about a hundred feet away from his son's gravesite, Art could make out another noise. It was low and indistinct, but there was something familiar about it—something that sent icy fingers encircling his heart.

Oh, my God, he prayed silently. *Please make Bernice stay in the car.*

He could never quite remember crossing that last hundred feet. He thought that he must have stumbled a couple of times because Charley had put a hand on his back to help guide him. But he had no memory other than that.

Because the next thing he knew he was hearing his son's voice. It was close, and it was saying, no, *growling*: "Got to make her pay. Make her pay for what she did to me."

Only it wasn't quite Andy's voice, Art told himself again and again. It was as though someone were doing a clever imitation of him. Like those nightclub comics are always doing of celebrities like John Wayne and Jimmy Cagney, he thought desperately. It's their voice, and yet it's *not* their voice.

And this was not Andy. Dear God, it couldn't be. Could it?

Art grabbed the flashlight from Charley's hand. The specter winced and squirmed away from the light. Art's trembling fingers lost their grip on the flashlight and the shotgun nearly slipped from under his arm. For he had seen his son's face, and, when the boy turned his head away, Art had caught a glimpse of the Minnesota Twins baseball cap Andy loved. More horrifying still, he had seen the dull metal gleam in his son's hand. The Walther.

"Andy!" There was a pleading note in Art's voice.

An answering grumble came out of the stillness.

And then Charley bent over and picked up the still-burning flashlight. He aimed the light on the figure kneeling on the mound of earth, and held it there.

Charley felt confused. His eyes must be playing tricks on him. He knew this couldn't be a ghost and yet it sure looked like young Andy. But wait . . . just hold on there . . . the boy's arms were too thin, and the hair was wrong; it looked as though it was pulled up into the baseball cap, and he could have sworn he could see tips of breasts under the white T-shirt. . . .

"Mr. Donahue!" Charley gasped. "That ain't your boy! That's your daughter!"

"No," Art said dully. "It can't be. Andrea's home in bed. The doctor gave her something to sleep. He said she'd be out all night." But he looked to where Charley was pointing the flashlight, jiggling it up and down as he talked excitedly.

"Look! Look at them arms," Charley said, as the apparition covered its face with its free hand. "That's a girl's arm or I'll be damned!"

For a second, Art felt the world spinning. When it stopped, he stood very still and gazed sadly down at his daughter's huddled body. "Turn off the light, Charley," he said. "It's hurting her eyes."

"No! Leave it on. I want to see this!"

Both men whirled, and the flashlight in Charley's hand made a thin arc of light that sliced through the night, flickering over gravestones, dying flowers, faded miniature American flags, until it came to rest on Bernice's stiff, white face.

She put up a hand to shield her eyes. "Give me the light, Charley," she said, extending her other hand to him.

Charley swallowed nervously and dutifully turned the flashlight over to her.

Bernice took a step forward and pointed the beam at the crouching figure. She held it there, using both hands to keep the flashlight from shaking. "Put that gun down, Andrea," she said, straining to keep her voice even, controlled. "You'll hurt yourself."

Andrea shook her head violently from side to side so that strands of her long hair slipped out from under the baseball cap. "No! Got to make her pay," she said in the voice that was so like Andy's that Bernice jumped, sending the beam of light shooting up into the trees.

Bernice drew in her breath. "Is that gun loaded?" she whispered to her husband.

Art hesitated, wiping his thick fingers over his sweat-covered forehead. "Could be," he said. "But I don't think so. I—I threw out all the ammunition for the handguns after—after Andy . . ."

"We've got to grab her and take her home, Art," Bernice said, keeping her voice low so that only her husband could hear. "She's crazy as a loon—"

"Don't talk that way!" Art cut her off. "I still care about her, even if you don't!"

Bernice spoke between clenched teeth, "You can't fight me on this anymore, and you know it. Something's got to be done about her and the sooner the better."

Art let out a long sigh. "You're right, I guess." His voice was barely audible.

"Of course, I'm right," Bernice said. "We'll talk about that later. First, we've got to get her out of here. I'll go and get the car. Do you think you and Charley can manage to get her into it?"

"Yeah." Art grabbed the flashlight out of her hand. "We've got to have this," he said. "You just bring the car." Then he gave her the shotgun. "We don't need this anymore."

As Bernice walked off into the darkness Art called out to Charley.

"Here I am." Charley stepped forward.

Art held out the flashlight to him. "Take this and when I give you the signal, shine it in her face," he said. "When she tries to cover her eyes I'll get the gun away from her."

Art dropped to his hands and knees and crawled across the grass until he was close enough to Andrea to hear her heavy breathing. "Now!" he shouted out to Charley.

The flashlight came on, its beam like a spotlight on Andrea's face. As she cringed in its glare Art lunged forward, groping for the gun.

But Andrea was too fast for him. She put the gun to her chest and tried to fire it. It didn't go off. She pulled the trigger again. Still nothing. And then she seemed to collapse, clinging to the gun, but Art wrested it away from her.

Headlights swept across them as Bernice drove up, and Art half-dragged, half-carried Andrea to the back seat of the Buick. He pulled her in after him and held her in his arms, rocking her tenderly—just the way he used to do when she was a little girl. "There, there," he kept repeating softly, "it's all right. Daddy's here. It's all right."

"Daddy?" Andy's voice was gone and in its place was a childish whimper. "Make Andy stop, Daddy. He's hurting me."

"Yes, yes," Art soothed. "I'll make him stop. I won't let him hurt you anymore." *I won't let anyone ever hurt you again.*

Bernice got out of the driver's seat and walked over to Charley, who was lingering in the shadows, uncertain what he was expected to do next.

"You won't say anything about this to anyone, will you, Charley?" she asked.

"Oh, no, ma'am," Charley said quickly. "Not a

word. Nothin' that would hurt Mr. Donahue—or you." He pulled out a handkerchief and blew his nose loudly. " 'Cause, you see," he mumbled, "Mr. Donahue's kind of been my idol ever since I was a boy—"

"I know, I know," Bernice said, her hand reaching out to Charley's sinewy arm and squeezing it. "And I wouldn't ask you to hide anything, Charley. But she's not really dangerous—not to anyone but herself, I think."

"Yep," Charley sighed. He stood for a moment looking into the backseat of the car. Then he shook his head and walked off into the night, muttering to himself, "It's a terrible thing for a mind to take—killin' someone you loved like that. A terrible thing."

CHAPTER ONE
New York City

He was back. In a way, Andrea had been watching for him, hoping he would return to the restaurant. When she saw his tall, angular frame come through the door she felt that tiny stab of pain in her chest again—just as she had the first time she saw him. That had been two nights ago. Monday.

It had been a slow night and few of her tables were occupied. She had just given Sam, the bartender, an order for drinks and she'd been standing at the end of the bar, idly looking over the customers.

He was about six feet away from her, his face in profile. She noticed that it was a nice profile— although his nose was a little too short for it to be classic. His fingers were absentmindedly drumming a tattoo on the polished mahogany surface of the bar, and Andrea's eyes automatically dropped to them. And then she saw it—the funny little birthmark on the tip of his right wristbone. A sudden, hot pain went shooting through her heart, and she grabbed the curved edge of the bar to support herself, knowing that the pain was a signal for another one of her blackouts. She hadn't had one in a long time. But as quickly as the pain had come it was gone. Her head stayed clear, and she was herself again. This time. She looked once more at the man's birthmark. No, it hadn't been her imagination—a perfect brown oval.

The fingers had stopped drumming, and she knew he was looking at her. She lowered her gaze and started to glance away—but she *had* to see his face. She raised her head, sliding her eyes up to his. They were deep, deep brown, and they were fastened on her flirtatiously. Andrea stared into them for a long moment, hoping—and afraid—that he would speak to her. Then Sam placed the drinks she had ordered on her tray, and with a combination of disappointment and relief, she headed across the room to her customers.

He had stayed at the bar for an hour. As often as she dared Andrea gave him covert glances—but never when she knew he was looking. When he finally left, she felt tempted to run after him. But she knew she wouldn't. As far as she knew, he had never come in before that night; he would probably never come in again. She had missed her chance.

But tonight he had returned and gone straight to one of her tables. Not wanting to appear too eager, she pretended not to see him.

Her tables were rapidly filling with the Wednesday night pre-theater crowd. Appropriately called the Center Stage, the restaurant was a hangout for actors, and consequently, for tourists avid to see actors in the process of hanging out. In the four months she had worked there Andrea had seen only three really big "names." But she wasn't surprised by that—it was just another one of many disillusionments she had had since her arrival in the city six months before.

She wished he hadn't picked this day to come in. She was feeling flustered, unsure of herself. She'd been late today, held up at an audition where she had given one of the worst performances of her life. She'd been the tallest actress there. When the casting director had made a crack about it, she had suddenly become a fumbling, awkward adolescent again.

That feeling was still with her, and the man's presence made her even more self-conscious. He was attractive—no, handsome—and she was sure he knew it. His brown eyes had a slight squint to them that probably meant he was nearsighted and refused to wear glasses. Vanity, she thought—unless he was an actor, too. Well, then he was probably gay—most of the good-looking ones had the hots for each other.

She walked by his table, carefully ignoring him.

"Waitress?" There was a tentative note in his voice.

She kept walking. Suddenly it had become very important to snub him, to keep the upper hand as long as she could.

"Hey, *Red!*" His voice was sharp and clear, with a ring of authority to it. It cut through Elton John on the jukebox, the low hum of conversations at the tables, muffled shouts from the kitchen.

She jumped at the sound of the name he had called her—and at the quick twinge of pain in her chest. Trying to recover herself, she swept her eyes over the sawdust floor, pretending to look for the invisible object that had caused her to stumble. *That name. All it had referred to was the color of her hair. Why should it upset her so much?*

She stole a glance at the bar. Sam, whose black eyes never missed a thing, looked up from the drink he was mixing, a half-smile on his face. "Andrea," he said out of the corner of his mouth, "don't keep the customers waiting."

She shot him a nasty look, and saw his quick, good-natured laugh. It was all part of a game they played, trading insults and riding each other. Sam was an actor too, and they often commiserated with each other about their frustrations in finding work in the theater.

Slowly, she turned around and walked back to Ol' Brown Eyes' table. He was looking at her expectantly.

"Did you want something?" she asked, trying to sound as cool and offhand as she could.

A flicker of amusement crossed his face. "Sure do," he said with more than a hint of a Southern drawl.

Wondering if the accent was put on, she pulled her pad and pencil out of her apron pocket. "What can I get you?"

"Fust of awl, Ah'd lak uh beyurr."

She found it hard to keep a straight face. "A 'be-yurr'?"

His eyes became very serious but his face was unreadable. "T-hass raht. Uh beyurr. Bee-ee-ee-arr." Each time he opened his mouth the accent became thicker.

Andrea lowered her eyes, momentarily confused. *Was he putting her on or was he for real?* Then she heard a low chuckle and she brought her gaze back up to his.

The brown eyes were filled with laughter, and looking into them she felt something quiver deep inside her. She smiled helplessly at him. He had paid her back with a deft touch.

His face broke into a broad grin. "Ma'am, I sure would appreciate it if you'd get that beer. I'm mighty thirsty." The drawl was still there, but now it sounded genuine.

"Oh." She started. She must have been gawking at him. "Oh, sure. I'll get it right away." She hurried over to the bar, her cheeks burning, and shouted to Sam for a draft.

Was it her imagination or did Sam give her a peculiarly penetrating look as he set the beer down on her tray? To avoid any questions, she frowned in concentration on adding up the bill for one of her tables.

When she was finished, she picked up the tray and scurried back to his table.

He smiled at her as she put the beer in front of him. She turned to go. "Hey," he said softly.

"W-what's wrong now?" He was making her feel

defensive, afraid of making a mistake in front of him.

"Nothing's wrong," he said smoothly. "I just wanted to know your name. Otherwise, I'll have to keep calling you Red—or 'waitress.' Mine's Bobby—Bobby Wilson—in case you're interested."

"I'm Andrea."

"Andrea what?"

"Donahue."

"Irish, huh? I might have known." He chuckled. "The hair."

A couple came in and sat down at the next table. Glad to have this excuse to get away from him, she turned away to take their order.

For the next fifteen minutes she raced from table to table fetching drinks, serving dinners, trying desperately to look as if she were too busy to notice him and too indifferent to try. But it was all a front, and somehow she had the feeling he could see right through it.

At last she could no longer ignore his empty beer stein. After all, he was her customer.

She approached his table. "Another one?" she asked casually.

"That depends." The brown eyes seemed to be appraising her.

She looked over at the bar. Sam was watching them, his eyes narrowed. *What did he think he was doing? He didn't own her.* He had asked her out once, when she first came to the Center Stage. But Sam's swarthy looks had kind of frightened her, so she'd turned him down. Now she considered him a buddy.

Bobby Wilson followed her gaze across to the bar. Sam turned away abruptly and began talking to one of the customers.

"Is that your boyfriend?"

"No. Just a friend," Andrea said quickly. "He kind of watches out for me."

"Ho, I'll bet you can take care of yourself." His eyes swept up her five foot nine inches.

She felt a hot blush rise. "Well, I-I haven't been in the city very long," she stammered. "That's what I meant."

"Listen," he said suddenly, "I hope you won't think I'm pushy, but I'd like to get to know you better. And I can see it's going to be kind of hard to do while you're working." He paused and smiled at her.

She was unable to repress an answering smile.

"So I thought," he went on, "maybe I could come back when you get off work." He nodded his head in Sam's direction. "Unless your bodyguard won't let you."

"Sam doesn't tell me what to do," Andrea said with bravado. "But I don't get off until one." She was sure he would not want to come back then.

"That's fine," he said. "I'll be back a little before." He started to get up. "Let me pay you for this beer now so you can get back to the hungry hordes." When he was on his feet, his eyes were only inches above her own. He grinned. "I like that," he said. "A woman I can look right in the eye."

He stuffed some bills in her hand, gave her a

wink, and was gone. She stood there a moment, looking after him.

Then she shook herself and went back to work, trying to hide her excitement—especially from Sam.

She succeeded, as long as they were both busy. But toward midnight when business started to slack off, he called her over to the bar.

"You goin' out with that guy tonight?" he asked.

"What guy?"

"You know who I mean. The creep who was in here before—the one who's been hangin' out here for a week, watchin' your every move."

"He has?" Andrea was surprised. She had only been aware of him once before.

Sam scowled at her.

"Why do you call him a creep?" she asked defiantly. "He seems nice enough to me."

"Yeah? What do you know? You're just a kid."

Andrea stared daggers at him. "I'm no kid," she said. "I'm twenty-four."

"Funny, I always thought you were younger than that," Sam said. Then he laughed, a cynical laugh, not at all like his usual easy humor. "And you're a real woman of the world, right? That's what I mean, honey. You don't know these hustlers like I do."

"What makes you think he's a hustler?"

"I got eyes, don't I?"

Andrea mustered up her best scathing look. "What makes you such a great judge of character?" The question came out sounding a little sharper than she had intended it to.

Sam regarded her for a moment, then shrugged. "Hell, I'm thirty-one years old and I haven't made it as an actor yet and I probably never will. But I put in a lot of time tendin' bar and that's one thing you learn from this job—people. And, baby, believe me, I *know* that guy. I've seen his type a million times before. He's all wrong for you."

Andrea looked away and then turned back, her blue eyes boring into Sam's black ones. "Why are you doing this, Sam?" she asked. "What's in it for you?"

Sam's gaze wavered. His right hand came up and began to stroke his thick, dark beard. " 'Cause I think you need someone to take care of you," he said. "You're too pretty, too fragile. People are going to take advantage of you."

Andrea laughed. "Me? Fragile?"

"I don't mean physically," Sam said. "I'm talking about being emotionally fragile."

Andrea suddenly tensed. She didn't want to hear what he was going to say next.

Sam stared at her, puzzled. "Did I say something wrong?" he asked.

"No," Andrea said sharply. "I just think I'd better get back to my customers." She turned and walked away.

Sam shrugged his shoulders and turned back to the bar. Hell, he'd *never* understand Andrea. She was a mystery to him. Maybe that was why his feelings for her wouldn't go away, feelings that he now took great pains to hide from her—although they sometimes showed through, as they had just now.

Why couldn't he just give up, admit that she was

a lost cause? He would have done that with any other woman long ago.

But not Andrea. From the first day she walked into the Center Stage she had touched something secret within him, a tenderness that he had nearly forgotten was a part of him. He could still remember her standing there at the bar, asking about a job—and looking as though just one harsh word would shatter her into a thousand tiny pieces.

She was just another shy, frightened kid off the streets, Sam tried to tell himself. He'd seen dozens like her. Yet there were inexplicable depths of emotion in her blue eyes, depths that he suddenly had a longing to explore. He couldn't let her go without any hope of seeing her again.

So he had taken her name and phone number, even though they hadn't needed any waitresses then. But the following week when one of their waitresses quit he had given Andrea's name to the manager and told him to give her a call.

When she came to work, Sam still hadn't known what to make of her. He had met lots of girls fresh out of the Midwest and still unblighted by the city—but she wasn't like any of them. He had an image of her—it was corny he knew—that she was like a flower. Maybe it was the perfume she wore that smelled like a summer garden or maybe it was the poppy color of her hair. Whatever it was, all he knew was that every time he looked at her he thought of blossoms tightly furled, not yet open to the sun.

She had enthralled him. She was so different

from the tough, sophisticated women he was used to—and thought that he preferred.

So he had befriended her. When he found out she was living in a fleabag hotel he had gone out and found a furnished apartment for her.

He had tried to help her out in other ways, teaching her things about the city, advising her on acting classes and auditions. She began coming to him with her problems, her disappointments at finding work as an actress, and he always listened sympathetically. He had the feeling he was her only real friend in the city.

She needed someone to watch out for her, and in the beginning that's what he told himself he was doing. But as time went by he had to admit that his feelings for her were more than just brotherly, and he wondered if she felt the same way about him.

One afternoon on his day off he stopped by her apartment on the pretense of dropping off a magazine article about the theater that she had wanted to read. She was glad to see him and invited him in. It was the first time he'd been in her apartment since he'd helped her move there.

He looked around the little room and was pleased to see how immaculate she kept it. Even the air smelled fresh and sweet with the faint fragrance of her perfume.

He sat down in the solitary chair and Andrea perched on the studio couch. "Can I get you something to drink?" she asked.

"You wouldn't happen to have a beer, would you?"

Andrea looked apologetic. "No, just some ginger ale."

"I think I'll pass."

They both fell silent. She seemed nervous, and Sam guessed that it was because she was alone with a man in her apartment.

"The place looks good," he said, trying to ease the tension in the air.

Andrea smiled. "Thanks. I haven't done much to it."

"Do you feel safe here?" Sam asked. "I mean, you're not afraid at night, are you?"

"Oh, no," Andrea said blithely. "Nobody ever bothers me. The hotel was a lot worse than this—there were always creepy characters hanging around."

"You know, I worry about you going home at night alone. I wish you'd let me walk you."

A flicker of irritation crossed Andrea's face. "I've told you before, Sam. You don't have to. I can take care of myself—besides it's only three blocks."

Sam laughed. "Where'd you learn to be so independent? I'll bet it was bossing all those cows around."

"Well, they could be pretty ornery sometimes," Andrea said, her eyes softening with amusement. "You had to be tough with them."

Sam chuckled softly. "Hell, I never even *saw* a cow until I was in junior high school. How's that for deprived?"

"You don't know what you missed," Andrea said, a slow grin spreading across her face.

Sam watched her. She was more at ease now; maybe he could do what he had come here for. "Listen, Andrea," he said, clearing his throat.

At the change in his tone her smile faded.

"Uh, how would you like to have dinner with me tonight?" he asked, then added quickly, "Maybe we could see a movie—or even get tickets to a play."

Andrea's eyes fell to a spot on the floor near his feet. "No, Sam. I can't."

"Why not?" he said. "I know you don't have to work tonight—I checked the schedule. Do you have something else to do?"

Andrea chewed at her lip. "Yes—no. I—" She waved a hand helplessly in the air.

He had to know why she was turning him down. "Is there a reason?" he asked. "Or maybe you just don't want to go out with me. Is that it?"

Andrea frowned. "I thought we were friends, Sam. I-I never thought about you in any other way."

Sam found that hard to believe. Had he been so cool that she had missed the signals he gave her? "Well, sure, I'm your friend," he said. "But maybe we could be a little bit more to each other."

That had been the wrong thing to say. Her eyes got a kind of panicky look to them.

"What's the matter?" he asked. "Are you afraid of me?"

She spoke reluctantly. "I guess maybe I am a little. You're—well, you're not like anyone I've ever known before."

What the hell did that mean? "Christ, Andrea.

I'm just a man," he said. "I'm no different than any other man."

She looked almost ashamed. "Maybe that's it," she said. "You see, I haven't known too many men—just a lot of boys."

"What's the difference?"

She suddenly stood up. "Please, Sam. I can't explain it to you. Can't we leave it at that?"

He stood up too and took a step toward her. She backed away, her wide eyes blinking rapidly. What did she think he was going to do to her?

"Okay," he sighed. "Forget it. I'll leave you alone." He turned and crossed to the door. "I hope you still think of me as your friend—because I am," he said over his shoulder. "See you tomorrow night."

He lumbered down the stairs, feeling rejected and confused. How could he have been so wrong about her? And how the hell could he face her at work and not let her see how much she had hurt him?

Yet the next day she had acted as if nothing had happened, and he had taken his cue from her behavior. He went back to playing the buddy-buddy role with her—all the while hoping that someday she would realize what she was missing.

That had been three months ago. In the meantime he had kept his eyes open, on the lookout for any guys hanging around her. There hadn't been any whom she'd responded to—not until that clown tonight. Well, she'd see through *him* soon enough.

But in spite of all the time that had passed nothing had changed in the way he felt about her. He still cared—too damn much.

He stood watching her now, wondering what it was that had upset her so, that had made her eyes grow so wide and glassy and the pupils diminish down to mere pin pricks. Seeing her like that he suddenly had the feeling he didn't know Andrea Donahue at all.

Bobby Wilson came back at ten minutes to one. Andrea had been so worried he wouldn't show up that when he walked through the door she broke into a grin and started to rush toward him—until she caught herself and slowed her pace.

Out of the corner of her eye she saw Sam busily cleaning off the bar. She could hear him clearing his throat to catch her attention. She ignored him and walked straight to Bobby.

"Hi," he said, reaching for her. Then he hugged her and brushed his lips against her cheek, as if she were an old friend. "You ready?"

Andrea pulled away from him. "No, uh—not quite yet," she said, flustered by his show of affection. She was sure Sam was observing them from the bar, and she wished Bobby had been a little more restrained in his greeting. "Sit down and wait for me while I finish up."

She steered him to a table across the room from the bar, hoping that would discourage Sam from striking up a conversation.

It didn't. By the time she had collected her things and was ready to go, Sam had enticed Bobby to the bar with a beer and was drawing him out.

Andrea watched them with a pang of annoyance. Bobby was so busy talking to Sam he didn't seem to notice her approach—or the fact that she had let down her hair, knowing how long and beautiful it was and how well it framed her face.

"Yeah, William Morris is handling it—" Bobby said as he looked up and acknowledged Andrea.

"I know a lot of people at William Morris," Sam said pointedly. "Who's handling you?"

But Bobby had turned to Andrea. "Hey, pretty lady," he said, climbing off his stool, "let's go."

"That's fine with me," Andrea said a little too brightly, glancing over at Sam.

"Goodnight, ol' buddy," Bobby said to Sam. "Thanks for the beer."

"Don't mention it." Sam's eyes riveted on Andrea's. "Take care, baby," he said softly to her.

"Goodnight, Sam." Andrea's voice was tinged with ice. She walked to the door with Bobby.

When they were outside he grabbed her hand. "I like your hair that way," he said. "I have a particular weakness for long hair—especially when it's as gorgeous as yours."

Andrea managed to mumble something in reply. Being alone with him brought back all the feelings of awkwardness. Suddenly she found herself tongue-tied. She desperately searched her mind for something to say. She was wondering if she dared ask him what he had been talking to Sam about, when he suddenly spoke.

"Do you like French food?" he asked.

"Sure."

"Good. Because that's where we're going."

"At this hour? Is any place open?"

He smiled smugly. "*I* know a place that's open twenty-four hours." He was hailing a cab, then helping her inside. "Fifty-third, off Park. The Brasserie."

When they got out of the cab, he stood on the sidewalk, gazing up, and Andrea followed his example. He took her hand again. "Do you know what building this is?" he asked.

Andrea shook her head.

"It's the Seagram Building—one of the most beautiful skyscrapers in New York. It was designed by Mies van der Rohe and Philip Johnson."

"Oh. Who are they?" She had a feeling from the way he said their names that she should have known who they were.

"Just two of the world's greatest architects," Bobby said. But he seemed pleased that she hadn't known, that he could impart some of his superior knowledge of the world to her. "C'mon," he said, "I'm starved."

Andrea looked at him shyly over the onion soup, studying his face. The brown eyes were downcast, intent on his spoon as he separated a strand of melted cheese from the top of the soup. But she could still feel their pull, the almost magical way their brown depths seemed so familiar, so *right*, igniting warm, wonderful feelings in her—just as the birthmark had done. His lashes were short and fine, but very black, ringing his eyes like ebony curtains. The rest of his features were broad, yet delicately drawn. Like the eyes, they had an ever so faint Oriental cast to them. She liked the wide, thin curve of his lips, and watched them as they closed around a golden brown morsel of cheese. She wondered what they'd feel like pressing against hers . . .

"Hey, Red." The lips suddenly opened and spoke to her.

A split second's pain again. She braced herself for its full force. Oh God, don't let it happen here, with him. But it retreated. "What? Oh, I'm sorry." He was staring at her, the dark eyes flashing. Curiosity? Alarm? She couldn't tell. What a fool he must think she was, gawking at him like an over-grown adolescent. And yet, that was how he made her feel.

"Give you a quarter for your thoughts. I'm a big spender." The brown eyes were laughing again.

"No, no. You don't want to know them. They were dumb," Andrea murmured. She could feel the blood rising in her face.

"Do you mind me calling you 'Red'?" The laughter was gone, the eyes were almost serious now.

"No, it's kind of nice. Nobody's ever called me that before." That was true. Nobody had ever called *her* that but someone—oh, it was so hard to remember back that far—someone somewhere had used that nickname. Something tugged at her memory. *Andy.* That was it. The basketball team used to call him "Big Red." Not her—never her. So why did she feel as if she had just told Bobby a lie?

"That's funny," he was saying. "Where I come

from anybody with red hair is automatically called 'Red.'"

"Oh?" Andrea said, taking her cue, "and just where is it you come from?"

He smiled. "The Tar Heel State."

She looked blank. "I don't know which one that is."

"North Carolina." He seemed pleased that once again he had been able to educate her.

"I went through there on the bus on my way to New York," Andrea said, proud that she could say something about his home state. "It was very pretty."

Bobby's brow furrowed. "I don't understand," he said. "How could you go through North Carolina on your way to New York? You're not from the South—I'd have sworn your accent was straight out of the Midwest."

Andrea nodded. "Wisconsin. But my mother moved to Florida a couple of years ago. I lived with her there for a little while. When she remarried I decided to come to New York."

"Are your parents divorced?"

"No." Andrea looked down at her soup and slowly swirled her spoon through the brown liquid. "My father's dead. He—he died in a plane crash on his way home from visiting me. I was at . . . school."

"How long ago was that?"

"Three—no, four years ago." Andrea felt a tiny fluttering in her stomach as she readied herself for his next question.

But instead he looked thoughtful. "That's

rough," he said. "I know how it is. My mother died about a year and a half ago."

Her stomach relaxed and Andrea gave him a look of sympathy. "What happened to her?"

"Cancer." There was pain in the eyes now. "It was awful."

They sat for a moment in silence. Then he shrugged, as if trying to shake off his unhappy memories. "Enough morbidness," he said. "I want to hear about you. How long have you been in New York?"

"Six months."

"Then I've been here twice as long as you have. That makes me practically a native."

"Mmm. You seem to know your way around town much better than I do."

"It's called survival." There was an edge of bitterness in his voice.

"Yeah, it can be pretty hard sometimes," Andrea said. She sighed. "I don't know what I'd do if I didn't have my job. At least waitresses never have to worry about starving to death."

"Sure, but that's not what you really want, is it?" The eyes were zeroed in on her, refusing to let her look away.

Andrea shook her head. "No, actually I'm an actress."

"I thought so." Approval registered in the eyes.

Andrea bit her lip. "Or should I say 'frustrated actress'? I haven't been on a stage since I've been here—except for auditions." She frowned. "I went to one today. I felt like such a fool . . ." Her voice trailed off as she remembered how the casting director had looked at her, rolled his eyes, and said something snide about their not needing a drag queen. She hadn't even realized what he had meant until later—that because she was so tall she would look like a man impersonating a woman in this particular role. Well, he didn't have to be so nasty about it. Why didn't he just tell her she was too tall for the part?

Bobby was nodding his head. "I know what you mean. I've gotten so many rejection slips I could paper my apartment with them." Then he brightened perceptibly. "Only now, things may be changing."

"You're a writer?"

"Guilty as charged. But until now the operative adjective has been 'unpublished.' "

"Is that what you were talking to Sam about? Is the Morris Agency handling you now?" She was pleased that she could let him know she wasn't entirely ignorant—at least she had heard of William Morris, one of the biggest talent agencies in the business. He must be pretty good to have such an important agent. She had tried for months and couldn't even get a run-of-the-mill one.

"So they tell me. They have my manuscript and they're very excited about it."

"Hey, that's great. What is it, a book?"

"Yep. A novel."

"What's it about?"

He leaned back in his seat and lit up a cigarette. "Well, it's rather complicated to explain in twenty-five words or less. But"—his eyes narrowed in concentration and focused on a spot just over her head—"it's about a young man from the South who has struggled—successfully, he believes—to throw off his racial prejudices. He comes to the North and meets and falls in love with a black girl, only he doesn't find out she's black until later because she has very light skin. It's not that she's ashamed of being black, but she wants to test him—"

"That's not very nice of her," Andrea interrupted.

He smiled tolerantly. "No, but that's beside the point. She has her reasons. Anyway, the man has to wrestle with himself to decide what he's going to do—give up the girl or not."

"But what's the problem?" Andrea asked innocently. "He'll choose the girl, right?"

He puffed on his cigarette. "Not necessarily. Remember he's from the South, and those racial hatreds die hard."

Andrea thought he obviously knew what he was talking about. She'd better shut up before she revealed just how ignorant she was. "It really sounds interesting," she said. "I'd like to read it sometime."

"Oh, I think that can be arranged," Bobby said, his hand reaching out for hers.

He brought her home to her apartment on Ninth Avenue. At the door—he didn't ask to come in—he kissed her goodnight, held her very close, and then turned and walked away.

Andrea was excited. She flopped herself down on her studio couch and thought about the evening. He had even said he wanted to see her again.

She had been worried about that. He was plainly so much smarter and better educated than she was—she was afraid he would think she was stupid. Of course, in the school she had gone to education had merely been a by-product—though the years of drama therapy had taught her she could act. "School!" A polite term for a private clinic for disturbed adolescents—a "mink-lined loony bin" some of the kids had called it. Her father had sacrificed to send her there. But he had told her that last time that it had been worth every penny. *You're so much better, sweetheart.* Tears had glinted in his eyes. *The doctors say you'll be coming home very soon.*

It was the last time she had seen him. The plane that was flying him back to Wisconsin had crashed, taking away the last person who really loved her. She had gone home for his funeral with a terrible sense of *déjà vu*; it was just like when Andy died. Except that now there was no Daddy to comfort her. There was nothing except her mother's ice blue gaze: *You killed him, killed your brother and your father, too.*

Oh, my God! Andrea sat up and stared at the calendar on the wall. *Today was the anniversary of Andy's death!*

Though she still thought about him often it was strange how little she actually remembered of that day. Random flashes of it came back to her occasionally, but sometimes it was even hard for her to realize that Andy was dead. She still had dreams about him—strange, wonderful dreams of Andy smiling at her with that crazy, crooked grin of his.

Then he'd laugh and start running away, calling out to her to catch him. Although she'd run as hard as she could, he was faster, never quite within her reach. "Stop, Andy! Stop!" she'd beg him when she could go no farther. But he'd only laugh and keep on running. . . .

So close. In those dreams she'd almost found it again—that marvelous feeling of completeness she'd always had with him. When they were growing up they had talked about it a lot and decided it was because they were two separate halves of one personality. When they were apart they were incomplete, when they were together everything was right and whole.

How she longed to feel that way again. It had been so many years and miles and memories ago. Maybe this time it would happen—maybe Bobby was the one. He had to be. The birthmark had shown her—it was the sign.

CHAPTER TWO

Bobby groaned in disgust and threw his pencil down. The graphite made a sharp gray mark where it hit the paper he'd been working on, and the pencil bounced across the desk top, coming to rest against his ashtray. Rubbing his gritty eyes with the fingers of one hand, he reached for his cigarettes with the other. Empty. He tossed the pack in the direction of the wastebasket. It missed by a good two feet.

He hoisted his tired body out of the chair and walked over to the window. Nineteen floors in the air, it fronted onto yet another glass and steel sky-scraper. Bobby's eyes swept across the glittering façade of the neighboring building: so many windows, and behind each of them someone was doing a job—most of them unimportant, insignificant, unrewarding jobs.

It amazed him to think that in that one building

right now were probably three or four times as many people as he had grown up with in his hometown. That thought always quickened his heartbeat. Because this was it: the Big Apple, the big time. The place where dreams came true. If he was going to make it as a writer he could do it here. He *had* to do it here.

So what had happened? Was this as far as he was going to get? Managing editor of a trade magazine for supermarket managers. Supermarkets! My God, what had become of his dreams: a staff job on *The New York Times*. Contributing editor to *The New Yorker*. And would he never be able to stroll past the Fifth Avenue bookstores, seeing his book on display in every window, the number one bestseller?

Bobby stared down at the tiny figures scurrying about in the August heat on the streets far below. Was he just like them? No different, no better? He twisted away from the window and exhaled sharply. Hell, he'd show them—someday he'd show them all.

He sat back down at his desk, but could not pick up his work. Today it seemed duller and more tedious than ever. Whoever said that life wasn't fair just wasn't kidding; it sure wasn't turning out the way he had planned. Nearly twenty-nine years old and what had he accomplished? That other North Carolina boy, Thomas Wolfe, had published *Look Homeward, Angel* when he was twenty-nine. Bobby would have a hard time eclipsing Wolfe's memory with such a late start. But there had been so many distractions, so many things that had gone wrong that weren't his fault.

Like his marriage. What a joke that was. Cynthia had seen to that. Tall, lovely Cynthia. Beautiful, heartless Cynthia. What had changed her from the simple, loving girl he had married into the cold, relentless bitch she was now? That question was always there, unanswered, buzzing at the back of his mind. Maybe he was afraid to answer it.

They had been happy in the beginning, he was sure of that. They'd lived only for each other—until Jennifer was born, and she had completed that perfect circle of their love. Life was so good then, he had wanted nothing else.

But a restlessness began to creep into their relationship—a foreign element that he did not know how to deal with. Cynthia grew away from him, and nothing he tried could bring her back. He became desperate, but that only seemed to increase her resolve to torture him. Finally, in despair, he'd fled to New York.

At first, that only made it worse. He was afraid that it made him seem weak in her eyes, that he had run away because he couldn't take it. So he tried to cut her out of his life, not to think about her—as if somehow that would get back at her.

Occasionally it worked and the memory of Cynthia would become a blur. That usually happened when he was with other women—in the beginning, before they turned him off. Because New York women drove him crazy; they were like the neon lights ringing Times Square—gaudy, flashing, brightly colored, and enticing, but shedding little light and no warmth at all.

In those first, lonely weeks in New York he had taken to hanging out in singles bars, and before the evening was over he would always find himself attracted to some woman—madly, intensely, he must have her. Possessing her body usually turned out to be easy, but then he would discover there was really nothing much else she had to offer that he wanted. In the past few months he had found fewer and fewer women who were able to attract him—even to that initial stage of one-more-notch-on-the-bedpost lust.

Except for that girl last night—Andrea. He had spotted her the first time he went into the Center Stage and he had gone back again to check her out. To be certain. She reminded him of Cynthia; they were both tall, and the redhead had that same air of being unaware of her own attractiveness that Cynthia had had when he first met her. Cynthia had long since lost it. Now, she knew only too well how gorgeous she was—and how to use it.

Andrea had another appeal, too. She was quiet and shy and sweetly feminine—even though in those moments when he embarrassed her she blushed and mumbled like some awkward teen-ager.

She was not as beautiful as Cynthia, yet that actually made her even more alluring. She was approachable—and very touching in her vulnerability. She seemed so young and impossibly innocent.

Of course, it wasn't likely that she was as untouched as she looked. Was anybody past the age of twelve still a virgin in this day and age? He frowned to think of his own daughter being seduced by some pubescent Lothario. Well, he still had quite a few years before he had to worry about that—he hoped.

Even so, Andrea must have been around enough to have gotten herself laid—at least once. She'd said she'd been to college, hadn't she? And he'd never known a college girl yet, who'd been a virgin.

But Andrea was, well, something else. The word "androgynous" kept coming to mind. He had never known anyone whom the term had fit before, and he had always thought it was synonymous with "sexless." But not this one. No, she was very sexy—in spite of the slightly boyish quality to her face and body. Her features were clear-cut and regular, strictly all-American, but her figure seemed somewhat underdeveloped—as if she were stuck at some point just in the middle of puberty. Her breasts were pancake-flat and her hips were narrow, like a man's. Yet with that mane of red hair swinging free she was as voluptuous as any movie star.

Besides, she made him feel—what? Important? Looked up to? No, more than that. She *believed* him, and that made everything true. The trust and utter lack of cynicism in her eyes was like a Midas touch, a precious gift of alchemy that could transmute the shabby reality of his existence. In Andrea's tender blue eyes he really was all he said he was—and more.

Yet there was something else about her, something he couldn't quite define. Something mysterious. It wasn't there all the time—only in those moments when her eyes took on a guarded quality, as if there were some dark secret lurking behind them. It made her all the more intriguing.

Last night he had restrained his impulse to try to get her into bed. He hadn't made a move, careful not to frighten her away. A girl like Andrea needed to be brought along slowly, cautiously—but he kind of liked that; it made him feel more masterful.

Thinking of her, he made up his mind. He drew his wallet out of his pants pocket and searched through it for the scrap of paper he had scribbled her telephone number on.

As he punched out the digits on the push buttons of his phone he longed for a cigarette. Damn, why hadn't he bought another pack at lunch?

The phone rang twice. "Hello?" Her voice sounded flat, tentative—as if she were afraid of finding out who was on the other end of the line.

"Hi, Red. It's me, Bobby." He laughed nervously. "Remember?"

"Of course." There was more energy in her voice now, but still no hint that she was glad to hear from him. And she made no attempt at repartee—maybe she didn't like to talk over the phone. He wished he could see her face.

"Are you working tonight?" He had hoped to be able to chat with her for a few minutes before getting to the point, but her silence had made him feel self-conscious—and he couldn't think of anything the least bit clever to say.

"Uh-huh. I have to start getting ready pretty soon."

"Would it be all right if I dropped by again tonight?" He could feel all his pretense at any sort of urbanity rapidly slipping away.

"Sure." Her voice sounded curiously tense, as if her throat muscles were stretched taut.

"Well, what I mean is, when you get off—like I did last night."

"Fine."

Still tight as a drum. "Do you get off at one?"

"Mm-hmm."

"Okay." Might as well end this strange non-conversation. "See you then."

"Bye."

Bobby put down the phone and frowned at it. They had a date for tonight, but he wasn't at all sure she wanted to see him again. Still, she had said she would, hadn't she?

Funny how she had affected him. Last night he had been smooth, in command. Today she had gotten the better of him—mustn't let that happen again.

How withdrawn she had been on the phone. Was that just the way she was or—the thought suddenly crossed his mind—was it possible that she had someone else with her? A man maybe? Could be. *Nobody* could be as innocent as she looked.

Shafts of afternoon sunlight sifted through the single window in Andrea's apartment. They reached just to the head of the bed where the telephone was. Although she had been glad to hear from Bobby she felt slightly put out. His call had interrupted the afternoon ritual.

She lay watching the motes of dust in their slow, haphazard descent through the sun-brightened air—much as she had as a child. Then, she had imagined the motes were fairies and she would lie on her bed in absolute stillness, for fear that the fairies would catch her spying on them. She would stay that way for long minutes at a time—until the earth moved and the sun was no longer shining in her window.

Andy.

Andy never believed in magic. He would laugh at her every time he found her "fairy staring"—as he called it. Then he would run into her room and jump on the bed, creating wild whirlwinds of dust that sent the fairies skittering for cover.

Even though she felt sorry for the fairies and complained noisily so they would know she wasn't responsible for the chaos, she had always secretly loved it when Andy came crashing onto her bed that way. Then, whooping and yelling, they would wrestle and tickle each other until Bernice came running to the foot of the stairs, shouting at them to be quiet. They would wait until she walked away and then, exchanging mischievous glances, they would carry on as before—only in silence—rolling over and over, arms and legs wrapped around each other, their bodies squirming and straining into one indistinguishable being. So absorbed, they would never hear their mother come in until she was standing over them, pulling them apart, scolding them, telling them they shouldn't play with each other like that.

Why not? Andrea had always wanted to ask. But even then she thought she knew the answer; it had something to do with the way Andy's body made her feel—especially when she wrapped her legs around him and rubbed up against him. It felt so warm and nice—down *there*. . . .

"Mmmm," she sighed.

"It feels good, doesn't it?"

"Oh, yes," Andrea responded dreamily.

"Want me to go on?"

"Yes! Don't stop."

"Like this?"

Andrea's lips parted and she let out a low moan. The warm fingers on her flesh were gentle but insistent as they moved back and forth across the most sensitive part of her body. "Oh, yes," she panted, "I love it." Then the rhythm began to build, faster and faster—bringing her to the point of aching excitement. Suddenly she felt the first wave of ecstasy rush over her. "Yes!" she cried. *"Yes!"* as her naked body writhed in pleasure. And then a jumble of words sounding like an incantation came rumbling up from the depths of her throat: *"AndyAndyAndypleaseAndypleaseplease-Andeeee . . ."*

Several minutes later Andrea rolled over and picked up her watch from the bedside table. "Damn!" she said, swinging her long legs reluctantly to the floor. She couldn't afford to be late again today; she'd better get a move on.

She stood up, stretching sensuously, delaying the

moment just a little longer. Suddenly she remembered her date with Bobby. Better straighten things up in case he wanted to come in. Bending over, she hastily smoothed out the covers of the empty, rumpled bed.

CHAPTER THREE

He didn't come. I should have known he wouldn't,
Andrea chided herself as she watched the hands of
the clock over the bar advance. Ten minutes past
one.

She looked quickly away, avoiding Sam's gaze.
She had not told him she had another date with
Bobby, but she was sure that he suspected it. He
had been watching her constantly for the past half
hour. Every time she glanced at the door or the
clock she could feel Sam's eyes on her, could sense
their disapproval.

When she had come into work earlier that evening, Sam had been right there, his eyes full of
questions. He waited for her to say something.
When she didn't he asked, with obvious annoyance, "Well? What happened? Wasn't I right
about that guy?"

Andrea had leaned toward him teasingly. "Not a

bit," she said, her voice taunting and deliberate. "He didn't make one false move."

Sam's eyes had narrowed then and he looked as though he wanted to say something. Instead he turned on his heel and abruptly walked away. He hadn't said a single pleasant word to her all evening.

Andrea didn't care. She resented Sam's attitude—as if she were a *child* who didn't know what was best for her. She had already decided that if Sam was going to be that way, then she no longer wanted him as a friend. And if the job got too awkward, well, she could probably find another one.

At thirteen minutes past one the door flew open and Bobby loped in, looking sheepish. "Gosh, I'm sorry, babe," he said, rushing over to Andrea. "I fell asleep in front of the tube." He kissed her cheek. "Forgive me?" he asked, his brown eyes signaling that he knew she would.

"Sure," Andrea said. She wanted to add, "Just don't do it again," but she was too happy that he had come after all. Besides, she thought it might sound presumptuous—as if she were so positive that they would be seeing each other again.

"Ready to go?" he asked.

Andrea nodded. She had been ready since 12:30, determined that Sam would not have a chance to be alone with Bobby again.

"Then let's do it," Bobby said, steering her toward the door. He said goodnight cheerily to Sam, but Andrea did not even glance in Sam's direction.

Outside, Bobby looked at her quizzically. "Aren't you and the bartender on friendly terms?"

"Not anymore."

"What'd he do? Come on too strong?"

Andrea shook her head. "It's not worth talking about."

"Okay, then," Bobby said, grabbing her by the hand. "Let's talk about *us*."

Andrea looked into his laughing eyes and smiled herself. *Us.* He had said *us.* She was part of a couple again. *Oh, God, it had been so long.*

He took her to an after-hours bar. But the place was noisy and smoky, and after half an hour of peering at each other through the cigarette haze and trying to shout over the din of the crowd and blaring rock music, Bobby suggested that they go to his apartment.

Andrea panicked. She didn't dare refuse. That would seem prudish. But if she went with him he would want to go to bed with her. And she didn't know how to deal with that; she had only had sex once before in her life—the circumstances had been very different then. Yet she could feel something stirring inside her every time he touched her. If it was going to be anybody, she wanted it to be Bobby. . . .

"Okay," she said, not daring to look at him.

They barely spoke during the cab ride. Andrea sat in the corner staring fixedly out the window as the cab raced up Eighth Avenue, around Columbus Circle, and on up Central Park West. Bobby seemed to sense her anxiety and he took her hand and gently stroked it.

His apartment was in a nondescript building a

few blocks from Lincoln Center. Brownstones lined the rest of the block. Some had been renovated with smart, new façades; Bobby's building stuck out in the plainness of its utilitarian lines.

There was no doorman, and as Bobby let them into the lobby with his key he continued the monologue he had begun after they left the cab. "You know they filmed *West Side Story* where Lincoln Center is now," he said, pressing the button for the elevator.

"Really?" Andrea responded. Her thoughts were racing. It was an effort to concentrate on what he was saying.

"Have you ever been to Lincoln Center—to a performance, I mean?" he went on, guiding her into the elevator and pushing the button for the fourth floor.

Andrea shook her head.

"Well, we'll have to do something about that," Bobby said. "What do you like best? Ballet? Opera? The Philharmonic?"

"Oh, it all sounds wonderful," Andrea said as the elevator stopped and they got out. She hoped he wouldn't notice the rising tension in her voice.

Bobby turned to the right. "Then just leave everything to me," he said. They walked down a short hallway and halted in front of a door marked "4-F."

Bobby got out his keys. "Isn't that something?" he laughed. "Putting an old soldier like me in 4-F."

Andrea laughed—a little too brightly.

The key in the lock, Bobby glanced sideways at

her. "Hey, you're really nervous, aren't you?" he asked. "Listen, if you'd rather go somewhere else that's okay with me—"

"Oh, no," Andrea said quickly. "This is fine."

"Well, I thought it'd be easier to talk here," Bobby said, pushing the door open. He looked at Andrea again. "You sure?"

"Sure," she said emphatically.

He reached in and turned on the lights and then stood back to let Andrea enter.

For a moment, disappointment stabbed her. The apartment was . . . ordinary. Not at all the swinging bachelor pad she had fantasized for him. The furniture, a faded wingchair, an overstuffed sofa, a scattering of mismatched chairs, seemed to have been chosen haphazardly. And it was cluttered; books, magazines, and old newspapers were stacked on top of nearly every flat surface.

"Now you know how a writer lives," Bobby said wryly. "I call this style Early Thrift Shop."

Andrea smiled wanly. "I suppose it suits your needs."

"I have more important things to do with my time and money than to furnish an apartment," Bobby said, turning on the air conditioner in the front window. He plopped down on the couch and gestured to Andrea to join him.

She sat down at the opposite end. "Is that where you do your writing?" she asked, pointing to a battered steel desk in the corner. It was piled high with reams of paper. A streamlined electric typewriter sat in the center of it.

Bobby nodded. "Guess that gives you some idea

of my values. The typewriter is the only thing in this apartment that's worth anything—except for the TV and the stereo system."

The television set, directly across from the couch, was an expensive Japanese color model. Above it, on a shelf, was the stereo system—it didn't look cheap either.

"I'd play some music," Bobby said, "but my amplifier's broken—can't even listen to the radio."

"That's okay," Andrea said. "I'd really rather just talk."

"Got any particular subject in mind?"

"No, I—uh, not really." Andrea lowered her eyes and was dismayed to see that her palms had left sweat marks on her skirt where she had been unconsciously gripping her knees. She leaned forward, glancing sideways at Bobby. "What was that you said before about being a soldier?" she asked, catching his eye so she could unobtrusively wipe her moist hands off by rubbing them against her bare calves.

"Yeah, that's right," Bobby said. "Once upon a time I was an officer and a gentleman."

"In what—the Army?"

"Yep." He frowned. "But I wasn't in it for long. The Army and I had a parting of the ways. I never even saw any action . . ." His voice trailed off and he looked away.

Andrea took advantage of the moment to sneak a glance at her lap again. She was relieved to see the sweat stains were drying.

"Hey," Bobby said, rousing himself. "I'm sorry I

drifted off like that. You should've poked me to wake me up."

"Oh, are you tired?" Andrea said. *God, she must be boring him.* "Maybe I'd better go." She started to get up.

Bobby's arm shot out and pulled her back, closer to him. "I'm not tired at all," he laughed. "I told you I took a nap earlier."

"But don't you have to get up to go to work in the morning?" Andrea was hardly aware of what she was saying, his touch and the nearness of his body were fogging her brain.

"Yeah, sure. But that's no problem. I can come in late if I want to."

"That sounds a lot better than my job. If I'm late, I get docked. What do you do, anyway?"

"Not much." He gave a short laugh. "But it pays well. That's about all I can say for it."

"But what do you *do*?" Andrea wondered why he was being so evasive about his job. He had been that way last night, too.

Bobby shifted his eyes. "I'm, uh, managing editor on a trade magazine."

"What's a trade magazine?"

"A publication directed at the people in a single industry—it's not sold to consumers."

"Oh, so I couldn't go out and buy a copy of your magazine then?"

"Not unless you became a supermarket manager."

"A *what*?"

Bobby looked vaguely apologetic. "That's who my magazine is for—I mean *whom*. Got to watch my grammar, it's a function of mine as an arbiter of editorial rectitude."

Andrea thought briefly that he might be making fun of her, trying to talk over her head. Well, that was pretty easy to do.

"No more talk of my job, please," Bobby said. "I have enough of it eight hours a day. Why don't we talk about you?"

"Me? I'm not very interesting."

"Whah ma'am, how kin you say a thang lahk that?" Bobby drawled, dropping to his knees dramatically. He took Andrea's hand in a mock gallant gesture, "Thass jus' not true at all—quite the contrary in mah humble opinion."

Caught off-guard, Andrea at first recoiled from Bobby's play-acting. But then she felt inspired. If he was going to try his hand at acting then she would just have to show him how much better she was at that particular game. *Scarlett O'Hara, eat your heart out.* She lowered her eyelids and fluttered her lashes. "Whah, suh," she said, magnolia blossoms in her voice, "how kahnd of y'all to take notice of l'il ol' me." And then she pouted, "Whah, Ah do declare! You're turnin' mah haid."

Bobby roared and rocked back on his heels. "That was pretty good," he said, "for a Yankee. Except you made one mistake. It'd be a dead giveaway—you could never pass for a Southern belle."

"Why not? What'd I do wrong?"

" 'Y'all' is never used in the singular. It's plural, it means 'you all' collectively. Any *true* Southerner knows that."

"Well, I'll have to remember that next time I'm in the South."

Bobby stood up. "Listen, I've got just the thing to give you a real taste of the South—right here." He made for a doorway at the far end of the room. Andrea could make out some kitchen fixtures beyond it.

"What's that?" she asked playfully. "Grits?"

"Oh, ho," Bobby said, spinning around. "Making fun of Southern cooking now, are you? Just for that I ought to force you to eat a bunch of chitlins."

"*What?* I've never heard of them."

Bobby's eyes gleamed mischievously. "Oh, they're a great delicacy. I'll have to make them for you some time."

Andrea didn't say anything. She hoped he couldn't see on her face how pleased she was at all these plans he was making for their future.

"Actually," Bobby said, starting for the kitchen again, "I thought we might have a bit of Jack Daniel's. Do you like it?"

"I've never had it before."

Bobby disappeared through the doorway. "A Jack Daniel's virgin, eh?" he said as he came back, carrying the bottle of whiskey and two shot glasses.

Andrea started at the word "virgin." Just for a second, he seemed to be studying her to see what effect it had made. Did he think she was a virgin? Was it possible she appeared to be *that* innocent?

Bobby sat down beside her and poured out the two shot glasses; he handed one to Andrea. "This is the way we drink it down home," he said, putting the glass to his lips and tossing the golden liquid down in a single swallow.

Andrea was appalled. Even though she served it to her customers all the time she barely liked the taste of liquor and had never drunk it straight before. Besides, it was so unfeminine to drink it that way. "I don't know," she said. "Can't I at least have some water with it?"

Bobby shook his head. "Just sip it a little. If you don't like it you don't have to drink it."

Andrea brought the glass to her mouth. Even the fumes of the alcohol seemed overpowering to her. How could anybody drink this stuff? She looked at Bobby and he smiled back at her, so she took as small a sip as she dared with his eyes watching her. The bourbon burned her mouth slightly, but by the time it got to her throat it just felt warm. "Hey, that's actually not bad," she said, surprised.

Bobby chuckled. "You know, you have potential. You just might make it as an honorary Southerner yet."

Andrea smiled and took a few more sips. She discovered that the faster she let the whiskey go through her mouth the less it burned. And she liked the way it made her feel: a little less nervous about being alone with Bobby, more relaxed and talkative—even a little bit sexy.

She decided she wanted to know more about him. "If you love the South so much, why did you leave it?" she suddenly asked, startling herself with the boldness of her question.

Bobby seemed somewhat taken aback, too. He

turned away from her momentarily and reached for the bottle. "I had to," he said ominously, pouring for them both.

Puzzled, Andrea did not even notice he had taken her glass to refill it. She was afraid to ask what he meant. What was he running away from? The law? Creditors?

Bobby laughed at the expression on her face. "It's not as bad as what you're thinking," he said, downing his shot. He poured himself another and emptied it again. "Actually, it's rather prosaic: I had to get away from the clutches of my wife."

Married! Andrea gulped at her own drink. Oh, God, she should have known—all this was too good to be true.

Bobby's eyes were on her. "But she's going to be my ex-wife very soon—if everything goes right," he said.

"I see," Andrea murmured, looking away.

"No, you don't," Bobby said. He put a hand under her chin and turned her face toward him, forcing her to look into his eyes. "I wanted you to know the truth. I didn't want to lead you on, because—for the present at least—I am a married man."

He held her face there for a moment longer and then let it go.

Andrea's eyes dropped to her empty glass. "Do you have any kids?"

"Yes. One—a daughter. She's three."

"Where is she?"

"With my wife. In North Carolina."

"How often do you see her?"

"I don't—I haven't seen her in over a year. Sometimes I'm afraid I'll never see her again."

"Why?"

Bobby reached for the bottle. "Because of the way things are between my wife and me. It's going to be a very bitter divorce. And if my wife doesn't get what she wants she may run off with my daughter someplace where I can't find them."

"But—but how could she do that?" Andrea burst out. "It's so awful!"

Bobby laughed mirthlessly as he poured himself another drink and drained the glass. "Believe me, Cynthia is capable of that—and worse."

Andrea looked at him, horrified. "What kind of woman *is* she?"

Bobby shook his head. "I really don't know. She's changed so. When I married her she was the sweetest little thing. . . . Now, I don't even recognize her as the same person. She's become hard— the proverbial bitch. And I don't understand why—"

Outside in the street a siren wailed, drowning out Bobby's voice as it passed under the window. "Hear that?" he said as it faded off down the block. "The song of the city. Somebody got knifed or mugged or beat up his wife. Can't blame the poor joker, not if he found her in bed with another man—like I did."

From somewhere deep within her Andrea felt a long-damped fire flare up: it was as if Bobby's betrayal were her own. Without thinking she found herself reaching out her hand to touch his arm, to let him know that she understood his pain.

Bobby put his hand over hers. "I can still see them," he said in a hollow voice. "I close my eyes and they're still—"

"No, don't." Andrea put down her glass and took the empty one out of his hand and set it beside hers. She leaned toward him. "Don't torture yourself like that."

"We were so happy," Bobby went on ruefully. "Jennifer was born and it seemed like we had everything. Then Cynthia just seemed to change—and she went and spoiled it all. Broke up our little family . . ." His eyes misted over and he covered them with his free hand.

Andrea could feel the terrible tension within him. She knew there was nothing she could do, yet she wanted to show him more than lukewarm sympathy; so, quivering with her own audacity, she brushed her lips against his cheek.

Bobby pulled his hand away from his eyes. "Is that because you feel sorry for me?"

Andrea slowly shook her head. "No. It's because I wanted to."

Bobby said nothing. His eyes fixed on hers. Then, trembling, he took her face in both his hands and gradually, hypnotically, leaned forward to kiss her.

When his lips touched hers, Andrea felt as if she had found something that had been lost a long, long time. There was something so familiar about the way Bobby kissed her, and she found herself matching the intensity of his kiss as it mounted, as his tongue probing her mouth became more passionate, more demanding. There would be no stopping now. Once more, she could give herself—completely.

Soon they were lying on the couch, their bodies entwined, her clothing heaped on the floor. The world was gone, left behind as they explored one another as if each were a new planet the other had just discovered.

Bobby's hands were all over her, building her excitement to such a feverish pitch that his very touch felt like fire. She longed to feel his flesh against hers, his mouth crushing hers, then moving downward, to touch the hollow of her throat, and kiss her bared breasts.

She moaned as his tongue flicked back and forth across her erect nipples. Each stroke echoed through her entire body.

She felt herself losing control, as if she were exploding inside. "Please, please," she gasped out. "Do it now. I can't wait. *Please!*"

Bobby drew back and looked at her. Then, seeing the desperate longing written on her face, he stood up and unzipped his jeans. "Are you protected?" he asked.

Andrea did not hear him. She was staring at his swollen penis, her mouth agape. "What?" she said, confused. "Yes, yes. It's okay. Please just do it. I can't stand it any longer." Her arms were reaching out to him, grabbing his legs, pulling him on top of her.

Then he was inside her and she wanted him to stay there—forever. With each thrust she groaned and sighed as her feeling of fulfillment doubled and redoubled. . . .

But suddenly something was wrong. Instead of pleasure she felt pain—sharp pain in her chest. It was stabbing her, cutting off her air so she could not cry out. Just when she thought she was surely going to die, merciful blackness engulfed her. . . .

Bobby rolled from the couch onto the floor, pleased with his conquest and utterly spent. After a moment he glanced up at her. She was lying still, eyes closed, chest rising and falling regularly. She looked on the verge of sleep. The skin around her mouth and chin was still red from his bruising kisses.

She had been a surprise to him—a very pleasant surprise. She would be good for him—it had been so long since he had had a woman appreciate him in bed that much.

"Hey, Red," he said softly. "Don't fall asleep on me. If you want to stay here, let's go into the bedroom."

No response.

"Red?" Bobby said, rising up on his elbow and jiggling her arm.

Still no reply, not even a movement.

Bobby sat up, suddenly worried. Now he could see that she was unnaturally still, too quiet for just having gone through a violent sex act.

"My God." He stood over her, shaking her, gently slapping her face. Then her eyelids fluttered, and he sighed in relief.

"Red, come on, wake up."

Andrea opened her eyes and stared blankly at

him. "Whad you say?" she asked, her speech heavily slurred.

"My God, what happened? Did you black out?"

Andrea looked dazed. "Guess so," she said dully.

"Has that ever happened to you before?" Bobby asked, sitting down on the edge of the couch.

Andrea passed a hand over her eyes. "Yes," she said. "Too many times."

"What causes them—it's not sex, is it?"

Andrea smiled weakly. "No, it's not sex. Nobody knows what it is. I've been checked out by a lot of doctors and they could never find anything wrong."

"But can't you take something to prevent it?"

"Not really," Andrea sighed. "Usually I have a warning, though. I get a sharp pain in the chest and I know that in a few seconds I'll probably pass out. Sometimes, though, I get the chest pain without blacking out."

Bobby nodded, as if to signal her that he understood. But he didn't understand at all. He had always found physical handicaps somewhat repulsive—not that Andrea's was that obvious. But what could it be—some kind of epilepsy? Such a shame, she was really so sweet. Too bad she was flawed.

CHAPTER FOUR

That night Andy came back. Just as Andrea had known he would. He came walking toward her, smiling, his arms open. She hesitated briefly, just to make sure that it really was Andy, then ran to him, tears of happiness coursing down her cheeks.

They embraced and kissed, and she knew that he had forgiven her. Life was beautiful again.

But after several minutes Andy started to pull away from her.

"No!" Andrea cried, clutching at him. "Don't go. Don't leave me again!"

"I'm not leaving you," Andy said, shaking her off. "I can't. I'm inside you, I'm a part of you. How can I ever leave you?"

Andrea started to protest, but Andy silenced her. And then he held out his hand, his index finger extended, and touched the tip of it to her chest—just above her left breast.

At the moment of contact Andrea screamed—for Andy's body had turned vapory and distorted, like a figure dimly seen in flickering candlelight.

"No! Andy, come back!" she cried, reaching out for the image that was becoming more and more indistinct.

Then a faraway voice was calling to her. "Wake up! Wake up! You're having a bad dream. *Wake up!*"

"What?" Andrea opened her eyes to see Bobby leaning over her, his face creased with concern. She blinked at him. He smiled. "Sorry, kid. I'm not Andy—whoever he is."

Andrea was glad that in the semidarkness Bobby could not see the flush that spread across her cheeks. "Oh, did I call out for him?" she asked, willing her voice to sound nonchalant.

"You sure did. Are you okay now?"

"Yeah, I'm fine."

"Sure?"

"Sure."

"Who is this Andy, anyway? Someone I should be jealous of?"

"Not anymore."

"Mmm," Bobby murmured, kissing her shoulder. "Now how should I take that?"

Andrea turned to face him, letting her breasts press against his hard-muscled chest. "What do you mean?"

Bobby threw his arm across her and playfully ran his hand up and down her back, sending tingles of delight along the length of her spine. "Well, should I take it to mean that this guy's part of your past—or that he will be now that you've met me?"

Already, Andrea had forgotten about the dream. All she was aware of was the reality of Bobby's flesh melting into hers. "Take it any way you like," she sighed, bringing her mouth up to meet Bobby's.

After that, Bobby became Andrea's favorite pastime. When she wasn't at work she was with Bobby, usually at his place, sometimes at hers, and most of their time they spent in bed. It was as though she could not see him enough, touch him enough, feel his body close enough to hers.

One night, after they'd made love again and again, Bobby lay dozing, but Andrea was wide awake, her passion still aroused. She lay quietly on her side for several minutes, watching Bobby sleep. His mouth was slightly open, and she took her finger and traced the outline of his lips. Then, as he began to stir, she dropped her hand to his chest, rubbing back and forth across it in ever-descending movements. When she reached the hard flatness of his belly, Bobby's eyes opened. He groaned and pulled her to him. "You little nymphomaniac," he said, laughing. "You know you're killing me."

Andrea froze in his arms. His words were frivolous but they held a sinister meaning for her. "Don't say that—" she began but broke off as a shaft of unexpected pain shot through her. Her right hand automatically flew to her chest, with her left hand she grabbed at Bobby.

"What's wrong?" he cried, crouching over her. "Are you going to black out?"

Her head tossed back and forth on the pillow. "Don't think so," she gasped. Then the pain began to subside, and she closed her eyes and breathed deeply.

Bobby ran his hand soothingly across her forehead. "God, you scare me sometimes," he said. "These attacks, they're not right. You should do something about them."

Andrea opened her eyes. "Like what? I've already told you that lots of doctors have checked me out. They can't find anything wrong with me."

"Well, maybe you haven't been to the right doctors."

Andrea's eyes narrowed as she stared up at him. "You think I should go to a psychiatrist, don't you?"

Bobby studied her a moment. "No, not a shrink," he said pointedly. Then his voice softened. "But, baby, some of the best doctors in the world are here in New York—maybe you should go to one of them."

Andrea relaxed and she sighed. "The problem is those fancy specialists cost a lot of money."

"What about your mother? Wouldn't she give you the money?"

Andrea gave him a scornful look. "Are you kidding? I wouldn't ask that bitch for a dime!"

Bobby leaned back and propped himself up on an elbow. "That's a pretty harsh way to talk about your mother," he said. "Why do you hate her so much?"

"I don't hate her!" Andrea said vehemently. Then she added in a more subdued tone, "I just don't like her very much."

"Why? Because she got married again after your father died?"

Andrea frowned. "I suppose that's part of it, but my mother and I were on the outs long before that."

"I guess that happens a lot. Mothers and daughters sometimes just don't get along."

Andrea shook her head. "No, it was more than that with us." She wanted Bobby to *know*. "I-I did something that my mother never forgot—or forgave," she said. *And neither did I,* she added silently.

"Want to tell me what it was?" Bobby's voice was full of compassion.

Andrea stared into Bobby's brown eyes—so attentive, so caring. Would they still look at her in the same way if she told him the truth—that she had killed her own brother?

She didn't dare risk it—not yet. "I can't," she said. "Not now. Maybe someday. It's still too painful for me to talk about—even after all these years." She averted her eyes so he wouldn't see the tears welling up in them.

Bobby said nothing for several minutes. Then he drew her to him and put his arms around her. "My poor darlin'," he said soothingly. "You've had a hard life, haven't you? But that's all over now—you've got me to take care of you. And I'm going to do just that. So tomorrow you go back to your apartment and get the rest of your things and bring them over here."

Andrea pulled back and gave him a searching look. "You want me to move in with you?"

"Sure, why not? You're practically living here now, anyway. The only time you go to your own apartment is to change your clothes for work. It seems kind of silly, doesn't it?" He paused, then added slyly, "Unless you think there's something morally wrong in living with a man."

Andrea smiled at him. "No, how could I think that? Only I've never done it before."

"Then it'll be a new experience for you. How about it?"

Andrea snuggled back into Bobby's arms. "Okay. I'll tell my landlord tomorrow that I'm moving out."

"Mmm, why don't you hold off on that for a while?" Bobby said. "Don't worry, I'll pay your rent. But until my divorce is final it might be better for you to have your own address. That way my wife can't accuse us of living together. Is that all right, darlin'?"

"Of course," Andrea said. "I understand—you've got to be careful." But Bobby couldn't see the frown on her face. That awful wife of his—she could hardly wait until the day Bobby was rid of her once and for all.

Andrea looked around Bobby's apartment—*their* apartment now. She smiled with pride at what she saw. In the weeks since she had moved in with him she had done her best to turn it into a real home.

Bobby had told her repeatedly how pleased he was with her efforts, and even she thought she had outdone herself.

She had waxed and polished the floors and furniture until they fairly gleamed. Bobby's books and magazines now lined shelves she had put up on the walls, and the old newspapers had been thrown out. A collection of thriving, green plants adorned the windowsills or were hanging in ceramic pots. Bobby had helped her pick out several pictures for the walls and their real treasure, an antique mirror with a carved, wooden frame, hung over the couch. With a used sewing machine Bobby had bought her, she had even made a paisley slipcover for the wing chair with matching window curtains and pillows for the couch.

This morning she had done the laundry. All Bobby's underwear and socks were now neatly folded in his bureau drawers and his carefully ironed shirts were hanging in the closet. She had spent much of the afternoon chopping vegetables and browning the meat for a thick beef stew. It was in a dish in the refrigerator now, along with a tossed salad, and all Bobby would have to do when he got home from work was heat it up. His place was already set at the dining room table. There were fresh, fall flowers on the table, too, which she had dashed out at the last minute to buy from the corner florist.

Andrea glanced around the apartment once again, and decided there was nothing she had overlooked. Then she grabbed a scrap of paper from Bobby's desk and penciled quickly, "Hope you

like the stew. See you later. I love you. Andrea."
She left the note by Bobby's plate and hurried out
the door, determined not to be late for her job at
the Center Stage.

As she walked toward the subway stop she
thought about how easily she had written the
words "I love you." Oh, yes, she loved Bobby—and
he *said* he loved her. And she believed him—most
of the time. But she still had her moments of
doubt. Not because of anything *he* did, but because of her own fears. She was afraid of happiness,
afraid that it would be snatched away from her as
it had been before. Bobby loved her now, but
would it last? No, it was too much to hope for. All
her hopes and dreams had been lost forever. They
had bled to death on a rock in her father's
meadow.

She had still not told Bobby about that black
moment that had blotted out so many years. She
couldn't be sure that if she told him it would not
spread its bloodied stain into their future.

He had not pried much into her past, and when
he did she talked about the farm and small-town
Wisconsin life. Whenever he mentioned college
she deflected his questions, got him to talk about
his own college days, anything to keep him from
zeroing in on the fact that for her there had been
no football games or proms or graduations—only
endless hours with psychiatrists, group therapy, su-
pervised recreation.

Once, Bobby had asked her if she had brothers
and sisters. Andrea had been prepared for that.
Coolly, she responded that she'd had a brother; he

had been killed in a shooting accident. Bobby had been sympathetic and sensitive. He had not asked her any more about it.

He, on the other hand, seemed eager to talk about his past. She knew all the secrets of his parents and two older sisters and many more about his neighbors in the North Carolina town where he had grown up. He was completely open with her on the subject of his marriage and even seemed to enjoy discussing it with her. Andrea felt flattered by that; surely the breakup of his marriage had been the most painful thing that had ever happened to him, and yet he was willing to share it with her, to expose this still-tender scar to her scrutiny.

They were talking about his marriage one evening, when Bobby suddenly broke off the conversation.

Andrea grew increasingly uncomfortable as he sat silently studying her, his face an inscrutable mask. She tried to keep on talking, but his stony silence unnerved her.

"Why are you looking at me like that?" she burst out when she could take it no more.

Bobby grinned. "Does it bother you?"

Andrea shot him a look of annoyance and started to get up from the couch, but Bobby pulled her back down. "Hey, don't go away mad," he said. "I didn't mean to play games with you."

"Then what *are* you trying to do?" Andrea asked testily. When Bobby tried to put his arm around her shoulders she twisted away.

"Aw, Red," he teased. "I'll bet you wouldn't be

so upset if you knew what I was thinking about."

Andrea's lower lip pouted. "I don't want to know."

"Oh, I think you do, darlin'."

"All right, then. What?" she demanded, but the anger in her voice was put on for Bobby's benefit.

"Well, I don't want to tell you just like this," Bobby said. He reached over to the lamp beside the couch and switched it to a lower setting so that the light was more diffused, casting soft shadows over them both. "There. That's better." He encircled Andrea with his arms and tenderly kissed her cheek.

She smiled back at him expectantly.

"Darlin', you know how I feel about you," he began. His face was only inches from hers and Andrea was thrilled to see what looked like adoration in his eyes; she wanted this moment to go on forever, for Bobby to look at her that way on into eternity.

"I'm not very good at this." His voice sounded strange, unnatural. He suddenly seemed so ill at ease, and Andrea couldn't tell if he was sincere or only acting. "I really don't know how to say this." He hesitated, then gulped, "Well, I might as well get it over with—"

Andrea felt a roaring in her head. *Get it over with!* That could only mean one thing: *he's going to leave me!* Deep inside her she screamed silently. *I knew it was too good to last! That's not adoration in his eyes, that's pity!* She could still see Bobby's mouth moving, but she had willed herself not to hear the words.

Then she felt him gently shaking her, asking her, "Well, what about it, Red? What do you say?"

Andrea looked at him warily. "About what?"

Bobby slapped the palm of his hand against his head. "Shit! You mean you haven't been listening to me?"

Andrea lowered her eyes. "Guess not."

Bobby tipped her chin up so she could not avoid looking straight at him. "You little ninny," he laughed. "I was asking you to marry me."

Bobby kissed her speechless mouth. "I hope this doesn't mean that you're turning me down," he said with a mock sigh.

"No! B-But what—*how*?" Andrea sputtered.

"Wait," Bobby chuckled. "You're getting ahead of me. First you have to say yes, and then I'll tell you how."

"Yes! Yes!" Andrea cried. "You already knew what my answer would be!"

"Mmm, guess I did," Bobby drawled.

"But what about your divorce?" Andrea gasped out. "Did it come through?"

"Well, I'm probably being a little presumptuous," Bobby hedged. "It's not final yet, but I talked to my lawyer today and it looks like it's going to happen any day now. A few weeks at most."

Andrea threw her arms around him in a bear hug. "I can't believe it, it's so wonderful!"

"You'd better believe it, hon," Bobby said, pulling her left arm from around him. " 'Cause pretty soon I'm going to be putting a ring on this finger," he wiggled her ring finger, "and you're going to be Mrs. Wilson."

"Mrs. Wilson. Mrs. Andrea Wilson," Andrea repeated slowly, her mouth closing carefully around the words, savoring them as if they were a vintage wine.

For days after that, Andrea drifted in a fog. At work, she longed to tell Sam of her new happiness, but she feared his cynical reaction so she kept silent.

She briefly thought about calling her mother with the news, but decided against that, too. Maybe she'd call her after the fact: *"Hello, Mother. It's Andrea. Guess what? Your crazy daughter just got married. And you know what else? I'm not crazy anymore!"* Oh, yes, she would wait; the satisfaction that call would give her would be worth it.

She couldn't tell any of the other waitresses she was getting married. She was sure they would tell Sam. And she had no girlfriends, only some casual acquaintances she had made at auditions. There was no one she could exult to, no one to witness her triumph.

Until one morning when she stood kissing Bobby good-bye at the door as he went off to work. Out of the corner of her eye, Andrea saw a crack of light from the door to 4-C across the hall. And she was positive she could see an eye peering through the narrow space between the door and the jamb. *Busybody!* Andrea thought to herself, intending to ignore it.

But when she closed the door behind her, she had an idea. On an impulse she went into the bedroom, threw on some clothes, combed her hair, and put on a touch of lipstick. Then, eyes glinting, she strode down the hall and pushed the neighbor's doorbell.

"Who's there?" a thin, quavery voice called out. *An old lady, I knew it!* Andrea smiled to herself. "I live across the hall," she responded.

She could hear the sound of a lock being turned, and the door opened a crack. But the chain was still on and a pair of eyes peered cautiously up at her. "Oh," the small voice said, as if Andrea had just passed the test of recognition. "Just a moment."

The door shut and Andrea heard the chain being pulled off. Finally, it opened again and a gray-haired wisp of a woman, only about chest high to Andrea, stood looking expectantly up at her. "I know who you are," the woman said. "I've seen you with that young man over there." She pointed a gnarled finger toward the door of Bobby's apartment.

There was an ever-so-slight note of disapproval in her voice, but Andrea detected it immediately. She resented the implication that there was something immoral in her relationship with Bobby. She couldn't allow that. "Yes," she said, slipping her left hand into the pocket of her jeans, "we just got married."

The woman's expression softened. "How nice," she said.

Andrea did not miss the change in her tone. She

smiled. It was only a very small lie. A harmless lie.

"I wanted to introduce myself to you. I like to know my neighbors," Andrea went on, making herself sound bubbly and chatty, just as she imagined a new bride would be.

"Oh, that's lovely, dear," the woman answered. "Most people aren't like that. I've lived in this building fifteen years and I barely know another soul here."

"I don't understand that," Andrea said. "But maybe that's because I'm from out of town."

"Would you like to come in?" the woman asked, stepping back from the door. "I'll make some tea— or coffee if you like—and we can talk."

"That's very kind of you," Andrea said, moving through the door. "Tea would be fine." She felt as though she had just pulled off a small coup. This woman believed her.

The apartment was crowded with furniture—old-fashioned, ornate tables and chairs and love seats of dark wood with curved, spindly legs and heavy, brocaded upholstery. Andrea felt right at home here.

"I'm Mrs. King," the woman said as she gestured to Andrea to sit down. "And you're Mrs. — ?"

"Wilson. Andrea Wilson. My husband's name is Bobby."

Mrs. King made the tea. "Tell me," she said as she settled back with her teacup in her lap, "how long have you been married?"

Andrea smiled shyly. "Just five weeks."

"I can tell that marriage agrees with you," Mrs. King said. "You still have that glow."

Andrea felt herself starting to blush. "I didn't realize it showed that much," she said. "But I guess I've been like this ever since I met Bobby."

"Did you meet him here in the city?"

"Yes, through mutual friends."

"I see," Mrs. King said. She took a sip of tea, then asked, "Did you have a big wedding?"

"No, it was very small. Neither of us wanted anything fancy. You see, if we'd gone back to Wisconsin and had it there I would have had to invite practically everyone in town and it would have turned into a circus—and Bobby wouldn't have liked that."

"But what about your family?" Mrs. King asked. "Weren't they disappointed that you didn't come home for your wedding?"

"Well, there's only my father," Andrea said. "My mother died several years ago."

"Don't you have any brothers or sisters?"

"Oh, yes. I have a brother—but he's overseas. He couldn't make it to the wedding."

"Was your father able to come?"

"Yes. He took the train out here—he doesn't like to fly. It was a long trip, but he said it was worth every minute of it—just to be there to give me away."

"Where did you have the wedding?"

"Oh, that was the best part. Bobby has a friend who has a penthouse overlooking the Hudson River. So we had it there—in front of these huge picture windows. The sun was just setting, and the sky and the river were all pink and orange. It was breathtaking." She paused and added, "I think my father would have preferred to see me married in the Church—but, well, Bobby's not Catholic, and I haven't been to Mass in years."

Mrs. King said nothing, so Andrea went on. "We had this really terrific honeymoon, too. Bobby wouldn't even give me a hint where we were going. All he said was that I'd better pack my bathing suit. Of course, when we got to the airport he finally had to break down and tell me we were going to the Bahamas."

"How nice. I've been there several times myself. Where did you go—Nassau?"

Andrea nodded.

"Did you stay on Paradise Island?"

"Yes. Have you been there?"

"Oh, yes. Which hotel did you stay at?"

Andrea frowned as if she were trying to remember. "Gee, I really don't know. I'm not very good at names."

"Neither am I, but let me see—was it the one where the casino is?"

"Uh, yes. That's right. That's the one."

Mrs. King laughed. "The first time I was there I lost nearly all my pocket money at the slot machines. After that my husband wouldn't even take me into the casino. He said that God created slot machines for fools like me."

Andrea smiled. "That's very funny," she said. "He sounds like he has a sense of humor."

"Oh, he *did*," Mrs. King said somewhat wistfully. "He was a wonderful husband. He's been dead nearly eleven years, and I still miss him terribly."

Andrea didn't know quite what to say. She cradled her teacup in her hands and then looked up to see Mrs. King staring at her naked left hand. Mrs. King's eyes quickly shifted away. "Would you like some more tea, dear?" she asked.

"Oh, no, thank you," Andrea said. "I've really got to be going. I've got so many chores left to do." She set down her teacup with her left hand and, as she drew it back, looked at it and laughed. "Now isn't that silly of me?" she said. "I took my wedding ring off to do the breakfast dishes and I forgot to put it back on. I guess I'm still not used to wearing it yet."

Mrs. King smiled indulgently at her. "All new brides do things like that."

"Well, this new bride had better get home," Andrea said. She stood up to go. "Thank you for the tea. I've enjoyed talking to you so much. I just hope I haven't kept you from anything."

"Oh, no, not at all, dear," Mrs. King said, walking her to the door. "It's been my pleasure. I have so little company these days. Please come and see me again."

"Oh, I will," Andrea said. She walked across the hall to her own apartment and dreamily closed the door behind her. The wedding in the penthouse, the honeymoon in the Bahamas—how gloriously real they had all seemed. Real enough to believe in.

CHAPTER FIVE

"Listen, kid, I've got to talk to you."

"Oh?" Andrea turned and regarded Sam with her most disdainful look.

"Yeah. I do," Sam said, holding his own against her withering gaze. "It's important."

"Well, I can't talk now, I'm already late, and I've got customers waiting for me." Andrea jerked her head in the direction of a corner table, where a middle-aged couple, out-of-towners, sat; the man was furiously signaling for her attention.

"No, not now," Sam said quickly as Andrea started to walk away from him. "What I'm goin' to tell you will take a little time, and I don't wanna be rushed."

Andrea shot him a glance out of the corner of her eye without breaking her stride. She didn't like the ominous note in Sam's voice. That could mean only one of two things: she was about to lose her job or he wanted to warn her again about Bobby.

She worked through the next few hours, her body going through the motions while her mind was busy trying to figure out what Sam could have to say to her. She wanted to prepare herself. If it was the job—hell, it wasn't such a great job, anyway.

But if Sam intended to badmouth Bobby to her again, well, she'd shut him up plenty fast. After those first few times he had stopped trying to talk her out of seeing Bobby. But even though he had played it cool, she could see the resentment burning in his eyes each time Bobby came to pick her up.

Finally, the evening wore on and the crowd started to thin out, and Andrea could no longer ignore Sam's meaningful glances. She checked to make sure that her last few customers didn't need anything, then marched over to where Sam was standing at the bar.

"Let's get this over with," she said, doing her best to sound unconcerned. "What is it you want to talk to me about?"

Sam gave her a long, dubious gaze before he spoke. "Well, kid," he said at last, "what I have to tell you is gonna hurt." He let out a sigh. "Maybe you think I like doin' this but, believe me, I don't. It's about your boyfriend."

Andrea's heart lurched. *No!* She would not let Sam see that he had already gotten to her. "Really," she said, raising her eyebrows and hoping she looked sardonic and sophisticated. "I doubt that anything you could tell me would have the power to hurt me."

Sam shook his head gently. "Don't try to pull that shit with me, hon," he said, his voice deadly soft. "I can see right through it." His eyes were dark and fathomless.

Andrea averted her gaze, reining her temper. It was a war of nerves and she knew she had already lost to Sam. But she wasn't about to acknowledge his victory.

"Look, let me get right to the point," Sam continued, reaching for her arm. "I've been doin' some checkin' up on your boyfriend Bobby."

Andrea jerked her arm out of his grasp. "Whatever it is I don't want to hear it!" she hissed at Sam, muffling the sound of her voice, but not the venom in it. "It's probably all a pack of lies, anyway," she added, more to quell the rising knot of fear in her own stomach than to silence Sam.

"I'm not the one who's been lying," Sam said. His voice was level, but his eyes held an odd mixture of reluctance and triumph.

Andrea bit her lip, afraid to speak. She knew that if she tried to say the words, to deny the truth of what Sam had just said, her voice might crack, revealing to Sam how deeply he had cut her.

Sam waited for her to speak, watching her carefully. When she didn't respond, he leaned closer across the bar. "Remember what he told me about that book of his?" he asked.

Andrea shrugged and took a step back from the bar. "Sure," she said. Of course, she remembered. Bobby had just told her last week that a top publisher was on the verge of buying his book. A movie studio was interested, too—his agent was just holding out for the right price. And he had already promised her that when it was sold he'd quit his job and take her on a trip to Europe—their honeymoon. It was only a matter of time before the negotiations were complete. "What about it?" she asked, hoping her voice sounded casual. But her heart was beating wildly. Had Sam found out about the book deal? It was possible—he did know a lot of agents.

"Well, he told me that William Morris was handling him."

"That's right," Andrea said, letting her chin jut out a little.

Sam fixed his eyes on her. "I had my friend at William Morris check him out. They never heard of him."

Andrea exhaled sharply. "It's some kind of mistake."

Sam shook his head. "No. My friend is a real thorough guy. I'm telling you, no one there has ever heard of Bobby Wilson."

Andrea felt herself go cold. The jukebox was playing, and she forced her mind to zero in on the song. She couldn't recognize the singer, but it sounded as though he was saying, "You lied to me. You lied to me." Although she knew every song in the jukebox, she had never heard this one before. She had a fleeting sense of *déjà vu*, an image that flickered across her vision, then vanished; an odd sense of having seen and heard it all before. But it was cut short by a needle of pain in her chest. She faltered and felt Sam's strong hand grasping her shoulder.

"Are you all right?" he asked, his voice full of concern.

"Yeah. Sure," she said, hating the weakness of her own body, how it had betrayed her to Sam.

She shook off his hand and slid onto a barstool, all the while avoiding the curiosity in Sam's eyes.

He brought her a glass of water. As she drank it she wondered vaguely why water was always supposed to help people who've just had an emotional upset; it sure wasn't helping her.

Watching her, Sam tugged fitfully at his beard. "I'm really sorry I shook you up like that," he said. "But I figured you ought to know the truth."

Andrea slammed the glass down on the bar. "Truth!" she nearly shouted. Then, in a whisper: "Why should I believe you? Maybe *you're* the one who's lying."

Sam shrugged. "I could give you my friend's name at William Morris and you could call him up, but better yet"—he paused dramatically—"why don't you ask your boyfriend who's telling the truth?"

Andrea stepped off the barstool and drew herself up to her full height. "I think I'll do that," she said. "And then we'll just see who's the liar around here."

She waited until Johnny Carson had finished his monologue. It was her night off and they had spent a quiet evening at home. During the commercial she asked Bobby if it was all right for her to turn the TV off, she wanted to talk to him about something.

"Sure," he said, barely bothering to stifle a yawn. "I want to get to bed early tonight, anyway."

"What I have to ask you won't take a minute," Andrea said, trying to sound offhand as she got up to turn off the television. She watched the picture telescope to a single white line that finally disappeared, then she caught her breath and turned around. "Bobby, honey," she began, hearing the false cheer in her voice mocking the real affection she was trying to put into her words. What was she so afraid of?

Bobby swiftly lifted his eyes from the magazine he had picked up. "What is it, Red?"

Damn! His guard was up already. She had blown it. Now, no matter what she said it was going to sound like an accusation. She waved her hand aimlessly in the air. "Oh, it's nothing really. Just something Sam told me. I'm sure he got it wrong."

Bobby's eyes narrowed. "Sam? What's that old lecher been telling you?"

Andrea tried to laugh, but it stuck in her throat. Might as well come out with it. "He said he asked someone at William Morris about you, and they told him they'd never heard of you."

For a breathless moment the words seemed to hang in the air. Then Bobby suddenly vaulted from the couch, his arm swinging in an arc. Andrea took the full force of his blow on her cheek, and staggered back against the television set. She

grabbed out at the TV for support and by chance
hit the switch that turned it on. As she crumpled
to her knees, the sound of uproarious laughter
filled the room.

Bobby bent over her, his face twisted, his eyes
wild with rage. "You've been spying on me! You
and that scumbag, Sam!" He punched the television controls, killing the laughter.

Andrea pressed her hand to her burning cheek.
The pain confirmed what her mind could not
comprehend: she had never been struck by a man
before—only Andy, and that was when they were
children. Now she did not know how to react; she
was too stunned to cry, too confused to be angry.
"No, Bobby," she whimpered. "I didn't have anything to do with it."

"Like hell, you didn't." He was standing over
her, glowering at her. "Why would Sam do a thing
like that on his own?"

"I don't know." It was a whisper.

"Don't tell me that! He wouldn't do it without
good reason—and you know what it is, you bitch!"
He grabbed her roughly by the shoulders and began shaking her.

"No! Bobby, don't—please, you're hurting me—"

"What is it? Why is Sam out to get me?" Bobby
insisted. He stopped shaking her, but instead of
letting her go he dug his fingers into her flesh.

Andrea stared at him, transfixed. His face was
only scant inches from hers, and she could see an
artery throbbing spasmodically in his temple. She
had never witnessed such fury in a human being
before, and the suddenness with which it had ex-

ploded frightened her almost as much as the rage itself. "Please, Bobby, let me go," she begged.

He dug his fingers deeper into her arm. "Not until you tell me about Sam."

The pain was so intense that Andrea was not aware she had begun to cry until she tried to speak and found her throat constricted. "S-Sam doesn't like you," she gasped. "He wants me to break up with you."

Bobby uncurled his fingers from her flesh, but held her stiffly at arm's length. "Why?" he sneered. "So he can stick it to you himself?"

Andrea closed her eyes and let her head drop limply to her chest. "No. He thinks you're going to hurt me, that you're no good for me."

Bobby let her go and stood up abruptly. "What a bunch of bullshit! That guy is just dying to get into your pants—I can see it on his face every time he looks at you." He laughed to himself. "I should have known he'd pull a stunt like this—he's the type that'd stoop to anything."

Andrea lifted her head slowly to look at Bobby. He seemed to have forgotten she was there and was staring at the wall, smiling to himself and nodding slowly—as if she had just confirmed some secret knowledge that he alone knew.

She covered her eyes with her hands and wept silently, afraid to make any noise that would draw his attention to her again. She was already planning what she would have to do: pack her things and take a cab back to her own apartment. She and Bobby were finished; that was clear. But what wasn't clear was *why*. What had she done to make him hate her so? For that was what she had read in his eyes when he attacked her—sheer hatred. Never, never in her life had anyone looked at her that way before. Not even her mother. . . .

"Red?" Bobby's voice was surprisingly gentle and his hand was tenderly stroking her hair. She quivered at his touch.

"What?" she sobbed, not taking her hands from her eyes or raising her head in response.

"I'm sorry." Then he was on his knees in front of her, his arms around her, his lips kissing the backs of her hands, the top of her head. "Oh, God. I'm sorry," he moaned. "Did I hurt you? No, don't say it. I know I did. I . . . I—" his voice was cracking, "I don't know what got into me. I couldn't stop myself. Please, *please*, forgive me. It'll never happen again."

Andrea pulled her hands from her eyes and gaped at him. How could he be saying these things to her now? Wasn't he the same man who had struck her only minutes before?

There were tears in Bobby's eyes. "Oh, honey," he cried, "I know how hard it is for you to believe this after what I just did—but I love you." His voice died to a whisper. "I love you so much."

The pain in his eyes made her see that he was really sincere, and the image of that other side of Bobby—the Bobby who had hit her and hurt her and hated her so much—his image had already begun to disappear from her mind.

She let him kiss her on the lips—a long, plaintive kiss—and then closed her eyes while he kissed her tears away.

"Bobby," she said finally, opening her eyes to study his face, "What happened? Why did you get so mad at me?"

Bobby pulled back, his hands covering his face, his head jerking from side to side. "I don't know," he choked out. "I don't know what came over me." He dissolved into sobs.

Andrea put her hand out to comfort him, stroking his head, the veins standing out on the backs of his hands, the mark on his wristbone.

When Bobby's spasm of self-recrimination passed, he uncovered his face and wiped away the tears. Bloodshot and red-rimmed, his eyes sought Andrea's. "No, Red," he said huskily, "I *do* know why I did that to you." He paused and his eyes slid away from hers. "Jealousy. Nothing but jealousy. I couldn't stand it when I thought you'd take Sam's word over mine."

"But I *didn't*," Andrea protested. "I just told you what he said—that's all."

Bobby's eyes came back to hers. They were full of hurt again. "But you believed him enough to ask me about it, didn't you?"

"No! No, I didn't—"

"*He's* the one who's no good for you, Red. He sees that you're happy with me, and he can't stand that so he tries to break us up by making you think I've been lying to you!" Bobby shook his head. "He's a bad influence on you, darlin'. I think maybe you'd better quit that job."

"But Sam's been so kind to me. And I can't just quit—"

"Sure you can. Call them tomorrow and tell

them you won't be coming back. They can send
your check to you so you won't have to go in there
and see Sam—ever again."

"But what'll I do for money?"

"For now, I can take care of you. And then you
can start looking for another job. There are plenty
of places in this neighborhood where you should
be able to get one."

"Well, I don't know—"

"Sure you do. It's all settled. Call tomorrow—or
if you want *I'll* call."

"No, no. I'll call. I can't let you do *everything*
for me."

"Good. It's better that way." Bobby stood up
and pulled her up with him. "Come on, let's go to
bed. That's the best part of fighting—making up."
He gave her a winsome leer.

Andrea smiled wanly and let him lead her into
the bedroom. As they were getting into bed and
his arms wrapped around her, a thought occurred
to her. Bobby had not once actually denied the
truth of what Sam had told her. It was a trouble-
some thought. She immediately put it out of her
mind.

CHAPTER SIX

Andrea dutifully called the manager of the Center Stage the next day and told him she was quitting. She felt she owed him some excuse, so she told him she was getting out of acting and had decided to take a "straight" job as a secretary. He seemed to swallow her story and promised he would send off her check for the time she had put in that week.

She had deliberately called early in the afternoon before Sam came on. Still, she expected some kind of reaction from him when he found out she had quit her job. She wasn't surprised when the telephone started to ring the moment she walked into her own apartment later that afternoon.

Naturally, it was Sam.

"I'm amazed you've still got this place," he barked out. He hadn't bothered to say hello. "I would've thought you'd've moved in permanently with lover boy by now."

"Sam, no sarcasm or I'm going to hang up."

"Okay, okay. I just want you to tell me what the hell is going on."

"Nothing's going on. I quit. Period."

"Why?"

"Because I'm tired of being a waitress. Don't you ever get tired of being a bartender?"

"He made you do it, didn't he?"

"That's none of your business—"

"You just confirmed it."

"No, I didn't, and if you keep this up, I swear I'll hang up on you."

"Is it because you asked him about William Morris?"

"Damn it, Sam! Why can't you just give up?"

"Okay. You don't have to tell me I'm beatin' my head against the wall—"

"Then *stop* it."

"I will, I will. Only—promise me one thing."

"What?"

"That if you're ever in any trouble you'll come to me."

"I'm not planning on getting into any trouble, Sam."

"Please. I'm serious. I know you haven't got anybody else here in the city—"

"Yes, I do."

"No, you know what I mean—"

"No, I don't."

"Well, I just want you to know that no matter

what happens you can come to me—anytime. You hear that? *No matter what happens.*"

"Yes, Sam. I hear you, and I promise I will."

"All right. I won't bug you anymore, but maybe you could give me a call in a couple of months—just to let me know how you are. Or if you can't call, maybe you could drop by—"

"I will. I promise I will. I have to go now."

"I know." There was a long pause. "Well, good-bye, kid."

"Good-bye, Sam."

As Andrea put the phone back in its cradle she realized it would seem very strange not to have Sam around as her self-appointed conscience, and—oddly enough—it made her feel somewhat sad.

From that day on, the world began to shrink for Andrea. Bobby became its center and she was his satellite, spinning round and round him in a fixed orbit.

Bobby didn't seem to care too much that she couldn't find another job right away. "Don't worry about it," he'd say whenever she'd report another fruitless day of looking for work. "You'll find one eventually. These things take time."

But she couldn't tell him the truth—that she didn't really *want* to go back to work; she liked staying home and playing housewife. Yet she owed it to Bobby to at least try.

So she would force herself to go out and look for a job. There were dozens of restaurants in the area, most of them along Broadway or Columbus Avenue, or farther up Amsterdam Avenue. She would pick one of those streets and walk along it, sizing up each restaurant she came to.

She'd always look at the menu in the window. If the prices were fairly expensive she'd cross that restaurant off. Too fancy for her. Any place with even a faint ethnic flavor she also quickly eliminated, telling herself they'd only want natives working there.

But when she'd come to one that seemed approximate in character to the Center Stage, she'd grit her teeth and walk in and ask the bartender if she could speak to the manager. Sometimes that was as far as she got. The bartender would simply say, "We don't need anybody." Then she could walk out, feeling relieved.

She wasn't always that lucky. Whenever she got to see a manager, she had to go through the whole routine of saying that she was looking for work as a waitress, that she had experience, and did they have any openings? Some of them took longer to say no than others, and she would stand there *praying* that they weren't about to offer her a job. So far, no one had.

When she'd had two or three of these rejections she'd go home, satisfied that she'd done her duty, that she wouldn't have to lie to Bobby.

Back in the apartment she was in her own world once again, a world with no intrusions, nothing to mar the happiness she had with Bobby. There, she didn't need anyone else; the two of them were complete together.

She was glad that Bobby didn't seem to have any friends apart from the people he worked with—and he never socialized with them. That way she didn't have to share him with anyone.

And her only friend now was Mrs. King. But even that friendship was strictly limited to the hours when Bobby was away at work. She hadn't told him about Mrs. King, afraid that they would meet sometime and her elaborate lie would be found out.

For Mrs. King's benefit she had bought herself an imitation diamond and wedding ring set, which she slipped on when Bobby left for work in the morning. She'd wear the rings all day, telling herself that soon Bobby would replace them with real ones. Just before he came home she would wistfully take them off and hide them in a pair of socks in her drawer.

As she worked around the apartment, cleaning, polishing, washing and ironing, she'd remember how she used to grumble about doing these chores when she was growing up. Now she did them effortlessly, contentedly—nothing was too much as long as it was for Bobby.

Her afternoons were devoted to experimenting with new recipes with which to surprise him. She took careful note of his likes and dislikes. Any dish that met with a frown was never repeated. Whenever they went out to eat she would watch what Bobby ordered, and would frequently try to duplicate the meal at home—which pleased him no end.

She had noticed that Bobby usually ordered pecan pie for dessert whenever it appeared on the menu. But when he finished it he would shake his head and say, "Not bad—but not like I used to get down home. Still, I guess I shouldn't expect Yankees to know how to make pecan pie."

Andrea had taken that as a challenge. She had looked and looked until she found a recipe for authentic *Southern* pecan pie. But she was still nervous about it. She made a test pie and took it over to Mrs. King.

"I don't understand why you're worried about your husband liking this pie," Mrs. King said as she took a second piece. "It's absolutely delicious."

"Mmm, it is pretty good," Andrea said, swallowing a mouthful. "But I never made it before, and Bobby being a Southerner, well, he has this notion that nobody up North can make real pecan pie."

Mrs. King laughed. "I think you've disproved that." Then she added, "But I do have one tiny suggestion."

"What's that?"

"Well, I've made pecan pie a few times myself, and I always used to add a dash of dark rum or brandy to it— that seems to give it an even richer flavor."

"I'll have to try that," Andrea responded. "Just a dash, you say?"

"Yes, that's right." Mrs. King turned abruptly and peered at her grandfather clock. "Oh, dear," she said. "I hope you won't think I'm rude if I turn on the television, but it's time for my soap operas to start. You're welcome to stay and watch with me."

Andrea wasn't interested in the soap operas, but she did want to try another piece of pie. "Well, just for a while," she said.

Mrs. King switched on the TV and tried to fill her guest in on the background as the show progressed, but Andrea only half-listened. She was thinking that she would have to get home soon and bake another pie for Bobby. Suddenly Mrs. King pointed to a dark-haired young woman who was obviously in a state of distress. "See that poor girl," she said. "She just got out of a mental hospital. She's having a very hard time adjusting to life outside."

Andrea had flinched involuntarily. She glanced at Mrs. King to see if she had noticed, but the old woman's eyes were still glued to the screen.

Andrea turned her attention back to the TV. The young woman was listening to another, somewhat older, woman. "That's her sister," Mrs. King explained. "She wants to send her back to the mental hospital."

Andrea lurched to her feet. "I'm sorry, I've got to be going," she said to Mrs. King. "Please finish the pie. I'll get the plate later."

It took her a while to calm down before she could bake the second pie. The pie received raves from Bobby—but as much as she tried, she couldn't get that soap opera character out of her mind.

The next afternoon she tuned in to the show herself. And the next . . . and the next.

One day there was a confrontation between the two sisters. "You're still very sick," the older one said in a cloying, oh-so-concerned voice. "I'm afraid I'm going to have to send you back to the hospital. It's where you belong."

"No! I won't go!" the younger one cried. "You

can't make me go back there—I'm not crazy any-more!"

They went back and forth for several minutes. The scene brought tears to Andrea's eyes. It was a pale reminder of battles she'd had with her mother, battles that came back to her now in all their scorching vividness: her mother's face twisted with hate, her voice raging, "You're crazy! You'll always be crazy! I'm sending you back to the Clinic—and I'm going to tell them to lock you up and throw away the key!"

"I won't go!" Andrea would scream at her. "I'll never go back there again!" Then she would run, crying, from the room.

The Clinic had always been her mother's idea—maybe that was why it had been such a hateful place to Andrea. She knew that it tortured her father to visit her there, but he had come once a month—almost always without her mother—forcing himself to smile and ignore the pain in his heart, a pain that would have eventually killed him if the airplane crash hadn't destroyed him first.

It was only after he was dead that Andrea had heard the stories about herself—from her mother, naturally. Her mother even admitted that her father had explicitly forbidden *anyone*—not she, not the doctors, not helpful "friends"—to tell her what she had done to Andy.

And it was at her father's very burial that Bernice had begun the attack. Her father's gravesite was right next to Andy's, and Andrea's eyes were drawn to the simple stone marker that bore the inscription: "Andrew McKinney Donahue, 1954–

1968." Her mother, too, kept glancing over at Andy's grave throughout the service.

When it was over and the crowd began moving away, Andrea and Bernice lingered behind. Friends and relatives kept stepping forward to extend their sympathy to her mother, but Andrea could bear none of that. She turned away to stand by Andy's grave. She could not remember ever having seen it before, yet she *knew* she had been there. Her mind was so busy grappling with the attempt to recall *when*, that she was not aware that her mother was standing beside her until she heard her voice: "You're the one who put him there, Andrea," she said bitterly. "It's time you knew that."

Andrea felt as if her heart had stopped beating, as if the very blood in her veins had stopped flowing. She looked around for someone to help her, but all the other mourners had gone. She was alone with this figure in black—who surely could not be her own mother.

"You put him there," the voice said again. "You're a murderer—you shot him point-blank in the chest. But you got away with it because you went so crazy you couldn't even tell us how it happened. But *I* knew—your father wouldn't believe it. But you broke his heart. You killed him, too." Then she turned abruptly and walked away.

Andrea started to call after her, but no sound would come out. It was choked off by the sharp pain piercing her chest. The next thing she knew she was falling onto the grassy earth covering Andy's grave, and the last thing she saw was his tombstone, looming over her head.

The doctor had to come that night to sedate her, and the next day she went back to the Clinic. She had been shattered by her mother's disclosure, but it had also forced her to try and remember what she could of the day Andy died. Bit by bit, over long months, the doctors helped her to put together the pieces of what she remembered of the events of that day. Eventually she was able to recall everything—all except the moment when the gun went off; that split second seemed to be lost forever to her memory.

Then there were the long weeks of therapy sessions that always wound up at the same point: Andrea huddled in the chair across from her psychiatrist, mindlessly repeating, "I killed Andy. I killed him, I killed him."

"It was an *accident*," the psychiatrist would respond firmly. "The gun simply went off when you shook your fist at him. It was not an intentional act. You've got to believe that."

Then Andrea would cry out, "No! I can't!" and dissolve into tears of agony, breaking off any further discussion.

Session after session ended this way until one day Andrea listened once again to the psychiatrist telling her it was an accident, and she looked back at him levelly. "I won't get better unless I learn to believe that, will I?" she asked in a somber, controlled voice.

The psychiatrist shook his head ruefully. "No, Andrea. I'm afraid you won't."

Andrea fell silent. The psychiatrist watched her

face expectantly. Minutes passed and neither of them spoke or stirred.

Finally, Andrea said quietly, "Then I guess I'd better start believing it."

Her improvement was marked from that day. Months later, they said she was well enough to leave, and Bernice reluctantly agreed to let her come home.

Only by that time there was no home to go to. After her father died her mother had sold the farm and moved to Miami. There seemed to be no choice. Andrea went to live with her.

Her mother's place was a condominium, and after the spaciousness of the farmhouse it seemed terribly cramped—especially for two women who did not get along at all.

Andrea tried to stay out of her mother's way. Both to keep herself busy and to assuage some of the guilt she felt for being such a tremendous financial burden to her mother, she went out to look for a job.

Although Bernice barely seemed to notice, Andrea had thought she had shown tremendous initiative in even *thinking* of getting a job. Of course, thinking about one and *getting* one turned out to be two different things.

It was always the same story: they'd take one look at her application and shake their heads, "No experience. Sorry." She got so many rejections that after a while they didn't even bother her—much.

And then, in an amazing stroke of luck, she had simply fallen into a job. She'd been out pounding the pavement and, although it was only early after-

noon, she had already been turned down twice.
Feeling tired and discouraged, she decided to stop
for something to eat. She disliked going into restaurants alone so she kept walking until she found
a small luncheonette with no tables, just a long
counter. Even so, the place was busy, and Andrea
had to wait for her Coke and grilled cheese. The
only person working was the short-order cook and
when a couple of customers complained to him
about having to wait so long for their food, he exploded. He couldn't help it, he raged, his waitress
had up and quit on him that morning. He was
doing the best he could.

Andrea seized the opportunity. If the man was
really desperate, he might even be willing to hire
someone with no experience. But he was too busy
to talk to her. She decided to come back when he
wasn't so harried by the lunchtime crowd. So she
left and wandered around for an hour, wondering
if it was naive to think that this man might want
her. She nearly managed to talk herself out of giving it a try, but in the end she forced herself to go
back. And the man hired her—just like that, no
questions asked. At least, none that she couldn't
handle.

Even so, she didn't tell her mother right away
that she had a job. She was afraid it might not
work out and she would get herself fired. For the
first week, whenever she left the house she pretended she was still going out job-hunting.

Actually, she even surprised herself at how
quickly she caught on. The only part of the job
that gave her any problems was giving the orders

to Burt, the cook. The first few times, she would walk down the length of the counter to where Burt stood at the grill and give them to him in her normal speaking voice. Finally, he pointed out to her that it was a waste of her time and energy to come running down to him every time she had to give him an order; the best thing was for her to shout it out to him. Andrea realized he was right, but she still felt self-conscious and foolish the first time she bellowed out an order to him. Still, the next time it was easier, and soon she was shouting out orders right and left.

It wasn't long before she felt like an old hand at the job, and it pleased her immensely to think that she had actually become a contributing member of society. She had a *job*, just like a normal person; maybe that meant that someday she could forget she had ever been anything but normal.

Her life took on a comfortable predictability, and she reveled in it. She looked forward to going to work, to losing herself in the job for several hours as she rushed from customer to customer, seeing to *their* needs, not even thinking about her own.

That was important, because at that point in her life she had no idea what her needs were. Her mother never bothered to find out, and it seemed that the only one who cared was Burt.

A giant of a man with white hair and a disarmingly subtle sense of humor, Burt seemed to her to be the wisest and most interesting person she had ever known. He had been a cook all his life, in the kitchens of some famous Broadway restaurants (most of which were no longer in existence, he sadly explained) ; in the Army during the war (the highlight of his tour of duty was the meal he had once cooked for Eisenhower) ; on cruise ships and finally, here, in Florida. And for every job, every place he'd been, Burt had a tale to tell.

At first, Andrea just sat back as he rambled on, telling her story after story of his experiences—he loved to talk and she was an avid listener—but soon, at his urging, she began to talk, too.

It was difficult, because there were so many things in the past she had to hide—or simply could not remember. So she talked about the future, about what she wanted to do. She explained that acting was the only thing she felt she had any talent for.

It was a tough way to make a living, Burt said. He had known lots of actresses and few of them ever made it. But if she was serious, she should save her money to go to New York, where she could take acting classes and look for work in the theater.

The thought of going to New York terrified Andrea, and yet she knew Burt was right, only it would be impossible to do for quite a while because she hadn't saved much money and, too, it would mean leaving her new friend.

But still, Burt would talk about New York, telling her where to go when she got there, what she could expect, and just generally how to survive. Andrea always listened carefully, trying to visualize what it would be like.

Burt gave her plenty of other advice, too. Most

of it had to do with how important it was for a pretty girl like Andrea to be going out with lots of different boys, having a good time—but not *too* good a time, he always implied.

Every time an attractive young man came into the diner Burt would signal Andrea with his eyes: flirt with him, get him to notice you. Sometimes it worked, and resulted in a date. But they always seemed to expect that she would go to bed with them—at least by the third or fourth date—and, of course, she couldn't because she didn't feel anything for them.

Not that she was sure what she would need to feel in order to go to bed with somebody, but she knew she had to feel *something*—otherwise it would be no good.

One guy actually got angry with her and accused her of being frigid. Even though that hurt her, she consoled herself with the knowledge that she wasn't. She was tempted to shout back at him that, on the contrary, she knew—and probably better than he did—just how wonderful sex could be. But she didn't; it would mean taking something beautiful and besmirching it with vulgarity.

So she remained chaste, but not really by design. In the meantime, Bernice seemed to be making up for her daughter's lack of activity.

Andrea had been shocked by the change in her mother's behavior, but she resented her too much to even give her the satisfaction of seeing her disapproval. She tried not to think about how her father would feel, and just as her mother didn't seem to care what Andrea did, so did she pretend to ig-

nore her mother's sudden popularity with the
opposite sex.

She was pretty sure that Bernice was not actually
having sex with all the men she saw. After all,
some of them were probably just interested in
companionship. But still, it seemed as though half
the retired widowers in Miami must have her
mother's telephone number.

So she didn't quite know how to react when
Bernice suddenly announced that she was planning to remarry. The man she had chosen was nice
enough; in truth, Andrea found Paul only tolera-
ble, but he was rich and she supposed that was the
real reason her mother was going to marry him.
Bernice was too much of a cynic to believe in love
or romance anymore. Andrea didn't like to think
about that; she was sure it was that hot August afternoon years before that had frozen her mother's
heart.

Paul took her mother off on a brief honeymoon.
From the moment they returned and Andrea had
moved in with them into his condominium, she
knew it was a mistake. She realized that this marriage must have represented a new life for her
mother. Andrea's presence only reminded her of
bitter memories. She spoke to Andrea only when
necessary, but smiled and tried to put up a good
front whenever Paul was around.

One weekend her mother and Paul took a boat
trip to Nassau, and Andrea was alone in the apartment. She had both days off and no dates planned
so she spent most of her time by the pool perfect-

ing her tan or just sitting in the apartment reading or watching television.

Sunday afternoon there was an intermittent downpour that cut short her sunbathing and, since there was nothing she felt like watching on TV, she wandered about the apartment looking for something she hadn't already read. She knew Paul was an avid reader so she went into their bedroom to look in his bookcase. She had picked out a volume that looked halfway interesting and was about to walk away when she noticed a photo album sticking out from the bottom shelf. It looked oddly familiar, and as she bent over and pulled it out, she suddenly had an image of this same album sitting on the coffee table in the farmhouse living room.

Excited and a little apprehensive, she sat down on the edge of the bed and turned to the first page. It contained a single black-and-white photograph attached to the fading black paper by three corner tabs—the fourth had fallen off. It was of her mother and father, standing side by side and looking very young. Her mother was wearing a white dress and hat and holding a nosegay of flowers and her father was in uniform. Next to the picture was a yellowed newspaper clipping. It was dated September 25, 1945, and its headline read: "Arthur M. Donahue, Twice-Wounded Hero, Weds Bernice McKinney." Andrea read over the details of her parents' wedding ceremony, remembering how many times as a child she had read these same words. She studied her father's strong, handsome face briefly before she turned the page, and tried not to think about how much she missed him.

There were several more pages of photos of her parents—usually with friends or relatives. And then there was a birth announcement and a photo of two identical babies wrapped in a satin blanket and more interested in each other than the photographer. Andrea was sure she remembered being told that she was the baby on the left, but as far as she could see from the photograph the twins were indistinguishable from each other.

She continued through the book, turning the pages slowly and feeling long-fallow memories being revived by each picture. Most of them were of her and Andy, except for an occasional family shot. But whoever had taken the pictures had always focused the camera lovingly on those two shining faces, so much alike.

They were usually dressed dissimilarly and, past infancy, their hair was always cut appropriate to their sex, but those differences only seemed to emphasize how much they were alike, the male and female version of the same child.

Andrea felt tears stinging her eyes as she came upon a snapshot of her and Andy, eight years old, and dressed for a Halloween party in cowboy and cowgirl outfits. She was smiling demurely, but Andy was clowning for the camera, trying to twirl his play pistol on his index finger.

Andrea slowly shut the book as other images of Andy came flooding into her mind: Andy several years later—with his real guns, twirling them expertly on both hands, cleaning them lovingly, guarding them jealously from her alien feminine touch. The tears coursed down her cheeks as she thought of how it was that fascination with guns had been his downfall—and hers.

No! Stop! She mustn't do this, she told herself. Hadn't the doctors warned her about punishing herself this way? They had told her that yes, it was important for her to face the past, but that didn't mean she should persecute herself with it. Whenever she found herself doing that she must make a conscious effort to arrest those thoughts, think of something pleasant.

Wiping her eyes and determined to concentrate on the happy memories, she flipped the album open again, causing a letter-size piece of paper to fly out and flutter erratically to the floor. Curious, Andrea retrieved it and skimmed it hastily. It appeared to be the carbon copy of a letter from her father's lawyer to a judge in the Mapleton court, and the language seemed to her to be very official and stilted, until she glanced at the date at the top of the page: August 23, 1968! Right after Andy's death. Andrea began to read the letter word by word, paying more attention to what was implied than to what was actually said. Suddenly she found herself reading a description of horror and madness, for couched in those careful, legal phrases was the story of how her father and mother had found her at Andy's grave, dressed in his clothing; how, when she tried but failed to kill herself, they had reached the painful conclusion that she should be sent away for psychiatric treatment. It was a story Andrea had never heard before; but it had stirred dark, ominous memories that told her it must be true.

The words swam in front of her eyes, taunting her, reviling her with their ghastly images. And then, just when she thought she must surely be looking down into the abyss of madness once again, the pain came, saving her. It was white-hot as it went shooting through her chest, but she welcomed it for it brought with it a gray cloud to float her away to oblivion—but not before she thought she heard her mother's voice singing out a tormenting refrain: "Crazy, crazy, crazy! You'll always be crazy!"

That night she packed a bag, got out her meager savings, went down to the bus station, and bought a ticket north, planning to go back to the safety and security of the Clinic—the only place she felt she belonged now.

It was a long bus trip, and on the way Andrea had plenty of time to think. To keep her mind off the bizarre thing she had learned about herself she tried to concentrate on more practical matters. Who was going to pay for her stay at the Clinic? They certainly didn't take any charity cases and the few hundred dollars she had with her was barely enough for them to admit her. Of course, they would probably contact her mother and *she* would pay (gladly, Andrea was sure). But she didn't want Bernice to know where she was, and she vowed she would die before she'd ask her for anything. For in her heart she was sure her mother had *meant* for her to find that letter.

Yet, if she went back to the Clinic, wasn't she only *proving* that her mother was right—that madness like hers could never be cured? Did the doctors at the Clinic think that, too? Was that why they had never told her about what she had done after Andy's death?

But was there any other place she could go besides the Clinic? Well, there were Uncle Jim and Aunt Dodie in Wisconsin, but she remembered the way they had looked at her at her father's funeral—as if they were afraid she might contaminate them with her insanity. No, even though they might take her in, she would not be able to stay there long.

As the miles rolled past the pain and fear seemed farther and farther behind her too, and she began to think she might even be able to take care of herself. The thought was scary, but not overwhelming. After all, she was an adult now, and she had proved to herself that she was ready to make it on her own. Hadn't she gone out and gotten a job all by herself—and stuck to it, too? Surely she could do it again—somehow.

But the more immediate the problem now was, where was she going? Her bus ticket was good up to Boston, where she would have had to transfer to a local line if she were still going to the Clinic. But she wasn't, anymore—was she? Maybe she should just go to Boston, a town that she had always found attractive on her various trips through on her way to and from the Clinic.

As she weighed her decision, the bus moved relentlessly northward, passing through the small towns and cities of Georgia, the Carolinas, Virginia. Once, she thought she would get off in Washington, D.C., maybe find a government job. But when the bus pulled out of the Washington depot, she was still on it. They were nearly through the Maryland suburbs before something clicked inside her head. What had she been thinking of? There was only one place to go, and she should have known it from the first: New York.

The moment she made her decision she was able to relax. It felt right, and she knew she would not regret it. *New York.* That was where she could leave her past behind and become an actress. That thought filled her with hope: she would make a new beginning, a different life, a real career.

As the bus rolled up through Maryland and Delaware, her anticipation mounted with every mile. By the time they reached New Jersey, she could practically feel the adrenalin rushing through her, causing her nerve endings to tingle and making it difficult to keep to her seat.

And then, as they were approaching the Lincoln Tunnel, she caught a glimpse of Manhattan skyline, and her heart leaped into her throat. It was all too, too beautiful and wonderful, and the most incredible part of it was that *she* was there.

She was out of her seat before the bus had pulled to a complete stop in the Port Authority Bus Terminal. When she alighted from the bus she could hardly contain herself with joy; the diesel fumes smelled like perfume and the babble of raucous voices around her sounded like a heavenly choir. She wandered through the terminal, her eyes rapturously taking in the panorama of humanity in transit. Then she remembered all the tales she had heard: pimps frequented the Port Authority, on the lookout for young, tender, unsuspecting flesh from out of town.

So, carrying her single suitcase, she left the confines of the terminal for the exotic pavement of Eighth Avenue. Although she had had the foresight to put on a winter coat, she still shivered in the chill of the February afternoon, but more from excitement than the cold.

At Forty-second Street she turned right and felt as if she had suddenly come upon some vulgar carnival sideshow. She cringed at the tawdry sexual displays lining the block: row upon row of X-rated movie houses; sleazy novelty shops; disreputable-looking men hawking the delights of second-story massage parlors; prostitutes—male, female, and god-knows-what—slouching in doorways; and worst of all the pedestrians—some looking like rejects from freak shows, others more like predatory cannibals. Andrea desperately tried to avoid their eyes, lest one of them pounce on her.

Walking rapidly, she managed to pass through the gauntlet unscathed and arrived at the corner of Seventh Avenue. Here, she turned into Times Square, which was hardly an improvement over the block she had just come through. Steeling herself, she picked her way through the milling crowds.

What did they call Times Square? "The Crossroads of the World"? She wondered how long ago *that* phrase had been coined. And Broadway—"the

Great White Way" of legend—looked dim and
dingy in the fading afternoon light. But at Forty-
fourth Street she turned left, and sucked in her
breath. There, down the street, she could make out
the sign for the Shubert Theatre and across from
it, a simple green neon sign denoting Sardi's;
Mecca was in sight—perhaps even within reach.

She spent the next hour or so wandering up and
down Shubert Alley and the side streets, gawking
at posters, studying the photographs of featured
performers, searching the faces around her for one
she recognized.

After dark the area seemed to metamorphose,
taking on its rightful character. The theater lights
blazed on, pushing back the cheerless, sordid shadows, and soon the lobbies began to fill with well-
dressed people whose expensive perfumes, pungent
cigar smoke, and buoyant chatter drew Andrea
closer to their enchanted circle.

She slipped into the lobby of the Martin Beck,
and sidled up to a group. The women were nearly
her own age, perhaps five years more, and they
were polished and pampered looking. The hus-
bands wore their success with an air of self-
satisfaction. Andrea admired them all as she edged
closer and eavesdropped on their bantering conversation.

Suddenly one of the wives gave Andrea a side-
long glance and then nudged the woman standing
next to her. They both gaped at Andrea and began
to titter scornfully.

For a moment Andrea stood, rooted to the spot.
But when the whole group turned around to stare

at her, she bolted through the lobby doors. Blindly, she ran down the block, crashing into hurrying theatergoers.

How she hated them! Life and circumstances had conspired to cheat her out of her rightful place in the world. *She* should be one of them: swathed in furs, her belly full of sumptuous French food, prating on to an adoring husband about what so-and-so at the beauty parlor had said about the play they were going to see.

Then, as her fevered excitement drained away, Andrea suddenly felt the cold's harsh sting and remembered—too late—that she had nowhere to go and it had been hours since she had eaten. She ducked into a coffee shop for a cheeseburger and a cup of coffee. The cheeseburger was greasy and overpriced and the coffee was undrinkable, but good for warming her hands.

After this brief respite from the cold she hurried out into the night again, bent on looking for a place to stay. The frigid air began to penetrate bone-deep as she scuttled along, frozen fingers numbly gripping her suitcase and purse. Now that the magic spell had been broken, all around her she could feel eyes—watching her, seeing through her, divining that she belonged to no one and was therefore suitable prey. From somewhere in the dim past she recalled the words to a *Hail Mary*, and she repeated them to herself as she walked faster and faster along the alien streets.

At last she found a hotel on Fiftieth Street that seemed reasonable, clean, and safe. Andrea was aware that, even behind his tinted glasses, the desk

clerk's eyes were busy assessing her as she checked
in. She put down a phony address in Milwaukee as
her residence—it didn't matter, she had no home
anymore. Just her suitcase and the hotel room itself—paid for a week in advance.

The room was cramped and spare—a bed, a bureau, a musty wardrobe, one rickety chair and a
closet-size bathroom—but it was moderately clean
and at least warm, for an ancient radiator in the
corner was volubly giving its all. Andrea lay down
on the bed, huddling in her coat, shivering for-
lornly while she waited for the chill to pass.

The physical chill dissipated quickly enough,
but the emotional one lingered, forcing Andrea to
curl her body tighter and tighter into itself in her
efforts to get warm. The heat from the radiator
made her drowsy, and soon she drifted off to
sleep—and fitful dreams.

She was back on the bus, still going north she
thought, because it kept getting colder and colder.
The bus was filled with people like herself—all
strangers, all alone, nothing to say to anybody,
going nowhere. Suddenly the bus stopped and
everyone got off—except her. They wouldn't let
her off, her ticket wasn't good for this stop. And
then the bus began to fill with a new group of passengers, only this group was not so quiet or so sul-
len as the first. They were smiling couples, happy
families, all laughing and talking at once. Andrea
sat, surrounded by them, feeling more miserable
by the moment as she witnessed their joy, their
harmony, their love for each other. . . .

She jerked awake, angry with herself for dreaming about something she could not have. Forget it, she told herself. Forget about *belonging* to someone, forget about falling in love and getting married and having a family—not you. That only happens to normal girls—girls who haven't killed their own flesh and blood, girls who haven't spent nearly half their lives in a mental institution, girls who don't have a talent for pain and suffering. But *you* do, so use it—as an actress. Become a *real* actress, discipline yourself, study—maybe even someday you'll be a great actress. Starting now, make that your goal. Forget the other.

And somehow she managed to do just that. The next day she shrugged off her longings of the night before and went out to look for a job. She spent several fruitless weeks, but finally landed the one at the Center Stage. She waited until she was certain that the job was secure and then she used the last of her Florida funds to enroll in an acting class and to pay for the rent and security on the Ninth Avenue apartment, which her new friend Sam had helped her find.

Her life had quickly become highly structured, filled with a great deal of activity. She was always rushing to auditions or classes or work and in between she was so exhausted that she scarcely had time to think about the past or the lonely dreams that still haunted her nights.

Until Bobby.

He was the dividing line, for now she could look back on those first few months here and see how different she'd been then. She had been in New

York nearly a year now, and that time fell into two distinct periods: before and after Bobby.

For Bobby had changed the whole pattern of her existence. After she started seeing him she did not sign up for any new acting classes in the fall because she didn't want to spend any of her free time away from him. She did continue to go to auditions, but without much enthusiasm—until she quit her job, when she more or less stopped going to them altogether.

Because, frankly, she didn't care that much about acting anymore. The love she had found with Bobby had opened her eyes to the fact that she had only been kidding herself before about a career. Now she had what she had really wanted all along: a man who loved her and wanted to marry her. At last, she *belonged* to somebody.

And she was happy—really happy with the way things were. Only that final, *legal* commitment was important to her, and she was glad that Bobby wanted it, too. She realized it probably wouldn't change their life together all that much, but it still *mattered*. And lately she had begun to wonder just when it was going to happen—although she knew it would as soon as Bobby got his divorce.

She just wished it wasn't taking so goddamn long.

CHAPTER SEVEN

Bobby could see something was bothering Andrea, had been eating at her for days—weeks, possibly. He could see it in her face, he could feel it, too—whenever he kissed her, every time they made love. There was a difference somehow; she was holding back, keeping a part of herself from him.

Several times he had started to ask her what was wrong, but he stopped himself. He already knew what it was. Until Andrea could bring herself to say something to him he was willing to go on pretending that everything was all right. He was very good at that; he'd played the game much longer than she had.

But he knew it was coming sooner or later. When it did he wasn't surprised, just rankled that she did it the way she did.

They were sitting at the dining room table, finishing a spaghetti dinner. Andrea had had a vague, thoughtful look on her face all through the meal and had hardly uttered a word. When she put down her fork she sat for several minutes staring at her plate, until finally she looked at him and said, "Bobby, I've got to talk to you."

Uh, oh. Here it comes. He could almost see her marshalling her strength, steeling herself to bring up what had become taboo between them.

He took a sip of beer. "What about?"

"About—about your divorce."

So she finally got up the nerve. He finished off the beer and crushed the can in his hand. "What about it?"

"Well—what's happening with it? Have you heard anything from your lawyer?"

"Not lately. But don't worry your pretty little head about it, darlin'. These things take time."

"I know that. It's just—" Andrea chewed at her lip.

"Just what?"

"It's been *weeks*, hasn't it? Is something wrong?" She averted her eyes and hesitated a moment before blurting out, "Is there something you're not telling me?"

There was a nuance in her tone, the way she had asked the question, that triggered Bobby's anger. He leaped to his feet, knocking his chair over. "What makes you think that?"

"Nothing—"

"You think I'm holding out on you?" He came around the table and stood over Andrea. "Well, do you?"

"No, no. I—" Andrea turned sideways in her

chair to face him. Her eyes were guarded as they stared up at him.

There was something in that look that made him want to hurt her, some little spark of disbelief that he must extinguish. He grabbed her by the shoulders. "Answer me! Do you think I'm holding out on you?"

"Bobby—" Andrea pushed at his arms. "I don't know what to think!"

Bobby wrenched his right arm easily out of her grasp, then swung back and struck her directly on the cheek with the flat of his hand. Andrea's chin jerked up and her head flew to the right. Off balance, she began to fall and the chair went out from under her. Her left hand clutched at Bobby, but the impetus from the blow was carrying her down and her fingers snatched at air. Her head collided solidly with the edge of the table. Strands of her long hair caught her plate, sweeping it from the table and splattering the remains of her dinner over her. A dollop of spaghetti sauce clung to her hair as she slipped to the floor, already unconscious. The red of the sauce mixed with the blood which quickly began to collect in a puddle under her head.

Bobby watched as if from a distance—fascinated by all that his single blow had set in motion. He did not think he had hit her so hard.

When, after several excruciatingly long seconds, Andrea still had not moved, Bobby was suddenly seized by the terrible notion that he had killed her.

"Oh, dear Jesus!" he cried, dropping to his knees and bending over her, afraid to touch her.

But she was breathing; he could see the slight flare of her nostrils. The puddle of blood was growing bigger. Fingers of it ran along cracks in the floorboards.

"Oh, God! Oh, God! What am I going to do?" Bobby wailed, looking around frantically as if his needing it would automatically bring help. He had never been so frightened in his entire life. Andrea was bleeding to death before his very eyes. He had to do something to stop it.

He ran to the bathroom for a towel, and nearly fell on top of her in his hurry to see that she had not died in the few seconds he was gone. Thank God, she was still alive! Hands shaking, he turned her head just enough to make out a wound on her right temple. It was difficult to distinguish exactly where the blood was coming from, there was so much of it soaking the side of her head.

He dabbed the towel at her temple and was able to stanch some of the flow. While he was doing that, Andrea's eyelids cracked open.

"Andrea! Can you hear me?" His voice was quivering with desperation. "Oh, God. Please! Can you hear me?"

Andrea opened her eyes halfway and tried to turn her head away from the towel. "Hurts," she said in a small, petulant voice.

Bobby cradled her chin with one hand while he continued to press the towel to the wound with his other. "Yes, yes. I know it hurts," he soothed, his own voice barely a whisper as relief flooded through him. At least she could feel pain. That seemed to be a good sign.

His mind began working, trying to figure out what he should do next. Okay, she was alive for now. But at the rate she was gushing blood she wouldn't stay that way for long. He had to get help—better yet, get her to a hospital. But how? He could call the police, of course, but then they would come into the apartment, ask how this happened. What could he tell them—that she fell down eating dinner? He could imagine how skeptically that response would be received. And if he called an ambulance it would be the same story.

No, what he should do is get her to a hospital himself. Somehow.

Yes, that was the answer. Anyway, the wound probably wasn't as bad as it seemed. Hadn't he always heard that head wounds looked worse than they were because they bled so profusely? But if that were true, then she really *was* losing a lot of blood. Got to hurry, get her to a hospital right away.

If she died, what would they charge him with—murder? No, more like manslaughter; maybe negligent homicide. Whichever, they both amounted to the same thing—prison. Oh, *please* God, he would love Andrea, be good to her, if only she wouldn't *die*.

She seemed to be regaining consciousness. Her eyes blinked open and shut several times. "Andy?" she said in a childlike voice.

"Yes, yes," Bobby said. Careful, don't upset her. Better to let her think that he was this Andy character—whoever the hell *he* was.

"Don't tell—" Her brow furrowed and her eyes fought to stay open.

"No, no. I won't tell." Bobby was ready to promise anything just to keep her talking, make her stay awake.

"Good. Secret." A faint smile hovered about the edges of her mouth.

"Whoa," Bobby said as she tried to lift her head. "Here, let me put this around you." He removed the bloody towel and replaced it with a fresh one, winding it around her head. Then, wrapping her in a blanket he pulled from the bed, he picked her up and carried her to the door. He had to shift her weight in his arms in order to get enough leverage to turn the knob. As he opened the door she moved, and he felt himself going off-balance. The tail of the blanket caught in the door as it closed behind him, and they tumbled onto the hall carpet. He managed to hold on to Andrea but she let out a loud moan, and he cursed himself for his clumsiness.

Fumbling in his pockets for his keys, he unlocked the door and pulled the blanket out. Then suddenly the door across the hall opened and a withered old face peered out. "What—oh, my God! What's happened to her?" The woman started to come out into the hall.

Jesus Christ! This was all he needed. Bobby stared up at the woman. He didn't think he had ever seen her before. Then he heard himself shouting, "Get out of here! She's fine, she doesn't need your snooping around! Just get out of here. Leave us alone!"

The woman jumped at the sound of his shrill, angry voice. Then, eyes blinking, she gaped at him before she retreated behind her door, slamming it shut.

God, why did I do that? He was trembling and his body felt weak—as if all the energy had suddenly drained out of it. But he had to try and stand up. His legs quivered under him as he got up on first one knee, then the other. It took all his strength to lift Andrea and to push himself to his feet without dropping her. Then he carried her, stumbling, to the elevator.

He laid her carefully on the floor as the elevator descended, then picked her up again and rushed into the street, shifting the weight in his arms to frantically wave down a passing cab. The driver jumped out and helped him put her inside, across the backseat.

"Hospital. Quick." Then, meeting the driver's curious eyes, "She's epileptic. Had a fit and fell down. Cut her head."

The cab driver was sympathetic. He seemed to believe him. And why shouldn't he? After all, the story was almost true, wasn't it? She *did* have those strange attacks. And she might have hurt herself like this at any time.

Bobby perched on the edge of the seat as the taxi screeched downtown. Andrea clung to his right hand, her fingers tracing the mole on his wristbone, her voice going on and on in that high, childish babble.

He had stopped paying attention to what she

was saying and was trying to concentrate on what he would tell the hospital officials.

He decided to stick with the epilepsy story. It sounded pretty good to him. He seemed to remember that falling down and hurting themselves was one of the dangers for epileptics. He could make it sound vague, like he didn't really know what had happened to her. Yeah, that was it; he was in the next room and heard a crash, and when he came running he saw her lying on the floor with a gash on her head.

At the emergency entrance to the hospital he paid off the cab and started to gather Andrea up in his arms, but she pushed him away. "No. Want to walk," she insisted.

Bobby held tight to her arm as she maneuvered herself across the backseat and out the door of the cab. She was actually quite steady on her feet, and he had the fleeting impression that she was giving some kind of performance. But that vanished when he caught up with her and got a look at her face. It was pale, like a ghostly mask, and the sagging muscles around her eyes and mouth gave it a hangdog expression. She didn't look as if she were even aware of where she was.

In the harsh, fluorescent light of the emergency room, he could see that the towel was soaked through with blood. Where Andrea held the cloth to her head, the blood was beginning to ooze through her fingers.

A figure in white passed by. "Help us, please," Bobby called out. "She's bleeding to death!"

The woman stopped, gave him a scornful look,

and glanced at Andrea. "Is she registered?" she asked. "Can't touch her unless she's registered."

"I'll take care of that," Bobby said, putting on his best peremptory manner, "*You* take care of her." And he gave Andrea a gentle shove in the woman's direction.

The woman scowled at him, then shrugged her shoulders and motioned to Andrea to follow her.

Andrea looked at Bobby as if she needed his permission before she would go off with a stranger. "Go ahead," he reassured her.

He watched them as they walked toward a double set of doors. Andrea's fate was out of his hands now, thank God.

The nurse was walking briskly, and Andrea was having a hard time keeping up. She shuffled along, dragging the blanket after her, and nearly lost her balance a couple of times as she swayed back and forth precariously. The bloody towel had loosened and was starting to unwind from her head, slipping down over her eyes.

Jesus, she looks ridiculous, Bobby thought before he could catch himself. No, he mustn't think that way. It was *his* fault that she was in that condition. Of course, she was partially to blame. *She* was the one who started the whole thing in the first place.

The nurse went through the doors and held them open for Andrea. She stopped and twisted her head around slowly. The towel was now nearly covering her eyes and she had to push it up to look at Bobby. He gave her a feeble smile, but her face showed no reaction. Then the nurse said something to her, and the doors swung shut behind them.

Bobby looked around for the registration desk, and for the first time was aware of his surroundings. The waiting room was crowded with humanity in various stages of suffering: most were black or Puerto Rican, a few were old, a number were children, and almost all appeared to be poor. Some sat holding their heads or bellies; one man was hugging his chest tightly as he rocked back and forth in his seat; a couple of small children were crying and whining loudly; and one pathetic, elderly woman sat muttering to herself. Several pairs of dark eyes looked back at Bobby—some with hostility, others with numb indifference.

A very bored looking black man was sitting behind a counter under a large sign marked "Registration." Bobby went over to him and stood waiting while the man looked him up and down in a way that was at once casual and menacing.

Unnerved, Bobby reached into his pocket for a cigarette, then thought better of it.

"I'd, uh, like to register someone," he said, cursing his Southern accent. It had never sounded thicker, he was sure.

The man studied him idly and then picked up an official-looking form.

Bobby gave him Andrea's name and answered all the routine questions that followed. When it came to "Next of kin?" he made up an address and telephone number in Miami for Andrea's mother.

"Nature of complaint?"

That was easy. Bobby simply said, "Head

wound," and when the admittance clerk gave him a quizzical look he added, "She's an epileptic. She fell down and cut herself during a fit." That seemed to satisfy him.

The man went on. Hospitalization coverage? Medical insurance? Andrea had neither and Bobby was aware that he would have to be responsible for all her bills. What if they wanted to hospitalize her? That would cost a fucking fortune. Jesus, he hoped she wouldn't need it.

When the form was completed, the man waved him away. Bobby looked around for a place to sit, but the only empty chair was next to a mother holding a thrashing child in her arms. He didn't feel like making himself the target for the child's wildly kicking feet, so he moved across the room and leaned uneasily against one of the smudged green walls.

He smoked cigarette after cigarette and tried to ignore all the noise and commotion around him. Then, suddenly, he remembered the envelope that was folded in his pocket, and took it out. Before this evening, the appearance of this letter on his desk in the morning mail had been the most momentous event of the day. Until now he had completely forgotten about it.

He opened the envelope and took out the single sheet of paper inside and read it through for perhaps the tenth time. It was from Cynthia:

Bobby,
   I suppose you're shocked to hear from me, but you're going to be even more shocked by

what I have to tell you. I may be moving to New York to try my luck at a modeling career. Nothing is definite yet, but I have had a lot of encouragement from a local photographer. He says he has contacts in New York who might be able to help me. I haven't made up my mind for sure, but I probably wouldn't do it till some time in January. I want to spend Christmas with Jennifer. I wouldn't be bringing her with me; she'll stay with my folks. Then if things work out for me, I can come back and get her. I'll be in touch with you to let you know what I decide.

Cynthia

Bobby stared at the letter. He couldn't quite believe it. Cynthia coming to New York. What did it mean? Yet she said she wasn't certain, so why had she bothered to write? Still, he needed to know whether or not she was coming. But he'd better wait a while, let her think he didn't care one way or another what she did, then he'd give her a call and see what she had to say.

He folded the letter and put it away. He had more pressing things to think about for the time being.

Every few minutes he glanced at the double doors Andrea had gone through—half expecting her to reappear, a doctor in tow, pointing to Bobby, saying: "He's the one. He's the one who knocked me down and almost killed me."

He started every time the doors opened, but no Andrea and no doctor appeared. Finally, the

woman who had taken Andrea inside came
through, and Bobby hurried over to her. "Is she
all right? Is someone taking care of her?" he demanded.

"Who?" the woman asked, giving Bobby a wary
look as she was about to walk away. "Oh, *you*," she
said as she recognized him. "Yeah, she's down the
hall there—112. You can go see her if you want.
Did you get her registered?"

Bobby barely paused to nod to her as he pushed
through the swinging doors. The corridor was almost hushed after the hubbub of the waiting
room. But as he passed the open doors of treatment rooms he could see doctors and nurses busily
hovering over patients.

As he passed one doorway a large, white-coated
figure suddenly emerged and crashed right into
him. "Jesus!" the man said as he shoved Bobby
aside. "Get out of my way!"

Bobby reeled. *Fucking doctors!* he wanted to
shout at him. *Who the hell do you think you are?*
But he bridled his anger and kept moving down
the hall. At the door to 112 he hesitated.

Andrea was lying on an examining table, her
face turned away from him. She was still wrapped
in the blanket, but the towel had been removed
from her head. In its place was a large gauze pad
with a spot of red where the blood had already sat-
urated it.

He stepped closer and could see that her eyes
were closed. The expression on her face was
strangely peaceful—too peaceful. He leaned toward

her to see if he could detect any movement in her chest.

Just then he heard a soft footfall behind him, and he whirled to face a bespectacled young man in wrinkled whites.

"Oh. I was, uh, just checking to see if she's asleep," Bobby said, feeling that he had to explain to this stranger what he was doing.

The man paid no attention to him. He walked straight over to Andrea.

"Are you a doctor?" Bobby asked, moving out of the way.

The man gave him the briefest glance before he bent over Andrea. Pulling away the bandage, he examined the wound. "What happened to her?" he asked, his back to Bobby.

"Well—" Bobby swallowed nervously. "I'm not sure. I was in the next room when it happened. I heard a crash and came running. She—she was on the floor and it looked like she had hit her head on a table."

The doctor turned to face Bobby. His eyes were small and hard behind his rimless glasses. "Is she an epileptic?" he asked.

Bobby wondered if it was the thickness of the lenses or the doctor's suspicions of *him* that made his eyes look so beady.

"I think so," Bobby answered. "She has these—ah, blackouts every once in a while."

"How often?"

"Oh—every four, five weeks."

"Does she take any medication for them? Like

Dilantin? White capsules with orange stripes around the middle?"

Bobby shook his head. "I've never seen her take anything like that."

"She take any other drugs?"

"No."

"Pot?"

"No—she can't even stand the smell of it."

"How about alcohol?"

"She drinks beer with me sometimes and occasionally she'll take a shot or two of Jack Daniel's. That's all."

"I see." The doctor nodded thoughtfully. Then he gave Bobby another piercing look. "You her husband?"

"No. We sort of . . . live together."

"What's your name?"

"Wilson. Hers is Donahue. Andrea Donahue."

"All right, Mr. Wilson. I've got to give Miss Donahue a complete examination so go sit in the waiting room. I can tell you already, though, that she's going to need a few stitches and probably some X rays. And then, depending on what we find—and if we can get her a bed—I think we should keep her here at least overnight. Maybe longer."

"Sure. Whatever you say." Bobby glanced over at Andrea. Her eyes were open now but they had a glazed, faraway look. "Just make sure she's okay," he said to the doctor before he slipped out of the room and into the corridor, glad to escape the inquisition of those disbelieving eyes. Hell, maybe the guy wasn't really suspicious. Maybe it was just his own guilt that made him see everything that way.

He went back to the waiting room and flopped himself into an empty seat. An old man next to him was wheezing asthmatically. Bobby turned away from him. He couldn't help hearing the old man's struggles for air, but he sure didn't have to watch them, too.

Oh, God, he hoped he would never have to be that old and useless. Somehow he doubted that he would, for—ever since he could remember—he'd believed he would die young. Once (kind of as a joke, but also to pique her), he had even told Cynthia that he didn't think he would live to be thirty. Furious, she'd shouted at him not to talk that way, she didn't want to be a young widow. Of course, that had been years ago—before the breakup and before his thirtieth birthday was as close as it was now.

Yet this very evening he felt the chill of death surrounding him in that split second when he thought he had killed Andrea. As if it had not only come for her, but for *him*, too.

He really couldn't help himself; he never *wanted* to hit her, it just happened. He mistreated her, he knew it. Tonight had been the inevitable outcome of the numbers of ways—large and small— that he took advantage of her trusting nature. She was too good for him, he didn't deserve her, and that made him feel all the more miserable, even angry—at *her*. So he took it all out on her: his frustration with his job and with his writing, his bitterness toward women because of Cynthia. But it must never, *never* happen again, he vowed. Especially with that blackout condition of hers. God, what had he been thinking of? Just the other day on the subway he had seen how hypersensitive she was.

They had been riding uptown on the Broadway local, coming home from a movie. Seated directly across from them were three loud, unruly teenagers. Their boisterousness was annoying, and when a transit cop came along he made it his business to shut them up. The cop planted himself squarely in front of the kids and ordered them to be quiet. Bobby, intent on watching the kids' reaction to the cop, was unaware that something was wrong until he felt Andrea stiffen beside him. He glanced sideways at her: she seemed stupefied, her mouth open, her eyes fixed on the transit cop's revolver in its holster. Bobby started to ask her sarcastically if she had never seen a gun before, but before he could speak she flung herself back against the seat as if someone had punched her in the chest. Before he could even put out a hand to steady her, she had slumped to the side, unconscious, her right hand twitching against her breast bone.

Paralyzed by the suddenness of it, Bobby had gaped at Andrea's limp form until he heard a voice ringing with authority saying, "Move over, mister. Give her some room." It was the cop, taking charge. "Get up, please," he ordered two passengers on the other side of Andrea. They obeyed unhesitatingly. Then he stretched her across the seat. The cop was gentle with her, but quick and confident—as if he had handled many predicaments just like this one before. Bobby held back, watching him, feeling useless and in the way.

The cop squinted at him. "You with her?" He spoke loud enough to be heard above the noise of the train.

Bobby nodded.

"What's wrong with her? You know?"

He moved closer to the cop so he wouldn't have to shout at him. "She just blacks out—but she usually comes around in a minute or two."

"She be okay if we just leave her alone?"

"She always has before."

The cop stepped back, indicating that he was turning the situation over to Bobby. "Okay. We'll just let her lie there until she comes to."

A man suddenly tugged at Bobby's sleeve. "Hey! She's trying to say something."

Bobby looked at Andrea. Her mouth was working, but he couldn't make out her words over the rumble of the train. So he sat down next to her and leaned close to her face. "What is it, Red?" he coaxed. "What are you trying to say?"

She tried to speak again, only it was not Andrea's voice that came out. It sounded like a stranger's—deep and muffled, like a man's. Whatever words there were, were obscured by the sound of the train as it braked to a screeching stop at Columbus Circle.

The sudden halt seemed to rouse Andrea. Her eyes opened warily and gazed at Bobby. Sheepishly, she said, "I did it again, didn't I?"

"You sure did," Bobby said. "Only this time you had an audience."

Andrea yanked her head around and took in the subway car, the transit cop, the other passengers staring at her. "Oh, no," she moaned, her face turning ashen.

Painfully embarrassed, she spent the rest of the ride explaining to Bobby, to the cop, and to anyone else who would listen, how sorry she was, she didn't know what had happened to her, she hoped that she hadn't inconvenienced anybody. Most of the passengers looked away, their blank faces betraying no further interest, and that satisfied her—momentarily.

By the time they pulled into the Sixty-sixth Street station she appeared to be back to normal and insisted on walking the few blocks home without any assistance from Bobby. But when they got up to the apartment, she began to badger him about the incident on the subway: Did she fall down? Did she have convulsions? What did she *do*?

So Bobby tried to explain to her, step by step, just what had happened. How he'd first felt her whole body grow rigid beside him. "When I looked to see what was wrong," he went on, "you were staring at the transit cop's gun." At the word "gun" he was startled to see a lightning change in Andrea's face. She had been listening intently; he could almost see her straining to remember. Suddenly, concentration turned to stony terror. She almost looked as if she were having another attack.

He moved to her side on the couch. "Are you all right, Red?"

After a couple of seconds she passed a hand slowly over her eyes. "Yes," she sighed. "I'm fine."

She dropped her hand to her lap. "Now I know why I blacked out—it was the gun."

Bobby didn't understand, but he kept silent.

"I-I'm deathly afraid of guns," Andrea said tremulously. "I can't even stand the sight of them." Her eyes were tinged with pain, but as she turned to face Bobby he could see something else there: dread? resignation? It was as if she feared what was coming next but was willing to submit to her fate.

She was trying to tell him something, something significant, he could see that. Why couldn't she just come out and say it? And then it struck him: a shooting accident. That was how her brother had died.

"Because of what happened to your brother," he said suddenly. "Is that why guns frighten you?"

Nothing about Andrea's expression changed, but the pupils of her eyes almost disappeared. She nodded her head slowly.

"He was killed by a gun, wasn't he?"

Andrea looked away. "Yes."

Bobby hesitated. He could tell there was more. "Were you there?" he asked. "Did you see it?"

Andrea nodded mutely, and Bobby was struck by the eloquence of that simple gesture. He put his arms around her and drew her to him. "Oh, my poor darlin'," he murmured, "you never told me. I never knew it was so bad. To see someone you love—"

Andrea twisted out of his embrace. "No, don't say any more," she said. "I don't want to talk about it."

And they didn't, because he didn't want to see her upset. He didn't even mention the incident on the subway again until a few days later when he told her about the strange, deep voice he had heard. She just stared at him, a look on her face so blank, so disbelieving that he let the subject drop right there.

So even his sweet little Andrea had mysteries about her. It was hard to reconcile with that unassuming, wholesome, farm-girl face.

The thought of Andrea's face made him shudder. After tonight it might never be the same; she might be scarred. Oh, God, he would hate to be responsible for *that*.

Consumed by his guilty thoughts, he did not see the double doors fly open and the young doctor coming purposefully toward him, until he stopped and called out, "Wilson!"

Feeling as if he were being called in front of the principal, Bobby marched over to the doctor. Behind the rimless glasses the face was a mask, and Bobby feared the worst. "Andrea's okay, isn't she?" he asked breathlessly.

"Yeah, sure," the doctor said. "Nothing's broken. She's got a slight concussion and we had to put in five stitches. I'd like to keep her here overnight, but she doesn't want to. Think you can talk her into it?"

Bobby shrugged his shoulders. "I'll give it a try." He started toward the double doors.

The doctor grabbed his sleeve. "Your name Andy?" he asked.

"No. Why?"

"She kept asking me where Andy was, if he was all right. Know who he is?"

"An old boyfriend, I think. Are you sure she's lucid?"

"Yeah, she's fine—just a little dazed. I wouldn't worry about it. But try and get her to stay here."

"Right."

Bobby pushed his way through the swinging doors, feeling so relieved he didn't care *what* Andrea called him. But he wasn't going to try and make her stay in the hospital if she didn't want to. No, he would take her home. Where she belonged—with him.

CHAPTER EIGHT

Two mornings later Andrea got out of bed for the first time. The day before Bobby had stayed home with her, and she had been sorry to see that day end. He had been so gentle with her, so solicitous, so eager to respond to her every need. He had refused to let her get out of bed and she kept hoping he would join her in it, but he seemed to be afraid to touch her. She slept fitfully throughout the day and several times upon waking she found him sitting in a chair in the corner of the room, watching over her.

They hadn't talked much about what had happened. Her memory of it was very hazy, but she didn't really care about filling in those gaps. She knew that Bobby had hit her, but it wasn't entirely his fault—she had probably egged him on. Anyway, she was sure he hadn't hit her that hard—he had just knocked her off-balance and she had fallen and hit her head. Certainly he had never meant to hurt her like that.

She didn't remember the hospital at all—except for some bright lights and hands pushing and prodding at her.

"They put five stitches in your head," Bobby explained when she questioned him about the large bandage covering her temple. "They said you can take the bandage off in a few days, and you have an appointment to go back in a week and get the stitches taken out."

"Will you go with me?" Andrea asked. "I don't like hospitals."

When Bobby gave her a quizzical look she quickly went on, "I hope you're planning to go to work tomorrow, because I think I'll be able to take care of myself."

"I don't know. You'd better be careful," Bobby said. "The doctor told me you shouldn't move around too much—you might get dizzy."

"I'll sit down if I get dizzy. But I don't want you wasting another day at home with me."

Bobby sighed. "Well, if you really think you'll be okay."

"I promise I won't get out of bed unless I absolutely have to."

But the next morning, as soon as Bobby had gone, Andrea put on her bathrobe, checked herself in the mirror to see that she was suitably pallid, and then went across the hall and rang Mrs. King's bell.

The door opened immediately. "Good heavens!" Mrs. King said, pointing at the bandage. "What happened to *you*?"

"Oh, it's just a scratch," Andrea mumbled. Mrs. King was holding the door open.

"Are you sure? That looks like an awfully big bandage to me."

Andrea started to nod her head and was instantly sorry she had. Mrs. King's living room suddenly tilted crazily, and a spasm of nausea rose in her throat. She grabbed the back of a chair for support and, leaning on it, brought herself around and sank down into it.

"What is it, child? Are you all right?" Mrs. King hovered over her, tremoring hands reaching out to help.

When the dizziness subsided, Andrea was worried that she had upset Mrs. King. She grabbed the older woman's hand and squeezed it. "I'm fine now," she said. "It was just a little dizzy spell. So you just sit down and try to calm yourself down."

Mrs. King looked at her dubiously, but sat down in a nearby chair. "Scratch, indeed. What really happened to you, Andrea dear?" she asked, her voice somewhat chiding. "I do wish you'd tell me."

Andrea sighed. "All right, I'll tell you." She twisted her face into a grimace. "But it's not a pretty story."

"I haven't lived to be as old as I am without seeing a little of the bad side of life," Mrs. King said stoutly.

Andrea couldn't help smiling at her neighbor's forcefulness, and it suddenly occurred to her that Mrs. King was a lot tougher than she let on. *Why that old fox,* Andrea thought. *She's a bit of an actress herself.*

"Well?" Mrs. King was asking impatiently.

"Oh, I'm sorry," Andrea said. "I was just thinking about what you said—about how much of life you've seen. I suppose there's not much that shocks you anymore."

Mrs. King frowned. "No, most things in this world don't shock me—but that doesn't mean I have to like them."

"Oh, I know what you mean. Like what happened to me—I wasn't expecting it, but when it happened I wasn't surprised, just angry."

"Well, what *did* happen to you?" Mrs. King asked, with more than a hint of impatience in her voice.

"I guess I'm just avoiding coming out and saying it," Andrea said, lowering her voice and her eyes before she said hesitantly, "I was almost raped."

The unshockable Mrs. King's eyes bulged out. "No!" she cried. "How awful!"

Andrea clenched her jaw as if fighting to keep it from quivering. "Yes, it was," she said thickly. "I still can't quite believe that it happened—except for this." She pointed to the bandage. "I got this little souvenir when I was trying to fight them off."

"Them!" Mrs. King blurted out. "How many were there?"

"Two. A black man and a white man."

"And they didn't—"

"No, I got away," Andrea said, her eyes growing

wide as she considered her amazing escape. "I'm not even sure how I did it—except maybe that they were surprised that I fought back."

Mrs. King stood up abruptly. "Let me make us some tea, dear. I think we can both use it, and it'll only take a minute—the kettle's already on. And then I want you to start all over again. Tell me everything—from the beginning." She went into the kitchen.

Andrea could not help grinning to herself. Mrs. King was the most responsive audience she had ever had.

Mrs. King returned carrying a tray with two steaming cups of tea and a plate of cookies. "I baked these yesterday," she explained as she handed Andrea a cup of tea and offered her the cookies. "I wondered if you'd be over. When you didn't come, I *thought* something might be wrong—"

"I'm sorry," Andrea said as she took a cookie. "I should have sent Bobby over—he stayed home with me all day—but I just wasn't thinking too clearly."

"It's all right, dear," Mrs. King said. "Now that I know what the situation was." She patted Andrea's hand. "How nice of your husband to stay home with you. He must have been awfully worried."

"Oh, he *was*," Andrea said. "I don't know who was more upset—him or *me*."

Mrs. King leaned back in her chair and stirred her tea. "Now tell me the whole story." Her eyes glinted brightly. "And don't try to spare me. I can take it."

Andrea suppressed a smile. "All right," she said,

sipping carefully at the steaming tea. "From the beginning." Crossing her legs, she balanced the teacup on her knee. "Well, it all started in the morning when I saw in the *Times* that the *QE2*— you know, the *Queen Elizabeth*—was going to be docking that day. I'd never really seen a big ocean liner before—especially not up close. So, I thought I'd go down to the pier. It was a beautiful day and I wanted to get out of the house, I didn't have anything else to do—I knew you were going to the doctor's—and it seemed like a good idea at the time—"

Mrs. King started to speak, but Andrea waved her to silence. "No, don't tell me how dumb it was. I've heard it all from Bobby—a million times."

"He's right, you know. It's not a place for a young woman to go gallivanting around all alone."

"Yes, *now* I know. But—well, anyway I did go down to the docks. And I wandered around by myself, looking at the *QE2* and some of the other ships, and before I realized it, it was starting to get dark. I didn't notice it because the sky and the river were still pretty light, but when I turned around the streets were already dark. So, I figured I'd better get out of there. There weren't too many people around and it looked kind of spooky. I thought maybe the best thing to do would be to get a cab—but I didn't see a single one that was free. So then I decided I'd better take the bus, and I started walking toward Forty-second Street.

"I was getting a little nervous because by this time it was *really* dark, and I had to walk past all these doorways and alleys where somebody could be hiding. I was walking very fast, almost jogging, so I was really surprised when I heard a voice right behind me. I hadn't heard any footsteps so I looked over my shoulder, and . . . and there was this man practically stepping on my heels. Before I could even shout or scream a hand came out of nowhere and grabbed me by the face, clamping my mouth shut. Right then I was so stunned I probably couldn't have screamed anyway."

Andrea paused and looked at Mrs. King, whose eyes were wide and rapt.

"Then they said something to me that made me realize what they wanted—that they weren't just going to rob me," Andrea said grimly. "And that's when I started to fight back."

"What did they say?"

Andrea looked at her neighbor levelly, then lowered her eyes. "One of them—I can't even remember which one it was now—said to the other one: 'She's a big one, isn't she? I like 'em big. It makes it easier to do it standin' up.' " Andrea blushed. "Actually, they put it a little more crudely than that."

Mrs. King gasped. "How horrible! You must have been petrified."

"Yes, but when I heard that, I knew I wasn't just going to let them get away with it, and I started to struggle."

"Did they have a weapon?"

"Yes. One of them pulled a knife on me—"

"But they could have killed you!"

"I know. But I didn't really think of that then. I just thought about getting away. I knew that was my only chance. So I grabbed for the knife—"

"Oh, my God!"

"—and I nearly got it, but I wasn't quite quick enough. So he swung at me with the knife, and I ducked—but he slashed me on the temple with the tip of it. That's how I got this." Andrea pointed to the bandage. "I didn't even feel it at the time. Then I kicked at him and got him in the kneecap and he fell down and dropped the knife. I heard it fall, and I tried to find it but I couldn't see it in the dark. Then the other one grabbed me from behind. He had me by the throat and was choking me, so I bit him on the hand and when he let go I bent over and jabbed with my elbow with all my might—right in the groin."

"Wonderful!"

"And then I just started running. I never looked back. I just ran and ran until I saw a car, and I jumped in front of it to make it stop. At first the driver thought I was some kind of weirdo, but when he saw the blood on me—I didn't even know it was there—he let me in. He took me to the hospital, and then the police came and questioned me but I couldn't even describe the men—just that one was white and one was black—so there's no hope of catching them. Finally, Bobby came and took me home. And that's the whole story."

Mrs. King let out her breath in a long, deep sigh. "My dear, you are so lucky to even be alive. But I must say you were very brave to fight back the way you did. I'm sure I could never have done the same thing when I was your age."

Andrea allowed herself a tiny smile as she sipped at the now tepid tea. "It didn't seem like bravery at the time," she said. "But I do feel rather good about it now." As she set her teacup down her hand drifted up to the bandage on her temple. How proud of it she was; after all, it was her badge of honor.

After Andrea left, Mrs. King sat, musing over another cup of tea. It wasn't any of her business so she had not mentioned to Andrea the scene she had witnessed in the hall two nights ago.

But it didn't fit with the story Andrea had just told her. That hysterical young man had been carrying Andrea *out,* not in—she was almost certain of that. Of course, she had been so frightened by his angry outburst that she had not even dared to look through the peephole, so she could have been mistaken—perhaps he *was* bringing Andrea home from the hospital.

But why had he looked so guilty when she opened the door—as if she had caught him in the middle of some shameful act? And then when he had shouted at her, he hadn't been trying to protect Andrea, he was trying to protect *himself.*

Had Andrea lied, invented that story about being assaulted in order to hide the fact that her husband was the one who had hurt her? That poor girl was so blindly in love with him that she would probably say anything to keep someone from guessing the truth.

Mrs. King sighed and shook her head. There was no point in trying to tell Andrea that she knew things were not quite right in her marriage. All she could really do was hope that nothing awful happened to that sweet, innocent child.

CHAPTER NINE

Weeks went by and Andrea made no more mention of the divorce. Bobby was trying his utmost to treat her better, and that seemed to keep her satisfied. Occasionally, he lapsed and said something mean or hurtful, but the sight of the dark, pink scar on her temple just below the hairline always brought him around. Most of the time the scar was not visible because Andrea's long hair fell in front of it, but she had developed a habit of tucking her hair behind her ears whenever she wanted to keep it out of her face, and at those moments Bobby was painfully reminded of the disfigurement and how it had come to be.

Andrea herself hardly seemed aware of it, although he suspected that was just a ploy to make him feel even more guilty. As time went by, he began to notice that whenever he started to show any irritation with her, the hair always went quickly behind the ears. Whether it was a nervous, unconscious reaction or one of design, it served the same purpose—it kept him in line. But on the whole, he didn't mind the change in their relationship; it made their life together much more stable.

Time had passed so quickly for him since he'd met Andrea. Summer had turned to fall and now the first chills of winter were already here.

There had been no further word from Cynthia about her coming to New York, and he hadn't yet bothered to call her. Let her think that it didn't make any difference to him.

Then, with the holidays approaching, his thoughts began drifting back to Christmases past he had spent with Cynthia and Jennifer. He remembered their last Christmas together so acutely that he could practically smell the piny scent of the Christmas tree as he and Cynthia had sat under it, laughing at Jennifer's dazzled eyes and squeals of delight as she tore the wrappings on her packages into shreds; the gaily colored ribbons and bright, crinkly papers seemed to fascinate her more than the toys she found inside.

One Sunday afternoon he and Andrea had gone for a stroll down Fifth Avenue to see all the lavish window displays, but the sidewalks in front of each department store were thronged with parents and children. The sight of all those happy little faces with their pink cheeks and wonder-filled eyes nearly brought him to tears. He dragged Andrea into a bar, where he spent the rest of the afternoon bemoaning his disfranchisement as a father and growing increasingly maudlin with every drink.

When he went shopping for Andrea's gift he debated whether or not he should buy presents for Cynthia and Jennifer, too, instead of just sending them a check as he had done last Christmas. But the thought of sending them gifts that he wouldn't see them open—and that probably wouldn't be appreciated—decided him against it.

He already knew what he would buy for Andrea. She had once mentioned that she didn't have a really warm winter jacket and didn't see how she could afford one. So he had decided that a nice, down, ski parka would be the perfect gift for her—once the icy New York winter blew in she would get a lot of use out of it.

On Christmas Day Andrea was like a little kid herself when she opened up her package. "Oh, Bobby, I love it. It's fantastic!" she gushed.

"Well, it's just a parka," he said. "You'd think it was a mink coat the way you're carrying on over it."

She put it on immediately and danced around the Christmas tree she had insisted on buying because it was so spindly no one else would want it. "You'd better stop that," Bobby warned when she kept running her hands over the shiny blue fabric. "You'll wear it out."

She gave Bobby an expensive, leather-bound thesaurus and a new wallet. "That's for all the money you'll be getting when you sell your book," she said shyly. He was touched by this subtle way of letting him know that she didn't believe Sam's charges against him, a subject which neither of them had raised since she'd quit her job at the Center Stage.

Andrea's pleasure in her gift and her obvious good spirits were infectious, but even as he looked at her beaming face and saw the excitement glowing in her eyes as she told him about the splendid Christmas feast she was preparing for him, he could not help wondering how Cynthia and Jennifer were spending the holiday.

So, when Andrea went into the kitchen to put the finishing touches on their Christmas dinner, he told her he had to go out for a pack of cigarettes. Once outside, he ducked into a phone booth and called Cynthia.

"Hi, Cyn. Merry Christmas."

"Who is this?"

"It's Bobby. What's the matter, don't you recognize my voice anymore?"

"Well, it sounds strange."

"I'm in a phone booth. I was on my way out to have Christmas dinner by myself and I passed this phone booth. So I thought, 'What the hell, I'd like to say Merry Christmas to my daughter.'"

"Do you want me to get her?"

"No, not just yet. How is she?"

"Fine. I bought her a doll with the money you sent."

"What did you get for yourself?"

"Nothing yet."

Bobby hesitated a moment, then asked, "Cyn, what about that letter you wrote me? Have you made up your mind yet?"

"I wondered when you'd get around to that," Cynthia said somewhat smugly. "As a matter of fact, I was just going to write you—I should be in New York the second week in January."

Three weeks. "Hey, that's great," Bobby said, trying to sound as casual as he could. "Where are you planning to stay?" Could she possibly be thinking of staying with him?

"A hotel, I guess. Can you recommend any?"

"Well, what about a hotel for women? You'd probably feel safer there."

"Sure. Whatever you say. Just give me the name and address and I'll write to them for a reservation."

"Don't worry. I'll take care of it."

"Thanks. That's considerate of you." There was just a hint of archness in her voice.

"It's okay. Listen, when exactly are you coming?"

"The fourteenth, I think. It's a Sunday. I'm taking the train."

"Do you want me to meet you?"

"No. That's not necessary."

"I'd be glad to do it—"

"I told you, Bobby. You don't have to."

"Okay. Then you'd better take a cab from the station. I'll let you know exactly where the hotel is and how to get to it—and then you tell the cabbie that so he won't try and gyp you."

"Why would he do that?"

"Oh, Cyn, never mind. You'll find out about these things when you get to New York."

"Is it really that bad?"

"Yeah, some of it. You'll just have to learn your way around—but when you do, you'll love it.

There's so much to do and see here. I can show you the sights—"

"Bobby, I'm not coming as a tourist," Cynthia said sharply. "I'm going to be spending all my time trying to find work."

"So you're really serious about it."

"I don't know why you should be surprised. *You* used to tell me I should be a model."

"Yeah, but every time I said that you laughed it off. What made you suddenly want to do it?"

"It's a long story." Obviously she wasn't going to tell it to him.

"Well, you know *I* might be able to help you out, too—but I guess we can talk about that when you get here. Listen, I think my three minutes are about up so I'm going to go."

"Don't you want to talk to Jennifer?"

"No, she wouldn't even know my voice. Just tell her I called to wish her a Merry Christmas, okay?"

"All right."

"Yeah, well, I'll see you in three weeks. If there are any changes in your plans, just give me a call at the office—collect."

"I'll do that. Good-bye."

" 'Bye, Cyn."

Bobby hung up the phone and jerked open the door of the booth. The air was biting cold, but he needed to walk—and think.

Cynthia's coming to New York might mean that there'd be a second chance for the two of them. He had heard nothing encouraging in her voice, but she *was* coming here—and that had to mean something.

Maybe she was afraid to come right out and say it, maybe she was afraid that his feelings had changed. Well, he'd set her straight on that score. When he wrote to her about the hotel arrangements he'd tell her exactly how he felt. Then when they met they wouldn't have to go through all those tedious games.

But even so, Cynthia was a proud woman. She probably wouldn't take him back just like that. She'd keep him dangling for a while, waiting to see if he'd changed. Well, he could handle that. He'd been biding his time for so long now, that a few more weeks wouldn't matter.

In the meantime, what the hell was he going to do with Andrea? She was such a sweet kid, he really hated the idea of dumping on her. Of course, there was no reason—so far, anyway—that he should have to get her out of his life, just as long as he could get her out of his *apartment*. That was important. Cynthia might be able to understand his seeing other women, but living with one, well, he just knew she'd never be able to forgive that.

Of course, Andrea herself might not like the change in their cozy little arrangement, but that couldn't be helped. Anyway, he'd try to put it to her so she'd understand. But he couldn't do it today, it would spoil her Christmas.

So he went home and pretended to Andrea that nothing had happened.

But she knew. "You're in a better mood now, aren't you?" she said. "You looked kind of sad before you went out. I thought maybe you didn't like your presents."

"Oh, no. I *love* my presents," Bobby said, smiling. Especially the one Cynthia had given him.

He waited until the holidays were over to give Andrea her walking papers. Before he went home that night he stopped to have a couple of drinks, just to build up his courage a little.

When he let himself in to the apartment, Andrea ran up to him and kissed him, and in that moment he felt a little like a heel.

"I'll have dinner ready in half an hour," she bubbled. "One of your favorites—barbecued ribs."

Bobby tried to give her a smile of appreciation, but he could feel that it came out wrong. "Darlin'," he said tentatively, "before you finish making dinner, sit down. I have some bad news for you."

Andrea's face fell. "I knew it," she said. "I could see it the minute you walked in."

Bobby led her over to the couch. Her hand felt clammy as he squeezed it affectionately. There was no sense in beating around the bush. "I got a letter from Cynthia today," he said. "She's moving to New York."

Andrea's eyes narrowed. "Why? What does she want?"

Bobby wagged his head ruefully. "Who knows? She *says* she's coming here for a career in modeling—but I think she's coming here to spy on me."

"Why would she do that?"

"To screw up the divorce. If she can catch me at something, then she'll have ammunition to use against me in court."

"But, Bobby—" Andrea hesitated, struggling to find the right words. Finally, she said, "Why can't *you* just go ahead and get the divorce? After all, you're the one who caught *her* in—in adultery."

Bobby sighed. "I can't do that, Red. I don't want Jennifer to ever find that out about her mother."

Andrea fell silent.

"I'm boxed in," Bobby said. "It's got to be her way or no way at all. If I ever want to see my daughter again I've got to go along."

"But it's not fair!"

"I didn't say it was. But it's just the way things are—she holds all the cards."

Something glinted in Andrea's eyes. "I don't understand you," she said angrily. "Why don't you fight her? You're letting her get away with—" She suddenly broke off, unable to complete the sentence.

"What?" Bobby asked, his own voice rising with indignation. *Damn it. Why couldn't she just let it go?* "What were you going to say? That I'm letting Cynthia get away with murder?"

"No—no, not that," Andrea said, strangely subdued. "I didn't mean it, Bobby. I'm sorry. I realize you've got to handle this your own way."

Bobby wondered what had caused her to relent so unexpectedly. He felt cheated out of an outlet for the fury that had begun churning in his stomach. "You're right," he said. "It's *my* problem." He dropped her hand, got up abruptly, and went into the kitchen for a beer. After he'd taken several long chugs on it, he returned to the living room and stood in front of Andrea on the couch. He noticed that she had tucked her hair behind her ear while he had been out of the room. That wasn't going to work with him—not this time. "There's something you're going to have to do while Cynthia is here," he said flatly.

He could hear Andrea's intake of breath. "What?" she asked, her eyes fixed on his as if she were a small child about to be chastised.

"Move out." He said the words as if they were her punishment, what she deserved for having defied him.

She nodded dully. "I figured as much," she said softly. "When you said Cynthia was coming to town I knew I couldn't stay."

Suddenly Bobby felt sorry for her, sorry for the easy way she accepted his mistreatment of her. He dropped down beside her on the couch. "Red, believe me, I don't want it that way," he said, setting down his beer and grabbing her hands. "But if Cynthia found out I was living with another woman she'd have me by the balls—and she'd start squeezing."

Andrea managed a smile. "Well, we can't let her do that, can we?"

"That's my darlin'," Bobby said, stroking her hands. "And of course we'll see each other—only we'll have to be a little more circumspect about it."

Andrea nodded her head resignedly. "I understand," she said. "When do you want me to move out?"

"There's no rush. I'm not eager to get rid of

you. Cynthia won't be here for another two weeks. So, take your time—but it might not be a bad idea to take a few things with you every time you go back to your apartment."

Then he kissed Andrea tenderly, and when she started to withdraw from him he pressed harder, forcing his lips against hers, his tongue thrusting into her mouth. He held her like that until he felt her responding. Then he took her by the hand and led her into the bedroom.

Mrs. King screwed her eye to the peephole. This was the fourth time in a week she had seen Andrea carrying a suitcase out. The first time it happened she had opened the door and confronted her. "Oh, hello, Andrea, dear," she had said as if she were surprised to see her. Then she glanced at the suitcase. "Are you going somewhere?"

"Oh, no," Andrea said quickly. "These are just some old clothes I'm giving to charity."

Andrea wasn't as good a liar as she thought she was. Mrs. King had not missed the momentary confusion in her eyes, the nervous catch in her voice. Giving her clothes away to charity, indeed. What kind of old fool did Andrea take her for? Something was going on across the hall, something that Andrea was trying to hide.

So Mrs. King had listened and watched. And if she wasn't mistaken, that poor child was moving out.

But whenever Andrea came to visit she talked as if things were still perfect in her marriage. Yet for all her pretense, there was an air of unhappiness about her.

Several times Mrs. King had asked her if anything was wrong. Always she got the same answer: "No. Nothing's wrong. Everything's just fine."

Then why are you moving your things out of the apartment? she wanted to ask. But she couldn't let Andrea know she'd been spying on her. Unless the girl broke down and confided in her, there was nothing Mrs. King could do.

Little by little, Andrea had moved most of her things back to her own apartment. She was not at all pleased with the situation, but what could she do? Bobby was at the mercy of this woman, as long as he was still legally married to her.

Actually, she felt sorry for him. Just when it seemed that the divorce was finally going to go through, the wife came along and threw another monkey wrench in the machinery.

What an evil person she must be; it wasn't right for such a vengeful, hateful person to be raising a small child, either. She wondered why Bobby hadn't tried to get custody of his daughter.

She also wondered just how long this silly farce would go on before Cynthia would give up, go back to North Carolina and stop dragging her heels over the divorce.

She couldn't bring herself to be very sanguine about it because Cynthia's coming to New York showed just how persistent she could be—and the lengths she was willing to go to persecute Bobby.

The day before Cynthia was due to arrive,

Bobby helped Andrea pack up the last of her things, and together they carted them over to her apartment in a cab. He spent the night with her and then the next morning, Sunday, they got up late, had a leisurely brunch before Bobby went back to his own apartment to await the phone call that would herald Cynthia's arrival.

After he was gone Andrea felt a great emptiness. It had been so long since she had been alone on a weekend and that fact seemed to make this separation worse. She tried to read, but couldn't concentrate, and always her mind would wander to what Bobby was doing and if he was as lonely as she was.

After a few restless hours, she chided herself for letting her loneliness get the better of her. All she had to do was call him. He would certainly assure her that everything was all right.

When Bobby answered the phone his voice sounded expectant. Then he realized it was Andrea and the tones became clipped, almost as if he were annoyed. Yes, yes, of course, he missed her, but he wished she hadn't called just then because he thought it was Cynthia and he had been preparing himself all day to talk to her. He was sorry if he was being a little short with her but he wanted to keep the line free so he could get this thing over with Cynthia. Yes, he promised he'd call her later tonight—after he'd heard from Cynthia.

Something in Bobby's voice bothered Andrea. Why had he been so eager to get her off the phone? Even if Cynthia had called at that very moment, she would only have to wait a few minutes and then call him back. She didn't see what difference it could possibly make—unless Bobby was not being quite candid with her.

Suddenly the security she had known over the past few months with Bobby began to weaken; she had learned to trust him mostly because he hadn't given her a reason *not* to. As far as she knew he hardly seemed aware that other women existed. But Cynthia was not just another woman—she was still his wife and he had certainly loved her once. Maybe—in spite of all the bad blood between them—there was still a small spark of that love left. And then a thought struck Andrea that left her quivering with doubt: What if Cynthia had come to New York not to spy on Bobby, not to persecute him, but to get him back?

She paced the length of the tiny apartment, trying to work things out in her mind. But the more she thought, the faster her fears multiplied. Finally, she realized she had to *do* something, she couldn't just stay in her apartment all night, waiting for Bobby's phone call and brooding. So she grabbed her down parka and a warm hat and went out into the waning light of the January afternoon.

She began walking rapidly, her steps headed inexorably in the direction of Bobby's apartment. It was a little more than a mile away, straight uptown, and she covered the distance in fifteen minutes.

Across the street from his building she stood in the shadow of a doorway and stared up at his lighted fourth-floor window. The blinds were open, but she could detect no movement inside.

She was not even sure what she expected to see, but she stood in the piercing cold, stamping her feet and clapping her hands together to keep warm, and waited and watched.

So intent was she on her surveillance of Bobby's window and everyone who entered or exited the building that she scarcely noticed the passage of time or the fact that day had long since become night.

Once, a cab pulled up to the building and she was sure that her vigil had been worth it. For when the driver turned on the overhead light, she could see an attractive young brunette preparing to get out—and she was *positive* it was Cynthia, although she had only seen her once in a blurry snapshot. Then the brunette stepped out onto the sidewalk and Andrea realized she must be mistaken—this woman was too short; Bobby had described his wife as being nearly as tall as Andrea herself.

After that, she felt a little foolish. She knew she had been standing there for hours. If Bobby was going to meet Cynthia or if she was going to visit him, they surely would have done so by now—unless, of course, they had managed somehow to elude her. Maybe he had gone out before she got there, or maybe—the thought made her sick—Cynthia was up there even now, taking Andrea's place in Bobby's bed.

She debated what to do: Should she hang around here? Should she go up to Bobby's apartment and demand that he let her in—or better yet—let *herself* in with her own key, surprising them if they were together? But if Bobby were alone he'd be furious—no, the best, most direct course would be to phone him. After all, she had an excuse: he'd said he'd call her later. Since she hadn't been home all evening, what was more natural than for *her* to call him? She'd say she'd been to see one of her actress girlfriends—he didn't know any of them and could never check. Besides, it would be good for him to think that she wasn't just sitting around waiting for his call.

So, with one more glance at Bobby's window, she slipped out of the doorway and walked the few blocks to Lincoln Center.

Lights gleamed from Avery Fisher Hall. The concert had already started. Andrea crossed the deserted lobby to the row of phone booths.

This time Bobby seemed pleased to hear from her. "Where were you?" he asked. "I've been calling you all night."

"Oh, I just walked in. I went to see one of the girls I met in acting class," Andrea said. "Did you hear from Cynthia?"

"Yeah, she called from the hotel about an hour ago. Her train was late and she was really tired. We only talked for a couple of minutes."

"I'm surprised she didn't want to see you right away."

"Oh, she'll want to see me soon enough, all right—but only when it's convenient for *her*."

Andrea was gratified to hear the contemptuous tone in Bobby's voice. If Cynthia did indeed have designs on him, she was going to be up against a lot more than she knew.

"Mmm, darlin', I miss you," Bobby sighed.

"I miss you, too."

"I wish you were here. I think I'll have myself a couple more beers and then I'm going beddie-bye—only it's going to seem awful cold and lonely without you there."

Andrea waited for Bobby to ask her to come over. When he didn't, she faked a yawn and said, "Well, it's been a long day for me. Guess I'll go to bed early myself."

"Okay, darlin'. I'll call you tomorrow."

She left the phone booth and briefly entertained the thought of taking up her post outside Bobby's window again—just to make sure he did go to bed, alone. But the phone call had erased most of her doubts; so instead, she caught a bus downtown to her own apartment and went to bed—satisfied that for the time being she had nothing to worry about.

The next morning she waited until she was sure that Bobby had gone to work, then dialed his number. When there was no answer, she threw on her jacket and hiked up there again. Only this time she went right into the building and let herself into the apartment.

She looked around the living room and let out a disgruntled sigh. Bobby was such a hopeless slob. The Sunday *Times* was scattered across the floor by the couch, there were empty beer cans and dirty dishes sitting about on the tables, and the ashtrays were nearly overflowing. Even the air was foul with the smell of stale cigarette smoke.

Andrea's fingers were itching to get to work cleaning up the place, but she didn't dare do that.

Instead, she picked up an ashtray and poked through the cigarette butts, searching for any traces of lipstick on the filter tips. After that, she checked the beer cans and dirty dishes for lipstick smudges. Then she went through the bathroom and the bedroom, alert for anything that didn't belong there. Finally, she bent over the unmade bed, her eyes scouring the pillowcases for any hairs that weren't either hers or Bobby's.

When she was satisfied that Cynthia had not spent the night with Bobby, she went across the hall for her morning visit with Mrs. King—just as she had on all the other mornings when she had been actually living with Bobby.

Mrs. King did not seem to notice anything was amiss, which was just exactly what Andrea had intended. She wanted the woman to go right on believing that she was still married to Bobby and living happily right across the hall.

Every day she continued her pretense—furtively entering Bobby's apartment, paying her daily courtesy call on Mrs. King, then hurrying home in time for Bobby's usual late afternoon phone call.

She did not see Bobby for a couple of nights. One of them she knew he had spent with Cynthia. That night she went to a movie alone and sat through two shows. When she left the theater she looked back at the marquee. Strange, but she didn't remember a single thing about the film she had just seen.

Her fears were allayed the next night when Bobby appeared at her apartment. He swept her up in a long, exuberant embrace and refused to talk about Cynthia—"that cold bitch"—at all. *That cold bitch*. The phrase warmed Andrea's heart.

A few nights later Bobby asked her to spend the night with him.

"What am I going to do with you?" she said, feigning shock when she walked into the apartment. "This place looks like a pigsty. I can't stand it—I've got to clean it up."

Bobby laughed and shrugged his shoulders. "See how much I need you, Red? I just go to pieces without you."

She was in the bedroom and nearly finished straightening it up, when the phone rang. Bobby answered it from the living room. From the tone of his voice she knew instantly that it was Cynthia. Curious to hear her rival's voice, she breathlessly picked up the extension.

Bobby was talking; he sounded irritated. He was asking Cynthia why she hadn't consulted him before she moved out of the hotel. A honeyed voice replied that she hadn't liked the hotel, and a model she had met had told her about a furnished apartment. Then she gave Bobby the new address and phone number.

Shaking with excitement, Andrea noiselessly put the phone back in its cradle and jotted the address and phone number down on a sheet of paper, which she stuffed in her jeans pocket. Already a plan was forming in her mind.

After a couple of minutes she strolled out of the bedroom. Bobby was scowling into the phone and he waved at her to be quiet. Andrea simply sat down on the couch and picked up a magazine.

"Who was that?" she asked casually when he hung up.

"Christ! Who do you think it was?" Bobby snarled, storming into the kitchen. He came back with a beer in his hand.

"What did she want?"

He slumped down beside Andrea on the couch. "To tell me that she moved out of that perfectly nice hotel *I* found for her into some crummy furnished room some model told her about."

"Well, what difference does that make? Why should you care? *I* live in a crummy furnished apartment."

Bobby frowned. "Yeah, I guess it doesn't matter." Then a devilish smile crossed his face. "Maybe she'll get herself mugged staying in that place," he said. "It would serve her right."

CHAPTER TEN

As soon as Bobby left for work the next morning Andrea washed out their coffee cups, hurriedly dressed, and left his apartment. She stopped at Mrs. King's just long enough to tell her that she couldn't visit with her today—she had to go out and meet a friend and didn't know when she would be back.

Then she took the bus down to her own apartment, where she changed the jeans and parka she was wearing for a dress and her winter coat. She grabbed a scarf out of her dresser, put it on over her head, and slipped a pair of dark glasses on. Then she surveyed herself in the mirror. Not bad for an impromptu disguise. Anyone who knew her would recognize her, of course—but she had managed to conceal two of her three most distinctive characteristics, her hair and her eyes. The third, her height, she could do nothing about.

She was all set. Now all she had to do was wait. Sooner or later Cynthia was bound to show her face, and that was what Andrea was after—a good look at the competition.

The address was in the West Fifties, within easy walking distance. Andrea traversed the blocks quickly with her long-legged stride, hoping Bobby's wife was not an early riser. It was nearly nine-fifteen. Cynthia might have left already. It was a chance she would have to take—after all, what did she stand to lose besides a little time? She didn't really have anything better to do, anyway.

When she reached Cynthia's block she slowed her pace to a leisurely stroll while she checked off the numbers on each building. It was a nondescript block, no better and no worse than hundreds of similar streets in the city. The buildings were mostly four and five stories high, each of them almost identical to its neighbor. In tiny squares of earth set in the sidewalks a few scrawny trees had been planted, and their branches had been scraped bare by the winter wind. Either that or they were all dead, Andrea thought. A woman was out walking her Doberman pinscher. Just like every other block in New York.

The address she was searching for turned out to be a six-story, dark-brick apartment house, obviously built before the turn of the century in an era of refined yet opulent elegance. Its striking façade was adorned with lacy ironwork balconies at each window and its cornices were festooned with carved stone garlands. But as Andrea drew closer she could see that one of the panes in the leaded glass of its front door was cracked, and some of the wrought-iron scrollwork above the doorway itself was rusty where the paint had chipped away—everywhere was the air of a genteel lady down on her luck. Still, it looked like a fairly respectable building, not the tenement she had pictured in her mind when Bobby reacted to it.

She walked on, past the building to the corner on the opposite side of the street, where she still had a good vantage of the apartment house doorway and where she would look less conspicuous just standing around. She would wait an hour or so; if Cynthia hadn't appeared by then she would give it up and try again later.

Five minutes went by, then ten, and she began to feel less self-conscious as she realized that few passers-by took the slightest interest in her—they were all in too big a hurry to get to work or do their shopping or whatever else had forced them out at nine-thirty in the morning.

A bright winter sun was warming the air. Andrea barely noticed the cold. She stood in a patch of sunlight, facing west, feeling its warmth on her back. She thought about Wisconsin and how it would be on a day like this: the sky an azure blue, the sunshine blinding as it reflected off the snow-covered hills, and the air so clear and still that you could imagine you could hear the sound of clumps of snow falling off the trees in the woods.

With a pang of homesickness, she wondered if she would ever see Wisconsin again. Maybe she would ask Bobby to take her there someday—after they were married. Maybe that's how she would tell him the truth about herself—about Andy and the terrible tragedy that had scarred her life. . . .

The door of the apartment house opened and abruptly jerked Andrea back to reality. A woman appeared. Andrea squinted at her. She had dark hair and was tall and slender, but a wide-brimmed hat made it hard to see her features distinctly. She began walking in Andrea's direction, and as she drew closer, Andrea grew increasingly positive that she was indeed the woman in Bobby's snapshot.

Even from across the street she was dishearteningly beautiful. Her face was serene and composed and she held her head high and proud—even a little arrogantly—as she walked with brisk, fluid strides. Aside from the beige hat, she was wearing a stylish, taupe-colored cloth coat, and brown gloves and boots. In her left hand she was carrying a black model's portfolio; a brown leather bag was swinging from her right shoulder.

Andrea watched as she reached the corner and turned left, onto the avenue. She was sure that Cynthia had not noticed her standing on the opposite corner. Maybe it would be safe to follow her a little way—just to get an idea of where she was going. Maybe it would give her an inkling of whether Cynthia's story about coming to New York to look for work as a model was true, or if it was just a blind, designed to throw Bobby off his guard.

She gave the woman a head start before she set off, matching her pace. It was easy to keep her in sight, for the beige hat was like a buoy, floating above the heads of most of the other pedestrians.

Cynthia walked straight up the avenue to Fifty-seventh Street, then turned left at the corner, out of view. Andrea broke into a trot, rounded the corner, and stopped abruptly. Cynthia was standing at the bus stop, not twenty feet away from her—and she was staring right at her.

Instinctively, Andrea looked away, afraid that she had been discovered. But that was ridiculous—Cynthia had no idea who she was. She stole another glance. By this time, Cynthia had turned around and was facing down the street, watching for the bus.

With a sinking feeling, Andrea realized that even if Cynthia had looked at her only in idle curiosity, she didn't dare move any closer—and she certainly couldn't follow her anymore; Bobby's wife would know her face now.

So she started walking again, this time west on Fifty-seventh Street, away from Cynthia. When she was halfway down the block the bus passed her, going in the opposite direction. She looked back over her shoulder, and saw the bus stop at the corner and the beige hat disappear inside. Well, that blew it—she might never get another chance to see Cynthia Wilson in the flesh again.

As she walked home, she thought about the fact that Cynthia had taken the Fifty-seventh crosstown bus. She didn't like it. Bobby's office was near Fifty-seventh and Sixth—could Cynthia be on her way to meet him? Damn it, she wished she'd been able to follow her a little while longer—if only to see where she got off the bus.

But if Cynthia was meeting Bobby, there was always the danger he might spot Andrea—and jump to the conclusion that Andrea was following *him*. And she knew from bitter experience how angry he could become if he thought someone was spying on him. His reaction the night she had told him what Sam had said was proof of *that*.

No. Following Cynthia was just too chancy. She'd better give up the whole idea.

Discouraged, she arrived at her apartment building, let herself in, and listlessly began climbing the two flights of stairs to her room. At the bottom of the second flight she paused, her foot on the first step. *What about a disguise?* A disguise so different from herself that even Bobby wouldn't recognize her? Yes, that could work.

Excited now, she ran up the rest of the flight to her apartment, unlocked the door, and burst through it. She took off the scarf and dark glasses, slipped out of her coat, and immediately began going through her things to see what she might use.

There was an old mouton coat her mother had discarded when Paul bought her a new mink stole. Perfect! Bobby had only seen her wear it a couple of times. She could build the costume around that. She would need to cover her legs, and for that she would use an old pair of baggy black tights. For shoes there was a pair of scuffed loafers she found at the back of the closet floor. A dress and gloves were easily taken care of, and that left only her face and hair to be concealed. Of course, she could wear a scarf as she had done today, but it would be better if she could change the color of her hair completely. A wig? A cheap one since she had to be careful of her money. And the mousier the better for the character she was planning to play. As for her face, she still had some theatrical makeup left over from her acting classes. That would have to do.

She bought the wig in a store on Times Square, and rushed home to try it on with the rest of the outfit. Pleased with the overall effect, she got out her makeup to make the transformation. Greasepaint first, to give her normally rosy complexion a gray, washed-out look. Next, she took a gray eyebrow pencil and drew in dark circles under her eyes, deep furrows in her forehead, and smile lines from her nose to her mouth. With the tip of her finger, she carefully blended the edges of the penciled-in marks to make them look more convincing. Finally, she penciled in eyebrows to match the color of the wig. The face was complete.

She put on the coat and pirouetted in front of her full-length mirror. What she saw was not Andrea Donahue, but a dowdy, middle-aged woman. The exterior was finished, but she would still need to work on the character inside. How would a woman like that walk and stand, what sort of facial expressions would she use?

Andrea closed her eyes and tried immersing herself in the role: this woman was probably unhappy, she had no family or friends—only a menial job she hated. A woman to whom life had not been kind. When Andrea opened her eyes she saw that her face had assumed a weary, weight-of-the-world expression, her shoulders had hunched into a slight stoop.

Now that she had the basic posture, adding the walk would be simple—she need only to take shorter steps and move as if it was difficult to pick up her feet. When she'd practiced this for a while, she decided it was time for a dry run.

On the stairs she met one of her neighbors and almost spoke before she realized that the woman had gone on, completely ignoring her. Still, it wasn't a good test, the woman was frequently unfriendly. But a group of children playing around the corner knew Andrea well and always exchanged quips with her. Now, they barely glanced in her direction. At the fruit stand on the next block the man who usually waited on her gave her a dirty look. That was enough; he knew Andrea by name, and had once even tried to arrange a date with her for his son. The dress rehearsal was a smash. Tomorrow she would make her debut.

The morning was gloomy and overcast. Andrea was up and in costume early, pacing the room from the bed to the window and back, nerves taut. She was grateful for the cloudy skies—harsh sunlight might show her makeup off to disadvantage. The same layer of clouds that hid the sun kept the temperature mild for January, and that meant that the long hours she would probably have to spend outdoors would not be too uncomfortable.

In character, she walked the distance to Cynthia's block at a much slower pace than she had the day before, and took up her station again, at the same corner. She had only been standing there a few minutes when Cynthia appeared, wearing the same outfit as she had on the previous day. She retraced the same route, too, but Andrea stayed closer this time—not wanting to have to run after her the way she had yesterday.

Cynthia made straight for the bus stop on Fifty-seventh. Andrea arrived right behind her. As they were standing there, Andrea kept her face turned away, so Bobby's wife would not have a chance to observe it too closely.

When the bus came she held back, wanting Cynthia to take a seat first so she could place herself strategically to watch her quarry unobserved. Cynthia found a seat near the rear doors, but although there was plenty of room in the back, Andrea stayed closer to the front so she would not have to pass Cynthia to get to a seat. She squeezed in beside a fat man whose ample hips were overlapping the seat divider. He pretended that she wasn't there.

Cynthia was on the opposite side of the bus, several seats down—but close enough for Andrea to get a first really good look at her face.

It was a beautiful face. Andrea felt a sharp twinge of jealousy as she watched it. She was more than merely pretty, surprisingly sophisticated-looking for someone fresh from a small southern town. Her makeup had been so skillfully applied that it could almost pass for natural, and Andrea could see that she only used it to heighten her beauty rather than to cover up any facial flaws. For there didn't seem to be any: she had incredible bone structure, with prominent cheekbones that cast the planes of her jaw into soft shadows; her complexion was fine-pored and translucent; her large, wide-set eyes were a delicate hazel that Andrea thought would probably change color with whatever she was wearing; her nose was small and straight, and there was a slight, provocative pout to her mouth. She smiled briefly as a woman with a small child took the next seat. Her teeth were white and even.

Cynthia was the very picture of decorum. Her black model's portfolio and brown shoulder bag were resting on her lap, and her gloved hands were neatly folded on top of them. She appeared oblivious to her companions on the bus and the occasional, envious glances they sent in her direction, and was intently staring out the window opposite her. Probably watching the unfamiliar streets to see where she was, Andrea thought.

As the bus approached Sixth Avenue, Andrea braced herself to get off. But Cynthia remained in her seat, and Andrea smiled to herself with relief. At least she was not going to meet Bobby—not now, anyway.

Two stops later, at Madison Avenue, Cynthia rose, and Andrea—not looking at her once— followed. Once they were in the street she felt safer, for the sidewalks were crowded and Cynthia most likely would not notice a nondescript woman in an old fur coat tagging along behind her.

Finally, she turned into what appeared to be the doorway to a small office building. A few paces behind, Andrea followed.

She was waiting for an elevator, so Andrea made
a show of studying the building's directory, squint-
ing at it, as if she was having a hard time reading
it, while she watched Cynthia out of the corner of
her eye. When Cynthia looked vacantly at her, she
froze: Had she realized that this woman in the
mouton coat was everywhere she went? Apparently
not, for Cynthia turned back, studying the illuminated numerals above the doors as the elevator descended. Finally it came, and she stepped into it.
For a second, Andrea thought she might risk getting into the elevator with her, but no, the quarters would be much too close.

So, she let the elevator go and went back to studying the directory. When she saw the name of a
modeling agency she was sure that was where Cynthia had gone. Now the problem was, how long
could she wait around for her to reappear?

She knew she couldn't wait in the building itself—that would appear too suspicious. She had to
go back out to the street. But this disguise was not
entirely appropriate to East Fifty-seventh Street,
and she felt increasingly uncomfortable as she
drifted along the block, pretending to be gazing
into store windows while she was on the lookout
for Cynthia's emergence from the office building.
She was out of place among the well-dressed pedestrians, and although few of them looked at her directly, she could still feel their scorn.

Half an hour went by, then perhaps an hour,
and her legs were beginning to quiver with tired-
ness and tension. There was a hard, aching knot
between her hunched shoulder blades, which she

tried—unsuccessfully—to loosen by twitching her shoulders several times, as if she had a nervous tic. Finally, when the discomfort began to turn to actual pain, she knew she would have to give up soon.

She waited a few more minutes, and when Cynthia did not appear, took a bus home. She stripped off the hated disguise immediately and let herself sink into a hot tub, to soothe her aching muscles.

She leaned back in the tub, letting the warmth of the water float away all the kinks in her body, and thought about what she was going to do next.

The disguise, the nearness to Cynthia had been exciting—like something out of a spy novel. But now that she had seen Bobby's wife up close, a new fear had seized her. Few men, Andrea was sure, could be immune to beauty like Cynthia's. And Bobby was certainly not made of steel. If Cynthia decided she wanted him back, Andrea would hardly stand a chance.

Still, Bobby loved *her*—or so he said. And from what he had told her of his contacts with Cynthia, they had not been exactly pleasant. Could he be lying, not telling her what Cynthia was *really* after, just so Andrea wouldn't worry? Possibly, but then he was doing it to protect *her*. That would be just like him.

Or maybe Cynthia was just playing hard to get, making Bobby think she didn't care anymore so his male ego would be aroused. Now *that* was a very strong likelihood. Cynthia looked like the kind of woman who would play that sort of game, stirring a man's interest in her by remaining aloof, a challenge.

If she could keep following her—just maybe—she could find out. Yes, she had to keep trailing her, and Cynthia must never notice, never know.

The water in the tub had cooled. She got out, dried herself briskly and, wrapped in her old terry-cloth bathrobe, went to her closet. The clothes underneath wouldn't matter much, a skirt and sweater would be fine, and her winter coat would be okay—for a while. Cynthia probably would not remember it. Black low-heeled shoes would suffice until it snowed, and she had to exchange them for boots. But she needed to buy another wig. Her own hair color was just too flamboyant. Makeup would be easy—she'd put on gobs of mascara and eyeshadow and pencil in her brows to match the color of the wig.

When she went out to get the wig she went to a different store. This time she picked one that was not so obviously artificial. It was dark brown, almost black, in a frizzy style that looked quite natural, and it altered her appearance radically.

When she got home, she tried it on with the makeup and clothes. The transformation was amazing. She looked just like any of dozens of other girls one might see on the bus or subway during rush hour.

She glanced at the clock. It was after five-thirty; Cynthia must be home by now. Well, there was one way to find out.

*   *   *

Cynthia eased slowly out of her boots. Oh Lord, did her feet hurt. No one had warned her that "pounding the pavement" was such a literal phrase.

She made a cup of coffee to revive her and then sat down with paper and pen.

Dear Mama,

I'm sorry that I haven't written for a while, but I can't tell you how tired I've been in the evenings.

Nothing definite has happened as far as the modeling goes, but I'm seeing an awful lot of people. I just keep hoping that one of them will give me a break soon.

Bobby calls me every few days. He's being quite nice really, and seems concerned that I have enough money to live on. He's also arranged some appointments for me. None of them has panned out so far, but he says it's important just to let these people know my face.

I can't say that I really like New York yet, but it's not as bad as I thought it would be. It's so big—you can't imagine how many people there are on the streets, some of them quite bizarre-looking. The funny thing about New Yorkers is that they don't look at you; it's as if they were all wearing blinders. I'm trying to get used to that, but I don't like it. I guess I'm afraid of becoming like them—cold and unfriendly.

I know it's for the best that I didn't bring

Jennifer up here, but I miss her so much—
sometimes I don't think I can stand to be
away from her for another minute.

Cynthia put down her pen as an image of Jennifer floated before her eyes: soft brown ringlets
framing her chubby cheeks, her dark eyes round
with delight, her pink, bowed lips forming the
word "Mommy."

Tears sprang to Cynthia's eyes. Dear God, how
much longer would she have to be away from her
little girl? This whole modeling idea was starting
to seem crazy, maybe she ought to pack up her
things and go home. . . .

Suddenly the phone rang, and Cynthia looked at
it hopefully. Could it be her mother? Had she
somehow sensed her daughter's unhappiness even
across the miles?

She picked it up on the second ring. "Hello?"
she said, not bothering to hide the longing in her
voice. There was no response. "Mama?" Cynthia
asked, "Is that you?" The only sound was a click
and then the line went dead.

A knot of fear tightened in Cynthia's stomach.
Someone was playing tricks on her. Who? Not
Bobby—even he wouldn't stoop to something so
low. Or would he? She felt more alone in this
strange city than ever.

Andrea was at her post the next morning when
Cynthia came out of her building and headed for
another, similar office building. She gave her a

few seconds, then went inside. The lobby was empty.

Damn! She had been planning to follow her right into the elevator, see where she got off—now she'd have to resort to a backup plan.

She went to the building directory, found the name and location of a modeling agency, then picked the name of another firm on a different floor. She went straight to the modeling agency and pushed open the door.

Cynthia was sitting primly on a couch in the reception area, along with two other tall, lanky beauties. All three pairs of eyes turned to stare at Andrea, but the receptionist did not even look up.

Andrea walked over to her desk." 'Scuse me," she said loudly in a broad Brooklyn accent.

The receptionist raised her eyes haughtily. "Yes?"

"Can you tell me where the Richardson Employment Agency is?" Andrea asked. "I can't seem to find it."

"Two floors down," the receptionist said, dismissing Andrea.

"Guess I pushed the wrong button on the elevator," Andrea mumbled, turning toward the three women on the couch. She smiled feebly at them.

Only Cynthia returned her trace of a smile, and as Andrea left, she was perplexed by what she had seen in that fleeting expression on Cynthia's face. There had been warmth there and a pleasantness that Andrea had never expected to find in a woman who was supposed to be so cold-hearted. Still, she mustn't read too much into that smile; it was probably meaningless, a polite, *professional* smile that models could turn on and off at will.

She went back to the lobby, and took up her post. She had only been there about fifteen minutes when the elevator doors opened and Cynthia stepped out.

Andrea started, uncertain whether to stand there or walk away, for she could see that Cynthia had noticed her and recognized her. As she hesitated, the moment passed, and then she had no choice but to stay because Cynthia was already smiling at her.

"Hi," she said in a soft, sweet drawl. "Did you find that employment agency?"

"Uh, yeah," Andrea said, backing up a couple of steps.

"Good. I hope they had a job for you."

"No—no, they didn't. At least not now. That's why I'm standing here—trying to figure out what to do next." Andrea knew she was talking too much, but she couldn't help it.

Cynthia smiled breezily. "Well, good luck to you," she said, and walked away.

"Thanks," Andrea called after her. When Cynthia was out of sight she stretched out her hand to one of the lobby's marble walls to steady herself.

That had been much, much too close. She had forgotten that someone so new to the city might still be in the habit of talking to strangers. New Yorkers didn't do that; they always kept a safe distance.

And that was what she must do from now on. Stay well back, never let Cynthia see her face—

especially never let her hear her voice again, because voices were harder to disguise than faces.

There was no point in trying to follow her again today. She'd have to get herself a different wig and a different coat—maybe she could pick one up cheap in a thrift shop. She would try again tomorrow.

And so it went, from day to day. Always varying her disguises and keeping well out of her rival's line of sight, Andrea pursued Cynthia in her rounds of the modeling agencies.

When it became apparent that Cynthia really *was* in New York for a modeling career, Andrea realized that she was going to gain nothing more by following her. Finally, she was forced to admit to herself that she continued to do it for the thrill of it—the delicious danger that she might be caught was always there, and it filled her days with excitement, much as all the daytime TV shows she used to watch had done. Only this was for real—it was happening to *her*.

She no longer dared to invite Bobby to her apartment, afraid that he might come upon the odd assortment of wigs and various secondhand coats in her closet. For, if he questioned them, she knew she would break down and confess everything.

Whenever she spent the night at Bobby's apartment she would give up her surveillance of Cynthia for that day and instead catch up with Mrs. King, who acted a little put out that Andrea had not been visiting her as much, until Andrea explained that she had been out job-hunting—because she and Bobby wanted to save up some money to buy a house. Mrs. King seemed to think that was a laudable aspiration.

Although she told it quite facilely, that lie bothered Andrea because it was so far from the way things really were between her and Bobby. Just the night before, she had been forced to acknowledge how much their relationship had deteriorated in recent weeks.

As she was setting the table for dinner, Bobby had looked up from his newspaper and asked her, "How's the job-hunting coming?"

Andrea kept her eyes down and went on placing the silverware. "Oh, you know, the same old story," she said, drawing out the words casually. "Don't call us, we'll call you."

"Jesus, Red," Bobby said, his voice sharp with exasperation, "you'd think that after all this time you could find *something*."

Andrea shot him a glance. "But, I'm trying, Bobby. Really, I am."

"Yeah, well, I wonder about that," he muttered.

Andrea slammed down a knife onto the table. "What is that supposed to mean?"

The paper snapped and rustled in Bobby's hands as he turned a page. "I just don't know about you anymore," he said, shaking his head. "You've been acting awfully strange lately."

"*I've* been acting strange?" Andrea said. "What about *you*?"

"I don't know what you're talking about," Bobby said, his eyes riveted on the paper.

Andrea knew she should shut up, go back into the kitchen and finish dinner—but she couldn't help it. She had to bring up the subject that was always there—unspoken—between them. "Cynthia," she said. "That's what I'm talking about. You haven't been the same since she came here."

Bobby flung the paper onto the floor. His eyes were dark and narrowed when he looked up at her. "I don't want to discuss her with you," he said, the words coming out clipped and vaguely threatening.

"I know you don't," Andrea said, returning his gaze with one equally defiant. "You never tell me anything—whether you've seen her, whether you've talked to her—"

"I said I didn't want to discuss her!" Bobby was on his feet, coming toward her, his eyes blazing.

Andrea had not meant to anger him so. What was the matter with her? She didn't want him to know how jealous she was of Cynthia. "I'm sorry, Bobby," she said quickly. "I shouldn't have mentioned her. I know how upset she makes you."

Bobby stared at her coldly. "That's right," he said. "Just don't bring her up again." He turned and retraced his steps to the couch, sat down and picked up the paper. "Get a move on with the food, will you?" he barked. "I'm starving."

Andrea sighed and went dutifully into the kitchen. At least she had managed to forestall another fight, for now. But damn it, what she had said was true: Bobby had not been the same since Cynthia's arrival. But then, of course, neither had she.

It was ironic. She was spending more time with Cynthia now than she did with Bobby. She felt as though she almost knew the woman. Sometimes on the nights she was alone, Andrea would dial Cynthia's telephone number and smile silently to herself as she listened to Cynthia's "Hello?" then, with anticipation turned to fear, "Hello? Is anybody there?" That soft drawl of hers seemed so familiar, so gratifyingly unnerved, that Andrea was strongly tempted to answer, "Hello, Cynthia. You don't know me, but I know you. In fact, I know *all* about you."

But she never did. Instead, she hung up. Softly.

She tried not to call too often, for fear that she would drive Cynthia into getting an unlisted number.

On the rare nights when Andrea wasn't too tired from her daily travels with Bobby's wife, she staked out one or the other of their apartments for a couple of hours. Nothing ever happened, though one night she did catch Bobby leaving his building, and she followed him in the shadows. But he merely walked to the corner deli—probably for beer and cigarettes, she thought—and went straight home.

She began to wonder if there was anything going on between Bobby and Cynthia at all. But *something* was causing Bobby's growing moodiness, and she couldn't figure out what else it could be.

On the occasions when Andrea did see Bobby it seemed that anything at all became a bone of contention between them. If Andrea said, "Gee, Bobby, there's a new Indian restaurant up the street. Why don't we go there tonight?" Bobby would say, "Ugh. How can you eat that crap?"; if Andrea suggested going to a movie, Bobby would insist on staying home to watch a basketball game.

The only thing they didn't disagree on was sex. But maybe it would have been better if they did, Andrea thought. Their lovemaking had become such a dull, monotonous routine: Bobby would go through the motions of foreplay for a couple of minutes, then he would climb on top of her. After he'd reached his climax he'd roll over and go right to sleep, without so much as saying good night. Andrea would lie there, wide-awake and unsatisfied, wondering where all their earlier passion had gone.

But no matter how much they fought, Bobby had not struck her since the night she'd had to go to the hospital. He seemed to be afraid of his own anger, and she often used his fear against him.

"Bobby," she'd say, "I don't care what you want to do tonight, *I* want to go out. I don't like basketball, and I'm not going to sit here while you watch some stupid game."

Bobby would glower at her. "You know, Red, you can be a real bitch sometimes."

"Call me anything you like, but I'm *not* staying in tonight."

"Oh, yeah?" Sarcasm edged his voice. "What did you have in mind? Studio 54? Regine's?"

"Why not?" Andrea asked perfectly seriously. "Why can't we go to one of those places?"

"Who's going to pay for it?" Bobby jeered. "*You?*"

"What's the matter with you?" Andrea snapped back at him. "How come you've gotten so cheap all of a sudden?"

That had gotten to him. Andrea could see the rage boiling up within him as he glared at her. Muscles danced in his cheek from the clenched tightness of his jaw. Then his eyes seemed to cloud over—as if some painful memory had passed before them. Suddenly his face went slack and he looked away. "Okay. Let's go out," he said. Then he glanced at her sharply. "Only I'm not taking you any place fancy."

"Whatever you say," Andrea responded, trying to contain the note of triumph in her voice.

She liked having this small amount of control over him, and because of this she sometimes deliberately provoked him. One night they had just finished watching a movie on TV, and as Bobby was on his way into the kitchen for a beer Andrea got up to turn off the television set. She happened to glance at the typewriter on Bobby's desk. It had had the same piece of paper in it for weeks. Who did he think he was fooling? "Hey, Bobby," she said, only half joking, "What's happening with your Great American Novel?" Then, twisting the knife, she added, "I'm beginning to think Sam was right about you."

She could see at once that she had made a mistake. Bobby's eyes narrowed and his hands tightened into fists. She held her breath as he came across the room at her, and—almost without thinking—she pushed her hair away from her face, her fingertips grazing the jagged scar on her right temple.

Bobby's eyes followed the motion of her hand and lingered on her temple. He stood motionless for several seconds, and Andrea thought she had managed to curb his anger. Then he looked her straight in the eye. "No," he said, his voice hard and flinty, "I'm not going to hit you." There was something new in his eyes, something Andrea could not read, and when he stretched out his hand toward her head she winced.

But he did not strike her. Instead, his hand reached back and grabbed her hair and pulled it taut. "Listen to me," he said, jerking her head back. "Don't *ever* think you can say anything you want to me and get away with it!"

"Let go of my hair!" Andrea screamed, her fingernails clawing at his hand.

Bobby yelped in pain. "You scratched me, you bitch!" With his free hand he fought her off and then gave her hair a furious yank.

Andrea felt sick. She could actually *hear* her hair breaking off at the roots, but the more she squirmed the harder he pulled. "Bobby, Bobby, please! I'm sorry," she cried.

But he did not let go. "*Now* you're sorry," he said. "But you won't ever do it again, will you?" He tugged viciously at her hair. "*Will you?*"

"No!" Andrea screamed. "Never—I promise!"

Bobby let her go. A handful of hair came away in his fingers and he looked at it with a mixture of triumph and disgust. "Serves you right," he said, tossing it in Andrea's face and walking away.

Andrea bent down and picked up the red-gold strands from the floor, and began to weep bitterly over them. Bobby had chosen his torture well; he must have known that the loss of her hair would hurt her more than any beating he might give her.

When the wave of sobs passed, she went into the bathroom to inspect the damage. It was not as bad as she had imagined—most of the hair that was broken off had come from the front. She could cover it easily.

But that was *too* easy. No, she wanted a reminder—like the scar—to show Bobby what he had done to her, something to punish him every time he looked at her.

There was a pair of barber's shears in the medicine chest. She got them out and began chopping savagely at her hair. It took her longer than she thought it would, and when she was done she nearly cried again at the sight of thick clumps of red-gold hair in the sink and on the floor.

But when she looked in the mirror she felt avenged. Never again would Bobby be able to run his fingers through her long, lovely hair, for she had butchered it to a scant few inches.

She picked up most of the hair and set it aside while she washed her tear-stained face. Then, clutching the hair, she opened the bathroom door and tiptoed out.

Bobby was sitting at his desk, staring at his typewriter and nursing a beer. He did not look up as Andrea came into the room.

She walked over to the desk. "I've got a present

for you," she said, flinging the mass of hair down on a sheet of typing paper.

Bobby gaped at it. Against the white of the paper the hair was an even more vivid red—almost like blood. He shrank back from it. "Oh, my God," he moaned, his eyes straining upward. "I don't believe it," he said, fixing his eyes on her face. "You chopped it all off—"

"I had to," Andrea said, her voice caustic. "It looked horrible."

"It wasn't that bad." He was shaking his head vigorously from side to side. "I saw it—you could have covered it up."

"Like *hell* I could have. You'd better get used to me this way."

"God, no! I hate it." Bobby's eyes were dark and scornful. "You look awful—you—you look like a—a *man!*"

Andrea returned his look with one equally contemptuous. "Is that so? Well, I guess you don't want somebody who looks like a man sleeping with you tonight." She turned away from him. "I'm going home."

"Good. Get out of here—I can't stand the sight of you." Bobby crashed his beer can down on the desktop. "God, you must be *crazy!*"

For a moment, Andrea faltered. *Crazy.* He had said she was crazy. And the *way* he had said it—as if he had *known* how it would wound her. No, she was too sensitive on the subject. Bobby hadn't really known what he was saying. He couldn't have.

She slammed the door behind her.

CHAPTER ELEVEN

A man. He had said she looked like a *man*. Andrea contemplated her reflection in the mirror. It wasn't true, of course. But it *was* an intriguing idea. She smiled grimly at her image. She had been mourning the loss of her beautiful hair all day. Now she could see there was a bright side to the disaster. With some men's clothes, perhaps a mustache and sideburns, who'd look twice to see that she wasn't really a man after all? Besides, unisex was "in"—often you really *couldn't* tell the girls from the boys.

She worked on her costume all day in a fever of excitement: a mustache, sideburns, and eyebrows just a shade darker than her own hair, all purchased from a theatrical costumer; a wide-brimmed felt hat, a bulky turtleneck, gloves, and a pair of wire-rimmed aviator sunglasses, the kind that changed color in the sunlight.

She put on all her new purchases, pulling on a pair of jeans, her Frye boots, and down parka.

But something was not right; there was something missing, and she had to laugh when she finally realized what it was—she needed some padding in the crotch of her jeans. Not much, but just enough to suggest that the essential equipment was there. A handful of tissues took care of that.

Now she had to work on the walk. She tried taking bigger steps, adding a kind of swagger, and it seemed to work. She marched up and down the room several times, and then turned to walk toward the mirror—and stopped dead in her tracks. For in the glass she had seen the very image of Andy coming at her—Andy as he might have looked if he had lived.

It was uncanny what a difference the male disguise made. Female eyes swept over her with studied insouciance as she strolled down the street. They made her feel self-conscious. Surely they had penetrated her disguise and were glancing at her out of curiosity. Then she spied her own reflection in a store window and suddenly saw what an attractive man she made: women were looking at her in *admiration*.

Even Cynthia was not immune. At the bus stop her eyes seemed drawn, almost beyond her control, in Andrea's direction. Diffidently, Andrea returned her gaze, afraid that Cynthia had recognized her. But the look lasted a shade too long to be merely the casual glance of strangers in passing. Then Cynthia lowered her eyes, her dark, silky lashes nearly brushing her cheek, and Andrea realized that propriety had forced Cynthia to drop her gaze first—lest her look be interpreted as an invitation. It was the typical behavior of a woman with a man who appealed to her.

All right, she would take her up on it. If Cynthia really was interested in her as a man—and Andrea had not missed the potential for irony there—it would be the perfect opportunity to learn more about her. There would be more risk in this out-in-the-open surveillance. And more excitement.

They got on the bus, and Cynthia found a seat near the front while Andrea moved to the rear. Not once did she look directly at Andrea, but kept her head inclined at such an angle that Andrea knew she was in Cynthia's peripheral vision. She stared at her boldly, ready to encourage flirtation. But Cynthia did not respond. Either she had not tumbled to Andrea's brazen stare or she was playing it very cool. Yes, that was it.

After the bus passed Madison Avenue, Cynthia rang the signal for the next stop. She headed for the front doors, and Andrea went to the rear. As Cynthia was waiting for the doors to open she cast a furtive glance to the back of the bus, and managed to mask her surprise when she saw Andrea at the rear exit. Andrea smiled, but Cynthia turned her face away, concealing any reaction.

They descended simultaneously. Andrea hung back, letting Cynthia take the lead to the corner of Fifty-seventh and Park, where she paused to wait for the light to change. Andrea kept her pace to a stroll, timing herself to hit the corner just as the light turned green. She wanted to stay close to Cynthia—but not so close that the woman would have a chance to scrutinize her face. She was about twenty feet away when Cynthia suddenly swiveled her head and looked straight at her. Andrea smiled again, but a veil seemed to descend over Cynthia's eyes. She jerked her head around.

When the light changed Cynthia walked briskly across Park Avenue and then turned downtown. Andrea matched Cynthia's pace, but maintained a distance, disappointed that Cynthia kept striding purposefully ahead, as if indifferent to her presence. Had she read the wrong meaning into that initial glance? No, it was the kind of look she herself might have given to an attractive man. Perhaps Cynthia was just being coy.

After a block and a half Cynthia veered and turned toward the entrance of an office building. Andrea recognized it as one she had followed her to before. With her hand on the heavy glass door, she tossed her head around, her eyes sweeping over the sidewalk behind her. Andrea kept walking, as if she were going about her own business, but grinned at Cynthia and with a flourish touched the tips of her gloved fingers to the brim of her hat. Cynthia gave her a wan smile in return, then with a look that seemed both regretful and relieved, she turned, pushed open the door of the building, and stepped inside.

Did she know she was being followed? She still might think it was coincidence that this stranger had been heading in the same direction as she. She would be divested of that delusion soon enough.

Instead of trying to find an unobtrusive place from which to observe the doorway, Andrea simply walked a few more paces and casually slouched against the granite wall of an adjoining building. With her hands stuffed in her pockets and a rakish gleam in her eye for pretty girls walking by, she gave off the perfect air of a young man with nothing on his mind but a little harmless girlwatching.

Cynthia emerged from the building about forty-five minutes later, frowning and with her eyes downcast. She looked at her watch before turning to retrace her steps uptown. Andrea had been hoping she would glance in her direction, but she was preoccupied. Perhaps her interview had not gone well.

Andrea fell into step behind her, sometimes giving her as much as a half-block lead, closing the gap whenever traffic threatened to come between them.

The sidewalks were crowded and narrow; it became more difficult to keep Cynthia in sight. Once, she even thought she had lost her and, panicking, she jostled her way through sidewalk vendors and gawking shoppers. Then Cynthia's hat had come bouncing back into view, and Andrea fixed on it, determined not to let her get away again. She reached the corner of Fifty-ninth Street just in time to see Cynthia slip into the revolving door at Bloomingdale's. She sprinted across the street against the light, and a taxi screeched to a stop inches from her. The driver rolled down his window and shouted at Andrea's retreating back, but she ignored him and shoved through a throng of pedestrians waiting at the curb for the light to change.

It was nearly lunch hour and Bloomingdale's was already bustling. Cynthia was nowhere in sight. "Oh, no! I've lost her!" Andrea said out loud, and a woman at the jewelry counter turned to stare at her. But she raced up a flight of stairs to the cosmetics department and scanned the people riding up on the escalator. No Cynthia. She looked frantically around and thought she saw Cynthia's hat at one of the cosmetics counters. Bobbing and weaving through the busy aisles, she worked her way across the floor until she could see the face beneath the hat. Yes, it was Cynthia. She was engrossed in catching the eye of a salesgirl and had not yet spotted the stranger moving toward her.

Andrea stopped at the next counter. Suddenly Cynthia's whole body seemed to snap to attention and she pivoted her head in a swift, startled movement. Their eyes met, and Andrea gave her a broad grin. Cynthia's face went blank for a moment, but then an expression of annoyance crossed it, followed by one that Andrea was surprised to see—fear. For the first time it occurred to her that she might actually seem menacing to Cynthia, all because she appeared to be a man. She had never thought of her surveillance of Cynthia Wilson as anything more than a cat-and-mouse game. Now she realized that the rules had changed. A new element had been added—a threat. Andrea suddenly had a giddy sense of the power she now held over Cynthia, a power that she might as well play out. So, she gave her prey a wicked leer.

For a second, she thought Cynthia was going to
bolt, but then a salesgirl came to wait on her. Cynthia blinked at her several times before she bent
over the glass-topped case and pointed to something on a shelf below. The girl got it for her and
took her money. As she stood waiting for her
change, tapping the countertop nervously, Andrea
could tell she was watching her out of the corner
of her eye.

Her hands were shaking so that she dropped a
scattering of change on the floor as she was trying
to put it into her purse. She smiled apologetically
at the salesgirl and stooped to pick the money up,
overlooking some coins in her hurry. Then, grabbing her package off the counter, she took off in
the direction of the escalators.

Andrea had a hunch that Cynthia was going to
try to shake her now, try to lose her in the warren
of shops and boutiques on the third floor. She followed closely on her heels as Cynthia stepped onto
the crowded up escalator. Trapped! There were
too many people ahead of her to push through
and, Andrea thought gleefully, she was obviously
too polite to try.

Second floor.

Third floor.

Where was she going, anyway? She stepped off
on the fourth floor, and made a beeline for the
other side of the store, with Andrea close behind.
In tandem, they crossed the floor, taking a breakneck pace between the counters of sparkling crystal and silver, the colorful displays of luxurious
bedspreads, and on through the lamp department

with its myriad of glowing lights and sleek, modern pedestals.

At the women's shoe department, Andrea figured it out. Here, nearly hidden behind a display, was another set of escalators, and she was sure Cynthia was going to take one of them and run up or down to the next floor.

But no, she sailed right past the up escalator, then made a sharp left as she would if she were going to get on the escalator going down. Instead, she continued straight ahead. At last Andrea knew where Cynthia was going: the ladies' room, the only place that Andrea—at least in her present guise—could not pursue her.

Across from the ladies' room entrance was a row of pay phones. Cynthia made for one of them. She fumbled in a little black address book before dialing, and she was halfway through the number when she had to stop and check it again. Andrea was about twenty-five feet away as she completed the call, and could see her talking to someone, but she couldn't have exchanged more than a few words with her listener before she banged the phone back on the hook. She lowered her head and pretended to be digging for something in her purse, but Andrea could tell that under the brim of her hat Cynthia was peering at *her*. Then she closed her purse, did an about-face, and stormed into the ladies' room.

Let her stay in there as long as she wants. Andrea told herself. She was still going to be there when Cynthia came out. And if she had to, she would go off into a corner, pull off the phony

mustache and sideburns and march right into the
ladies' room after her. Anyway, how long could she
stay in there? It certainly wasn't the most comfortable place in the world to try to wait somebody
out.

She began to walk slowly up and down the aisle,
trying to give the impression of a guy patiently
waiting for his girlfriend. But long minutes passed,
and Andrea began to fidget. She drifted back toward the shoe department and gazed into one of
the designer boutique windows. On display were
several pairs of flimsy, impossibly high-heeled san-
dals. Andrea stared at them wistfully; she had always longed to wear dainty, feminine shoes like
those—but with her size ten feet and already gar-
gantuan height, she would never dare.

Suddenly she caught herself. For a moment, she
had slipped up, had stepped out of her role. A man
would never look at shoes like that, unless it was
with indulgence or disdain.

Carefully she resumed her character, pasting a
look of masculine superiority on her face again.
Then back she went to the area outside the ladies'
room, where she continued her anxious pacing.
Women streamed by, going in and out; one plump,
pretty blonde glanced in Andrea's direction, but
she was too distracted to even care.

She wondered what would happen if she just
went ahead, walked right inside. Would someone
try to stop her? Would they think she was strange?
Probably—and it might get her into trouble with
the store management. Then Cynthia would have
the last laugh. Forget that.

She had been in this ladies' room herself and she was pretty sure there was no other way out of it. Cynthia *had* to come out sometime. Most likely she had other appointments today. Maybe she was freshening up her makeup, taking her own sweet time about it, and hoping the stranger would give up and go away and leave her alone.

Not on your life. If Cynthia only knew how many hours her shadow had spent waiting for her already, she'd realize how hopeless it was to try and beat someone who was that persistent, Andrea told herself smugly.

She was so involved with her own thoughts that she almost missed her when Cynthia emerged from the ladies' room. And it took her a couple of seconds to react to what Cynthia was doing.

She was standing only a few feet away, her eyes blank and staring straight through Andrea. There was an almost imperceptible quiver to her lips, and she seemed to be lost in a fog of irresolution.

With sudden insight, Andrea realized that in the safety of the ladies' room Cynthia had steeled herself to confront her shadow. Only now that they were face to face, she couldn't go through with it.

As she watched her pitiful wavering, Andrea felt a stab of sympathy for her. What a nightmare this must be for her, her worst fears of the city come true. In the space of a few hours she had changed from an enterprising young career woman into a bewildered, unhappy victim—and now she even seemed to be losing her will to fight back, to protect herself from this invasion.

At last, Cynthia took a step forward. Her mouth

was set in a determined line, but when she opened it to speak the words came out in a faltering, timid voice.

"What do you want?" she asked of Andrea.

When there was no response, she swallowed hard and tried again. "Why are you doing this? What do you want from me?"

Andrea gave no sign of having heard her. She remained silent—not only because she was afraid that her voice might betray her, but because she knew that the unspoken threat was more sinister than any she might voice.

"Who *are* you?" Cynthia asked. The words were breathless, barely audible—as if she were not expecting to be answered.

Andrea just stared back at her, her face an impenetrable cipher.

Cynthia pulled her coat tight about her and side-stepped Andrea. "Leave me alone!" she cried, but it was an anguished plea, not the directive it was meant to be.

Andrea let her move a few steps ahead before she turned to follow her. Cynthia made straight for the down escalator and continued down the moving stairs to the main floor, where she walked rapidly through the men's department to one of the Third Avenue exits. Andrea hung back, letting her have the lead, but always keeping her close enough so that she could catch up quickly if she needed to.

Cynthia walked down two blocks to the crosstown bus stop, never once looking back, almost as if pretending that the stranger wasn't there would make him go away.

When the bus came, Andrea let a few people move between them before she boarded. As the bus lurched away from the curb, they did not look at each other—although Andrea was sure that Bobby's wife was painfully aware of her presence. She wondered whether Cynthia was on her way to another appointment. Or was she heading for cover, for the safety of her own apartment?

The bus made its way slowly across town in the heavy midday traffic, and Cynthia stayed on board. When she finally did get off it was one stop before her usual one, and Andrea realized that she thought her pursuer did not know where she lived. She was going to try to shake him off before she went home.

Heading downtown, Cynthia turned onto a street lined with small, renovated apartment buildings. Halfway down the block she suddenly darted up a flight of stairs and disappeared into the entryway of one of the buildings.

Andrea could not see into the dark cubicle behind the doorway. but she was sure that Cynthia was in there waiting, her body pressed flat against the wall, hoping the stranger would give up and go away, allowing her to come out and go to her own home—relieved that her ordeal was over now.

So Andrea played along with her. She paced up and down in front of the apartment house for five minutes and then, with a disgruntled shrug, turned and walked away—in the opposite direction from Cynthia's building. When she reached the corner she broke into a trot and doubled back, positive she'd be there first. Cynthia would not emerge from her hiding place until she was quite certain there was no more danger.

Andrea slipped into a dark doorway across the street from her quarry's building. After fifteen minutes she peered out and saw Cynthia coming up the block, walking at an almost leisurely pace, but still cautious, looking back over her shoulder every few steps. She waited until the woman was only about fifty feet from her own building before she stole out of the concealment of the doorway and began to cross the street toward Cynthia, not bothering to hide the smirk on her face.

Cynthia saw her at once and stopped, paralyzed as Andrea approached. Her face had turned chalk-white and her eyes were wide with shock and fright. Then, just as Andrea reached the curb only about ten feet away from her, she bolted and ran, cowering, into the sanctuary of her apartment house.

It had been a good day's work, Andrea thought, as she creamed off her makeup and fixed herself two overstuffed sandwiches—surprised at her ravenous appetite. She was still replaying all the details of the day's chase in her mind, congratulating herself on the masterful way she had handled each situation—especially the last confrontation at Cynthia's door. She kept seeing that look of terror on Cynthia's face when she realized she had not eluded her pursuer at all, and more: he even knew where she lived.

If Cynthia were scared enough she might even move out of that building. Andrea hoped that she wouldn't. She wanted to be able to keep tabs on her. Still, if Cynthia got *really* scared she might even leave New York. Now *that* was something to think about.

Worn out by the sheer excitement of the day, Andrea lay down to take a nap. She didn't wake up until several hours later when the ringing of the telephone broke into her dreamless sleep.

It was Bobby, and from the affectionate tone in his voice Andrea could tell he was feeling apologetic about their fight. He wanted to see her; could he come over?

"I don't know," Andrea hedged. "What time is it?" she yawned. "I was asleep."

"It's a little after six," Bobby said. "I just got home, and I thought I'd take you out to dinner."

"I'm surprised you want to be seen in public with someone who looks like me."

"Oh, c'mon, Red," Bobby sighed. "I really feel bad about that, and I want to try and make it up to you."

"That's just great. You think one crummy dinner is going to make everything all ri—"

"Forget the dinner. I just want to see you. Can I come over?"

"No. I, uh—the place is a mess."

"Then come up here. I'll order a pizza and we can talk. What do you say?"

"Oh—okay. But I'm not going to spend the night."

"Anything you want, darlin'. Just get up here as fast as you can."

Andrea hung up the phone, once again amazed at how mercurial Bobby's moods were. One day he loved her and the next he hated her. Today she was in his good graces again.

"You know, I felt really bad after you left the other night," Bobby said through a mouthful of pizza. "It was all my fault. I was edgy—but I shouldn't have taken it out on you like that."

"What were you edgy about?" Andrea asked, glad he hadn't mentioned her own part in the fracas.

"Nothing, really," Bobby hedged. "It was just a rough day at work. I had things on my mind."

Andrea wondered if one of those "things" was Cynthia. But she said nothing.

"Anyway, it didn't turn out so bad." Bobby winked at her. "You look kinda cute in your new hairdo."

"Thanks." Andrea smiled at him and quickly turned the conversation back to his problems at the office. She was uncomfortable talking about her haircut—especially after what it had inspired her to do today.

Bobby polished off half a six-pack with the pizza, and when they were finished eating he was in a very romantic mood. He took Andrea into the bedroom and began making tender, passionate love to her—the kind they hadn't had for weeks. Until the phone rang.

"Shit!" Bobby said. "Somebody's got great timing." He picked up the phone. "Yeah?"

Without even looking at Bobby's face Andrea knew it was Cynthia.

"Hold on a minute, Cyn," Bobby said into the phone. "I can't understand you, you're too excited." There was a long pause. "Some guy *followed* you? Is that all?" A shorter pause. "I mean did he *do* anything?"

Andrea rolled over on her stomach and picked up a magazine from the nightstand.

"I don't know," Bobby said. "He sounds pretty harmless to me. This is New York, you know. These things happen—"

Andrea looked up from the magazine. Bobby's forehead was furrowed. "What good would the police do? Look, Cyn, he's probably just one of your neighbors—that's how he knows where you live. Maybe he saw you on the street and liked you and just decided to follow you around."

Bobby glanced over at Andrea. He was leering maliciously. "I'm *not* being flip with you." A pause. "Yes, I can understand why it would be upsetting—but still, if he didn't *do* anything—" Another pause. "I'm sorry I wasn't there. Why didn't you leave a message? . . . Well, I'll be in the office all day tomorrow. If he shows up again just give me a call. Okay?" Bobby reached over and ran his hand down the length of Andrea's naked spine. "That's right. Don't get too close to him—he's probably scared to death of you, anyway."

Andrea closed her eyes as Bobby's hand lingered lovingly on her back. How odd it was that he should come so close to the truth. She wasn't "scared to death" of Cynthia, but wary of her—oh, yes, that was certainly true.

"Okay? You feel better now? . . . Good. Take it easy and don't worry about it. Talk to you tomorrow." Bobby hung up the phone, laughing softly to himself.

"What's so funny?" Andrea asked.

He shook his head. "Poor Cynthia. She's got some weirdo following her around and she's convinced he's a mad rapist or some crazed killer."

"Why doesn't she go to the police?" Andrea said. Indifferent . . . she must show complete indifference to Cynthia's problems.

"What for? This guy hasn't done a single thing to her. He's just *there*. She says he practically followed her into the can in Bloomingdale's—maybe he's a toilet freak."

Andrea turned her head away so Bobby wouldn't see the smug grin on her face. "I wouldn't be surprised," she said, suppressing a chuckle. "We've got every other kind of freak in this town."

Bobby kissed her shoulder. "Mmm—speaking of mad rapists . . ."

There was no more conversation between them.

Long after Bobby had fallen asleep Andrea lay next to him, mulling over the situation she had gotten herself into. Cynthia's fears excited her, but now she wondered how Bobby would react if she told him that *she* was the man following Cynthia.

Would he laugh, take it as a big joke? Or would he be suspicious of her, angry?

From his casual manner on the phone, Andrea guessed he might think it was funny—but she couldn't be sure. No, she didn't dare tell him. She would keep it inside her, another secret that she must not reveal until she could be certain of his reaction. Maybe after they were married—maybe then she could tell him everything.

When she'd made that decision she curled up next to him, her chest pressed against his back, her knees tucked behind his. But she remained oddly wakeful, uncomfortable sharing a bed with Bobby and—even more disquieting—vaguely uneasy in her own body. There was a nagging pain in her chest, so persistent she thought it must be indigestion from the pizza. After thrashing back and forth for what seemed like hours, she got up, looked at the clock, and was amazed to see that it was only a little before midnight. Fumbling in the darkness for her clothes, she managed to dress noiselessly. Then she tiptoed into the living room, turned on a light and sat down at Bobby's desk to write him a note. Minutes later she found herself still staring at a sheet of paper, her mind as blank as its surface. *My God, what was happening to her?* She grabbed a pencil and scribbled hastily, "Bobby—Sorry to leave you like this, but I couldn't sleep. Decided to go home. Love, Andrea." Then she shrugged into her jacket, went downstairs and hailed a cab. "Step on it," she told the driver. "I've got to get there fast."

CHAPTER TWELVE

"Where the hell did you sneak off to last night?" Bobby's anger raged in her ear. When the phone rang Andrea had been sound asleep, and she was barely able to understand what he was talking about. Finally, she managed to mumble something about not feeling well, maybe she was coming down with a cold, and that seemed to appease him.

It was only after she'd put down the phone that Andrea realized she had been sleeping fully clothed. Only they weren't the clothes she'd worn over to Bobby's the night before; they were the ones she had worn during the day—when she was following Cynthia. There was something odd about her face, too—she could feel the bristly hairs of the fake mustache and sideburns and the pull of the sticky adhesive against her skin.

She threw back the covers and leaped out of bed. She was in full male regalia.

When had she put it on? Her mind raced back and drew a blank. Her last memory was of leaving Bobby's, her chest still aching dully. The next thing she knew the phone was ringing and she was talking to him. There was no in-between, *nothing*.

She collapsed back onto the bed, weak with fear. There could be only one answer: she'd had a blackout. That had to be it. She'd been feeling strange when she left Bobby's; at some point after that, she must have blacked out. But why the disguise?

Suddenly her mind reeled sickeningly. There was another time she had done something like this. A scene flashed before her eyes: a graveyard at night, a young girl dressed like her twin brother, kneeling on his grave, trying to kill herself . . .

"*No!*" Andrea screamed. She leaped to her feet. "It can't be happening again. I won't let it!"

She tore off the disguise and dressed frantically in her own clothes. She had to get out of the apartment, out into the air, mingle with normal people.

Still shaking, she put on her parka, and stuffed her hands in the pockets, looking for her gloves. They were there all right, but they weren't *her* gloves, they were the men's pair that she used as part of her disguise. That didn't make sense. She could have sworn she'd taken them out of the parka the day before. Then she felt something else in one of the pockets and fished it out. It was a book of matches from a cheap Times Square bar, and she stared at it, horrified. They hadn't been there yesterday. Where had they come from? Where—or *who*?

Her stomach churned uneasily and, as a sudden
wave of nausea rose in her throat, she ran into the
bathroom and threw up. Then, feeling somewhat
calmer, she washed her face and went downstairs.
Angrily, she tossed the matches into a garbage can
in front of her building, and tried to toss them out
of her mind as well.

It was an unusually mild day for February—not
like the day when she'd arrived in the city a year
ago. The sun was bright and warm on her face, the
streets bustled with shoppers and strollers. To Andrea, her neighborhood had always seemed thriving and lively, a potpourri of exotic faces speaking
strange, musical languages. All along Ninth Avenue, there were fruit and vegetable stands and
macaroni factories jostling for space with bodegas
and Greek restaurants. Each block seemed to have
its own distinctive aroma, and sometimes she could
close her eyes and tell exactly where she was, just
by breathing in deeply.

She turned down a side street and came upon a
Con Edison crew, the men standing around on a
break. One of the men spoke cheerily to Andrea.
She gave him a grin and started to walk away when
she caught a whiff of something in the air. It was
not an unfamiliar odor, but it was so unexpected
in the midst of this concrete city: it was the smell
of freshly turned earth, and it made Andrea ache
with homesickness for the rich, dark soil of Wisconsin, soil where her father and brother lay in
their graves.

She looked back at the dark, rectangular hole,
the Con Ed crew had dug, earth and rocks heaped

next to it, and felt a sudden lurching in her chest. A grave. It looked like a grave. The last time she had smelled newly dug earth had been at a grave— her father's. And before that, it had been at Andy's. But that was a much dimmer memory.

She stared at the looming mouth of the hole and the piles of earth on either side of it, and suddenly had the most overwhelming feeling that she was looking into her own grave. Frightened, she whirled away from the leering eyes of the workmen and strode on, trying to shake off her awful sense of doom.

At the corner she turned and went into a grocery, forcing herself to concentrate on mundane matters. She rolled a cart up and down the aisles, filled it with everything she needed, and then took it to the checkout counter. The clerk rang it up. Ten dollars and twenty-one cents. Andrea knew she had a twenty-dollar bill in her wallet—she had seen it there when she paid the cab fare from Bobby's last night. But when she reached in to pull it out, there was no twenty—only four singles. Too embarrassed to explain to the clerk, Andrea dashed out of the store.

What could have happened to that twenty-dollar bill? She knew she hadn't spent it. Had she taken it out of her wallet without thinking and left it at home? Somehow, she knew she hadn't.

She didn't understand what was happening to her, why she suddenly had these jarring gaps in her memory. She kept telling herself that it must be because she had so much on her mind. That had to be it—the other possibility was too dreadful to even consider: that she might be *losing* her mind. Again.

Time had suddenly turned into her enemy because so much of it seemed to be slipping away from her—and she had no idea where it had gone. Each day became indistinguishable from the one before: she'd wake up in mid-afternoon, still tired, and always dressed in men's clothing, with the mustache and sideburns on her face. Odd items kept appearing in her pockets: ticket stubs from porno movie houses—she had never even seen an X-rated movie—and more matchbooks from sleazy dives where she would be ashamed to show her face.

Her cash seemed to disappear overnight, and when she checked her bank balance it was much lower than it should have been. When she questioned the bank, they told her that several large withdrawals had been made with her card from the twenty-four-hour automatic cash machines. That was impossible, Andrea said, because the bank card had a code number which only she knew—and she hadn't used the card lately. Nevertheless, the assistant manager responded, an odd look on his face, the code must have been used because the computer would not operate without it.

After the bank incident Andrea stopped going out. She stayed in her room with the curtains drawn, wishing she could blot out her tortured thoughts as easily as she did the sun. Something awful was happening to her, and there seemed to be nothing she could do to stop it. She began to dread waking up—afraid of what new horror the day would bring. And although she had no appetite and barely ate a thing, she didn't lose an ounce of weight.

Bobby called to ask how she was feeling. She longed to tell him everything, to open up her heart and pour out all the torrents of pain and anguish she had bottled up in there. But how could she tell him what was wrong when *she* didn't even know? Besides, she didn't dare mention the part about the disguise to him. So she lied and told him she was still sick.

Sometimes she thought she was being punished for what she had done to Cynthia, that God had singled her out for a special damnation. Waking up in the disguise day after day was her personal penance. Only God didn't work that way, did he? People did. *Cynthia.* That was it. Somehow Cynthia had found out about Andrea. She had stolen a key to her apartment and she came in in the middle of the night to put the disguise on Andrea.

But Andrea knew—even as she was thinking these thoughts—that they were absurd, the result of her own paranoia. Nobody else knew about the disguise—*nobody*.

She felt cut off from the world, from all hope and comfort. There was no one to turn to. Bobby was her only friend, and he couldn't help her now. Once, she had promised Sam that she would go to him if she were ever in trouble—but this was not the kind of trouble he had meant. No one—except maybe the doctors at the Clinic—could help with this.

Perhaps she ought to go back to the Clinic, let them take this terrible burden off her mind. But even if she could afford it—which she couldn't—how could she explain it to Bobby? Tell him that she had to take her once-crazy psyche back in for its yearly checkup? No, that would mean questions—with answers she doubted he would like to hear, and that she would hate to give.

There must be other doctors. Hell, this city was practically *infested* with shrinks. Every actor she ever knew who could afford it put in his obligatory time on the couch.

But shrinks cost money—and that was something she had precious little of these days. If it kept on disappearing the way it had, soon she wouldn't have enough left to live on, let alone pay for a psychiatrist. And getting a job was out of the question now—not with the state she was in.

But there was one place she probably could get some money—and she was desperate enough to give it a try.

She started to dial the telephone number but panicked and hung up before she had completed all the digits. Her mouth felt cottony and her palms were so sweaty she could barely hold on to the phone when she picked it up to dial again. This time she went through with it, scarcely able to breathe as she listened to the hollow, clicking sounds of the long-distance connection going through and then the mechanical hum of the phone at the other end ringing.

Someone picked it up after the third ring. "Hello?" a woman's voice said. Andrea was surprised at how good it felt to hear her voice again. "Hello?" Bernice Donahue repeated. "Is anybody there?"

"Hello, Mother," Andrea choked out. Her eyes were already smarting with tears and the words had caught in her throat.

"What? I can't hear you. Who is this?"

"It's Andrea."

There was a long pause. "Andrea. Where are you?" The voice had the tiniest quaver to it.

"I'm in New York. I-I've been here all the time."

"What are you doing there?" Her mother sounded a trifle put out.

"Well, I was, uh, working as a waitress and going to acting classes and trying to get work in the theater."

"It never occurred to me to look for you there—I never knew you were serious about being an actress."

"You tried to find me?" Andrea asked incredulously.

"Does that surprise you so much?"

"I don't know. I guess I never thought about it."

"Paul and I both tried to find you. He wanted to hire a detective, but I told him that was just a waste of money, that nobody could find you if you didn't want to be found, and that when you were good and ready you'd let us know where you were."

Andrea could not speak. If her mother had actually looked for her, maybe she *did* care—and maybe she could help her now. Andrea began to cry, softly at first, but then something broke inside her and the tears came pouring forth in a flood of despair and agony.

"Andrea, what's wrong?" her mother asked. There was concern in her voice but it came across as phony—as though she were giving a performance for someone. Andrea suddenly realized that Paul must be in the room with her, listening to her side of the conversation. For his benefit she was playing the part of a loving mother.

Andrea dried her tears. She should have known that even after all these months her mother's heart would not have softened toward her. Did she imagine it or could she really hear that shrill accusation "Crazy! Crazy!" echoing through the wires? "I-I'm okay," Andrea sniffled into the phone. "It's just that I've been having some problems lately."

"What kind of problems?" There was an almost imperceptible note in her mother's voice: I-told-you-so. But Andrea caught it, though she was sure Paul would not. She was not about to give her the satisfaction of letting her know that she might be right.

"Oh—money problems," Andrea sighed. Then, in a rush, "I had this job as a waitress, but I quit that when I got a part in a play. But then the play closed right away, and now I can't get another job."

"So that's why you called. You need money." Andrea heard Paul's voice in the background. It was several seconds before her mother spoke again.

"Paul says he'll send you a check," she said. "How much do you need?"

"But I don't want to take *his* money—"

"You'd better," her mother cut in, and Andrea could tell from the way Bernice said it that she would never send a penny of her own money. "How much do you need? A thousand? Two thousand?"

"A thousand, I guess."

Her mother must have put her hand over the mouthpiece because Andrea could only hear muffled sounds of conversation on the other end. Then Bernice came back on the line. "Paul says he doesn't want you to worry about starving. He'll send you three thousand."

"Oh, well, uh, tell him I really appreciate it and I'll—"

"Tell him yourself. I'll put him on the phone."

When Paul came on the line Andrea played the part of the penitent, wayward daughter. He was an old-fashioned, fatherly sort of man who sincerely believed in the virtues of the family, and Andrea knew that he would have been more than shocked to find out how much her mother detested her own offspring. Andrea was tempted to tell him what a hypocrite her mother was, but she bit her tongue and listened to him telling her how sick with worry they had been when Andrea disappeared, how happy they both were now that she had seen the error of her ways and had decided to come back to the fold.

It turned Andrea's stomach to think of the charade her mother must have put on for Paul's benefit—all the time she was probably exulting inside that she had finally gotten rid of the millstone around her neck.

Bernice came back on the phone and they talked a little more—mouthing empty phrases—and finally Andrea gave her mother her address to send the check and her telephone number and promised to keep in touch. But she knew she'd be damned before she'd ever call *her* again.

When she put down the phone, Andrea felt like flinging it across the room. *The bitch! The rotten, lying bitch!* If Paul hadn't been right there, she probably would have slammed the phone down the second she heard Andrea's voice. How naive she'd been to hope for any kind of comfort from her mother—not even money, it seemed.

But thank God for Paul. Now she could afford some help to get her out of this hell she was living in.

It was going to be all right.

But it didn't happen that way; the next day was a repeat of the day before, and she woke to find herself garbed in the male disguise again.

As she was getting dressed, she opened a dresser drawer to get out a sweater. The one she wanted was at the bottom of the pile, and when she reached under it to pull it out she felt something cold and metallic. Shaken, because she didn't remember ever hiding anything there, she lifted up the sweaters to see what it was. It was a small handgun, a revolver of some sort, and as Andrea gaped at it, horrified, she tried to tell herself that it must be a toy. She could not bear to touch it again, but somehow she could not tear her eyes away from it. Its dull, black surface was covered with tiny scratches and nicks and it appeared to be loaded, for Andrea could see the flat, brass ends of bullets in the chambers of its cylinder.

She let the sweaters drop back over the gun, and staggered across the room to the bed. Already a pain was mushrooming in her chest, and she knew she was about to black out. But her clouded brain grasped at the thought that someone was doing an awfully good job of driving her crazy, and whoever it was knew about her fear of guns and had to have a key to her apartment. *Bobby*. It had to be. But Bobby would never do anything like that to her. Would he?

CHAPTER THIRTEEN

The intercom buzzed on Bobby's phone and he picked it up. "Cynthia Wilson on line one," his assistant announced, and Bobby's heart turned over in anticipation. *Cynthia.*

"Okay, thanks, Angela," he said coolly, as he pressed down the button to take the call. "Hi, Cyn," he said, swiveling his chair back and propping his feet up on his desk. "What's happening?"

"Bobby, I've got to see you—right away." There was an urgency to Cynthia's voice that carried through the sounds of traffic in the background.

Bobby sat upright. "What's wrong?"

"He's back. That man—he's following me again. Please, can I come up to your office? I'm so scared."

Bobby thought for a second, trying to formulate a plan. Maybe he could trap this guy. "Wait a minute," he said. "I've got a better idea. Where are you?"

"I'm at a phone booth on the corner of Fifty-seventh and Fifth."

"Okay. Now listen—there's a bar on the corner of Fifty-seventh and Sixth. I want you to walk there as fast as you can and go inside and wait for me."

"But he'll follow me to the bar—"

"That's exactly what I want. Will he go inside?"

"No, he'll probably hang around outside waiting for me to come out."

"Good. Now tell me what he looks like."

"Well, he's about six feet tall, and he has sort of reddish hair and a mustache and he's wearing a hat and dark glasses and a blue ski parka."

"Okay, I guess I should be able to spot him. Now you just go into the bar and order a drink and wait for me."

"What are you going to do?"

"I'm going to leave the office right now—it's practically five, anyway. I'll get to the bar a few minutes after you do, and if this guy is there waiting for you I'm going to find out what the hell he wants."

"But he might be dangerous—"

"Let me worry about that. I can take care of myself. You just do what I told you—and don't leave the bar until I come to get you. Okay, have you got that?"

"I guess so," Cynthia said reluctantly. She hesitated a moment, then added, "Bobby?"

"What?"

"Please be careful. I don't want anything to happen to you on my account."

Briefly, Bobby wondered if she said that because she cared—or because she was afraid of losing her meal ticket. "Don't worry," he said. "Now you get going, and I'll see you in a little while."

Bobby hustled up Sixth Avenue and rounded the corner onto Fifty-seventh Street. Exactly seven minutes had passed. The guy was there, all right— he fit Cynthia's description to a tee—and he was looking in the window of the bar, hands in his pockets, one foot impatiently tapping up and down.

Bobby started nonchalantly toward him, intending to grab him before the man knew what hit him. But suddenly the man turned his head, looked straight at Bobby—and then like a shot, bolted down Fifty-seventh Street.

It took several seconds for Bobby to react. How in the hell had the man known he was after him? Maybe he'd seen him with Cynthia before. Christ, there was something familiar about him—but, shit, he wasn't going to catch him just standing here.

The man had a head start, but his progress was impeded by the hordes of office workers pouring out onto the sidewalk from the adjacent buildings. Bobby darted and shoved through the crowd, ignoring angry voices snarling at him. Then he heard someone shout, "He must be a cop!" and people began to step aside. The idea of being mistaken for a cop would have been laughable—if he'd had any breath left to laugh with. Bobby was gain-ing on him now, but his effort was costing him dearly; his lungs were already burning, and he knew he could never run another block at this breakneck pace. As a teenager he'd once run the mile in five minutes flat, but the years and the cigarettes had taken their toll.

In the middle of the block there was a walkway through to Fifty-sixth Street, and Bobby cursed as he saw the other man hurl himself toward it. He could hear the man's footsteps reverberating against the walls as he disappeared from sight. When Bobby reached the walkway there was no sign of the man, but he kept running—ignoring the constricting band around his chest as it grew tighter and tighter. When he emerged on Fifty-sixth Street he had to stop. Taking in great gulps of air, he looked up and down the street. The man had vanished.

"That fucker's got some kick!" Bobby said to no one in particular as he took off his gloves to wipe his forehead. Well, whoever he was, he was gone for now—and if he had any brains he wouldn't be back.

When his breath started coming in easier swells, Bobby turned to walk back to the bar where Cynthia was waiting. He was troubled; he couldn't figure out just where he might have seen that man before.

It was still early, but Sam could already tell this was going to be a slow night. After so many years behind the bar, he had a built-in sensor system about how a night was going to go—just like he had about people.

He usually didn't bother to look up whenever the door opened, but for some strange reason he happened to glance at it when the man in the broad-brimmed hat and bulky parka came in. In the dim light and with his face shadowed by the hat, Sam could barely make out his features—but he knew they reminded him of someone.

The man sat down at the far end of the bar, and as Sam walked down to him, an image came into his mind: a pretty, sunny face with freckles and cornflower blue eyes. *Andrea*. Now why the hell should this guy remind him of Andrea? Sure, there might be a strong physical resemblance, but this guy was obviously some street dude—probably spaced-out on drugs. Why else would he keep his dark glasses on inside?

At Sam's approach, the stranger tilted his head ever so slightly.

"What'll you have?" Sam asked, trying not to be too obvious as he studied the fellow's face.

"Beer." The voice was deep and muffled, but Sam thought there was something constrained about it, something . . . unnatural.

"Comin' right up," Sam said, and went to draw off a stein. He brought it back and set it down in front of the stranger. "Haven't I seen you in here before?" he asked with careful nonchalance.

The fellow took a sip of his beer and shook his head.

"Are you sure?" Sam persisted. "I know I've seen you somewhere. Are you an actor?"

Under the mustache there was a crooked grin. But again the head wagged out a negative response.

Sam regarded him a moment longer and then turned away. *Christ, the guy must be a real weirdo*—he hadn't even taken off his gloves to drink his beer. Yet, try as he might, Sam could not shake off the uncomfortable feeling the man gave him. His gaze kept straying to the end of the bar, watching the stranger drink his beer. Even behind the dark glasses he could feel the man's eyes, looking back at him, almost as if he were checking *him* out. Sam had the oddest feeling that the man was there for a reason, as though he was trying to read his mind or something. It gave him the creeps.

He made himself busy fixing refills for his other customers, and when he looked up again the stranger was on his feet, fishing a bill out of his pocket. "Don't you want another?" Sam called out, and as an inducement he added, "On the house."

But the stranger shook his head, threw his money on the bar and walked out.

Sam went down to the end of the bar and picked up the bill and the empty beer stein. Thoughtfully, he fingered the money and all of a sudden his head started to reel—*Christ, he must be going bananas*—but somehow he imagined he could smell an ever-so-faint hint of a cologne that Andrea always wore.

That did it. If he couldn't get her off his mind, he'd better do something about it. He already had the perfect opening line: "Hey, Andrea. I saw your twin brother tonight." She'd get a laugh out of that one—that is if that asshole Bobby didn't have her head so fucked up she couldn't think straight anymore.

Sam stepped away from the bar to the pay phone. Keeping an eye on his customers, he put his dime in and dialed Andrea's number. He had been wanting to make this call for a long, long time, had started to time and time again. He let ten rings go by before he hung up, disappointed. If he got the chance, maybe he'd try her again later. Or maybe he'd better wait till tomorrow.

Bobby watched Cynthia as she fiddled with the keys to her apartment door. Things were going better than he had dared to hope. When he met her in the bar after the chase he had basked in her gratitude.

She *needed* him, and he intended to capitalize on that. He had bought her a few more drinks and then dinner, and then he had insisted on seeing her home.

He was hewing a very fine line: alternately calming her fears about the stranger, and keeping her just anxious enough so that she would turn to him for protection.

So far, so good. She had not made a single murmur about his coming home with her. In fact, she had seemed relieved that she would not have to walk the dark streets and go into the gloomy apartment alone.

Now he was practically there. Once inside, he might even end up spending the night.

Cynthia unlocked the door, flicked on the

lights, and ushered Bobby into her apartment. It was just what he had expected, typical furnished-room decor. The cheap, Danish modern furniture was not actually shabby, just long past its heyday. The apartment was a single, boxy room, with the kitchen fixtures along one wall.

"Oh, *Cyn*," he groaned. "You left the hotel for *this*?"

Cynthia shrugged her slender shoulders. "I know it's not much," she said, "but it's quiet and private. I couldn't stand the noise in that hotel—and everybody wanting to know everybody else's business. It was like being back in the college dorm."

Bobby took off his coat and sat down. "Aren't you sorry you moved? I mean, with that creep following you around?"

Cynthia was pulling off her own coat. At Bobby's words her body seemed to give an involuntary shudder. "Don't remind me," she said softly. Then, almost to herself, she added, "If I see him around here one more time I'm leaving."

Bobby frowned. "Going where? Back to the hotel?"

Cynthia went over to the closet and hung her coat up. "Maybe—maybe not," she said. "I might just leave New York altogether."

"Come on, Cyn. You can't let one freak scare you into leaving town."

Cynthia didn't answer. She walked over to the sink and began filling a tea kettle from the faucet. "Would you like coffee?" she asked. "I'm going to make some."

"Sure, I'll have a cup," Bobby said automatically. His eyes lingered hungrily on her. Her dress, a soft green jersey, was clinging to her ass as she leaned over the sink. His palms started to tingle, almost as if they remembered and longed to experience again the feel of her flesh. Later, later, he told himself. He started to pull out his pack of cigarettes, then, remembering that Cynthia didn't like his smoking, put them back. Oh Christ, he wanted her so much. He *had* to talk her out of leaving. "Listen," he said in a slightly derisive voice, "you didn't answer my question before. Would you really leave New York just because of this guy?"

Cynthia didn't respond. She put the kettle on the stove and switched on the gas. She seemed fascinated by the blue flame curling around the blackened bottom of the kettle, and she stood motionless, staring into it dreamily.

"Cyn?"

She had turned her back on Bobby and he thought he saw her shoulders shaking. When she turned around to look at him he could see a glimmer of tears in her eyes. Without thinking he got out of his chair and walked toward her. "What's wrong?"

Cynthia's face twisted in pain. "God damn you, Bobby Wilson!" she exploded. "You did this to me!" Her hands were balled into fists and she shook them at him. "Oh God, how I wish I'd never met you!"

Bobby gaped at her, confused. What had he done to deserve this outburst? "Me?" he asked. "What do I have to do with it?"

"Everything." She was struggling to regain her composure, but the tears were already beginning to spill down her cheeks.

Bobby was torn between his urge to comfort her and his anger. How dare she accuse *him*. He opened and closed his hands at his sides and then, not knowing what to do with them, stuffed them in his pockets. "Yeah, sure," he said finally. "That's right, blame it all on me. Anything goes wrong in your life, it's good ol' Bobby's fault."

Cynthia glared at him through the tears. "You still don't know what you did to me, do you? You still don't understand."

"Oh, God," Bobby sighed. "Here it comes again. You never get tired of rehashing how I done you wrong, do you?"

Cynthia's cheeks burned red. "Very funny. It's all a big laugh to you, isn't it? All my pain and suffering are nothing but a joke."

Bobby wrenched his hands out of his pockets and doubled them up into fists. "I don't believe this! You're not the only one who's been through hell! You think I enjoyed watching our marriage go down the toilet? I did everything I could to save it!"

The kettle began whistling loudly, and Cynthia turned and shut off the gas. Then she took down cups and saucers and some instant coffee and measured it out. When the coffee was ready she brought the two cups over, handed one to Bobby and then sat down on the studio couch.

Her eyes were red but dry as she looked up at Bobby, who was still standing. "Sit down and drink your coffee," she said. "I don't want to talk about the past. There's really no point in it, is there?"

Bobby sat down opposite her. "I don't know, Cyn," he said tentatively. "It might help—maybe if I knew exactly where we went wrong I wouldn't make those mistakes a second time."

Cynthia cocked an eyebrow at him. "Why? Are you thinking about getting married again?"

Bobby looked at her sharply. *Was it possible she knew about Andrea?* "No," he said emphatically. "That's *not* what I meant." He watched Cynthia's face, and when she lowered her gaze to her coffee cup he knew she understood that he was talking about a second time with her.

"Don't, Bobby," she said. "It's no use."

"Why not, Cyn? Why won't you even give me a chance? I'm a different person now—I've changed an awful lot."

A bitter smile crossed Cynthia's face. "You mean you don't tell lies anymore?"

Bobby had not been quite ready for that one. He slumped back in his seat, nearly spilling his coffee. "I-I never did that to hurt you, you know," he said, surprised at how pathetic his own voice sounded.

Cynthia's eyes flashed up at him. "I suppose you feel that justifies it. You always said you couldn't help it, but you ended up hurting me all the same, didn't you?"

Now Bobby looked away. "I never lied about anything important. Not to *you*, anyway."

"Maybe not. But you sure did to other people, like the Army—"

"I don't want to talk about that—"

"Of course not! It's not everyone who has the distinction of being discharged from the Army as 'psychologically unfit'!"

Bobby squirmed in his chair and this time the hot coffee splashed onto his suit jacket. He ignored it. "So the bastards caught me in a few lies. But I'm not sorry it happened. I hated the Army. I was glad to get out."

"But that wasn't enough," Cynthia said tartly. "Then you had to lie to me about your discharge."

"I was just trying to impress you," Bobby said. "How do you think I felt? I had just gotten kicked out of the Army, and then I met you and you were this pretty little high school girl with big ideas about the anti-war movement—"

"So you had to tell me you left the Army as a conscientious objector, right? Because you knew that would appeal to me."

"What's so terrible about that? How was I going to compete with all those long-haired radicals you liked so much, if you had known the truth?"

"The *truth*," Cynthia sneered. "What do you know about the truth? I think you lied so much you never could remember what the truth was. Even when I found your discharge papers you tried to lie about that—just like you did everything else."

Bobby set down his coffee cup. "What else did I lie about? You make it sound like every word out of my mouth was a lie."

"Wasn't it? What about that book of yours that

was always just on the verge of being sold to a publisher? It took me years before I figured out that it was just another one of your lies."

Bobby shook his head forcefully. "That wasn't a lie, Cyn. My book *did* almost get sold—several times. I was so sure it would, too. But at the last minute the publishers always backed out. That happens all the time in publishing—"

"Stop it, Bobby! I've heard all that before. Your book never got sold because there was never any book. Maybe you wrote it all in your head—but you never got one word down on paper."

"Well, you're *wrong*," Bobby countered. "But there's no point in arguing with you, since you obviously don't believe anything I say."

"Why should I? Nobody can change that much—especially you. You're a liar, Bobby—a pathological liar. My doctor told me that—"

"Doctor? What doctor? Dr. Greentree? That old fart couldn't even pronounce 'pathological,' let alone diagnose it."

"No, a psychiatrist in Raleigh. You don't know him. I went to him a few times after—"

"You mean *my* money was paying for *you* to see a shrink?"

"You're damn right!" Cynthia snapped. "You're the one who drove me to it!"

"What the hell did you have to go to a shrink for? They're nothing but a bunch of money-grubbing parasites—"

"That's really ironic, Bobby," Cynthia cut in. "Nobody in the world could use a psychiatrist more than you, and yet you have the audacity to put me down for going to see one!"

"Don't tell *me* I need to see a shrink!" Bobby shouted. The bitch wasn't going to say that to him and get away with it. "Don't you ever tell me that again or I'll—" He lurched forward in his chair, as if to pounce.

"Or you'll what?" she scoffed. "Hit me? Like you used to?" Her eyes narrowed. "You lay one finger on me ever again and I'll call the police. And don't think I wouldn't press charges this time."

Bobby stared at her, and for a second he saw her face as it had looked the last time he had hit her—all purple and puffy. That was the last time—because she had called the police that night. When they came to the house he had been scared shitless, until Cynthia changed her mind and refused to press charges. Instead, the next day while he was at work, she had taken Jennifer and moved out. They had never lived together again.

He leaned back in the chair. "I'm sorry, Cyn," he said meekly. "I lost my head for a minute."

Triumph gleamed fleetingly in Cynthia's eyes. "You haven't changed," she said. "Not one iota. You *still* like to smack women around." She paused and then added, "I wonder if any of your New York girlfriends have discovered that side of you yet."

Bobby cringed, remembering the scar on Andrea's face, but he frowned in sincerity. "There haven't been any 'New York girlfriends.' I've gone out with a few women, sure—but nobody special. And I certainly haven't beat up on any of them."

Cynthia's eyes went hard again. "Maybe not. But don't tell me you haven't had any girlfriends," she said. "That's impossible, Bobby. You've always got to have a woman around—or two or three to build up your ego."

Christ, had Cynthia somehow found out about Andrea and the others before—and a couple since—his relationship with her? Bobby shook his head. "You're wrong again, Cyn. I've never been the womanizer you thought I was. Just because I cheated on you a couple of times—"

"A couple! By my count there were at least half a dozen, and there were probably more I didn't know about!"

Bobby forced a laugh. "You give me credit for a lot more stamina than I have."

"But you don't deny it!"

"Of course, I do! I made a couple of mistakes, that's all. You knew I was sorry about that—"

"The only thing you were sorry about was getting caught!"

"Jesus Christ, Cyn! What do you want from me? I told you over and over again how sorry I was, that it'd never happen again. And that's the God's truth!"

Cynthia sipped at her coffee. "I don't know why we're yelling at each other like this. It doesn't matter, anyway. It's all over."

"Not for *me*," Bobby said fervently. "It'll never be over for me. I'll never let you go."

Cynthia looked at him for a long minute, her eyes wide and staring. Finally, she said, "But we're *divorced,* Bobby. We've been divorced for over a year and a half."

Bobby shook his head slowly from side to side. "Not as far as I'm concerned—it's just a piece of paper," he said. "We took a vow, remember? 'Till death do us part.' Those words meant something to me."

Cynthia groaned and ran a hand across her eyes. "God, what a hypocrite you are! After all the lies you've told me, you expect me to stand by a meaningless vow like that. You must think I'm a fool."

"Not you, Cyn. Never you. You've always been one of the sharpest women I've ever known—"

"And you certainly have known a lot of women."

Bobby ignored her remark. "You know," he said, "if you and Jennifer moved up here, we could have a good life together. I'm making a pretty healthy salary now—"

"That's just great, Bobby," Cynthia sneered. "But I remember a time when I had to beg you for money to keep Jennifer in diapers—"

"I'm doing my best to make it up to you, aren't I? I've given you every penny you asked for, and I've gone out of my way to help you get started on your modeling."

"Forgive me," Cynthia said sarcastically, "did I forget to thank you? Anyway, it's only what you owe me after all you put me through."

Bobby jumped up out of his chair and raised his arms heavenward in a mock, supplicating gesture. "Lord, have mercy," he wailed. "I don't deserve to live after fucking up this poor woman's life the way I did."

"Go to hell." Cynthia glowered at him.

Bobby walked around to the back of his chair and leaned on it. "You really hate me, don't you?" he said. It was not a question, but more like a request for exoneration.

Cynthia chewed at her lip a while before responding. "Sometimes I felt I wanted to kill you," she said slowly. "Other times I felt like killing myself." Bobby started to speak, but she raised a hand to silence him. "Oh, I didn't try it—mostly because of Jennifer. But after the divorce I went through such a terrible period of depression. I'm pretty much over that now, but I'm still frightened."

Bobby looked at her hands gripping the coffee cup. Her knuckles were white. "Of what?" he asked.

For a moment Cynthia seemed not to have heard him, and Bobby was about to repeat the question when she stirred. Her eyes darted around the room before they came to rest on his face. "Men," she said in a near whisper, as if she were ashamed to say it out loud. "I'm afraid of men."

"*Men?*"

"Yes. I'm really frightened of them—especially the ones who try to get close to me. I-I'm still attracted to them, but when they move in I panic. I sometimes wonder if I'll ever be able to go to bed with a man again—let alone get married."

Bobby sat down, shaking his head in disbelief. "And *I* did that to you?"

Cynthia scowled at him. "Why do you find that

so difficult to accept? You—you completely destroyed my trust in you. Don't you think that would have a profound effect on my relationships with other men?"

Bobby shifted his weight in the chair. "I don't know, Cyn. I think you're overreacting a bit."

Cynthia swept the coffee cup from her lap and put it down on the table next to her. The cup rattled noisily in the saucer. "You're an ass, Bobby," she hissed. "A complete and utter ass."

Bobby fidgeted in his pocket for his pack of cigarettes, pulled one out, and lit it. He looked around for an ashtray and when he didn't see one, dropped his match in his saucer. Exhaling deeply, he said, "Go ahead, call me names if it makes you feel better."

Cynthia stood up. "Why don't you just go home?"

"You mean the audience is over, Your Majesty?"

"*Please,* Bobby. I'm tired. I've got a really important interview tomorrow morning and I want to get plenty of sleep."

"You could stay up all night and still look good, Cyn. You're more beautiful than ever." Cynthia barely managed an indifferent smile, but Bobby went on. "You sure you don't want me to stay here with you—just in case your secret admirer comes back, I mean. I could sleep on the floor—I promise I won't bother you—and then I could take you to your interview in the morning."

"No, Bobby. Just go home. Please."

Bobby dropped his cigarette into the coffee cup, where it sizzled a moment before going out.

"Okay, I'm leaving," he said, getting up. "But first, promise you'll call me in the morning so I'll know you're all right."

"Why?" Cynthia asked quickly. "Is there something you're not telling me?"

"Not at all. Actually, I'd be surprised if that guy showed up again," Bobby said confidently. Then he added, "But if you're still worried I could come by in the morning."

Cynthia rubbed her cheek absentmindedly. "I don't know," she said. "My interview is at ten-thirty."

"Fine. I can come by about ten and we'll take a cab over."

"But what about your job?"

"No problem. Angela can handle anything until I get in."

"Well, I'm not sure it's necessary. He probably won't come back—but can I call you in the morning and let you know?"

"Sure. Call me about nine, okay?"

"Okay."

Bobby got into his coat. He had an intense desire to see how Cynthia would react if he tried to kiss her, but he knew that would be foolhardy. Better to act like the perfect gentleman. He walked to the door with her following behind. "Don't forget to lock up," he said.

"I won't." Cynthia gave him a weary smile.

Bobby looked longingly at her beautiful face. The evening had not ended at all as he had hoped. There were still so many things he wanted to say to her, but this was not the time. Perhaps tomorrow—maybe he'd see if he could meet her for lunch. "Well, goodnight, Cyn," he said, his voice husky with emotion. He pulled open the door and walked through it, not daring to look at her face again. He felt like a condemned man as he marched to the stairwell, and pounded down the steps to the lobby.

He burst through the front door of the building, and the cold night air felt good as it stung his face. The sky was overcast, reflecting the city lights below it with a rosy glow. Street lamps illuminated most of the block, but here and there against the buildings were inky shadows. Bobby started walking and then stopped abruptly. Was it his imagination or was there really a man standing in the doorway of the building across the street—a man in a wide-brimmed hat?

He took a few steps, still unable to distinguish between shadow and substance. But as he stepped off the curb and began to cross the street, he was suddenly sure he spied some movement in the doorway. Cautiously, he approached the building, and then jerked open its outer door.

Nothing.

He stepped into the tiny vestibule and tried the inner door.

Locked.

There was a window in the top half and he peered through it. He could see a long hallway with a stairway leading off to the right. They were both empty.

Puzzled, he studied the names on the mailboxes on the wall to his left—as if a name there might ring a bell and give him the solution to this mystery. Maybe he *had* been right. Maybe Cynthia's stranger lived in this very building. That meant he was probably just some lonely guy who had seen her in the street, developed a crush on her, and started following her around.

Bobby went back out on the street again and looked carefully up and down the block. There was no one about and it was quiet, except for the noise of traffic on the avenue. He turned to go home, certain that Cynthia was safe for the night. Still, he thought he'd give her a call when he got home—just to let her know he was watching out for her.

CHAPTER FOURTEEN

Cynthia was slipping into her nightgown when the downstairs buzzer rang. Her first instinct was not to answer it—at this late hour it must be a mistake. But when it sounded again, she realized it was probably Bobby. She looked around the room, but couldn't see anything he might have left behind. Still, she wouldn't put it past him to use that kind of excuse.

She pressed the talk button on the intercom. "Who is it?" she asked guardedly.

"It's Bobby, Cyn." The intercom gave a tinny quality to his voice, but his North Carolina accent came through.

"What do you want?"

"I forgot to tell you something. Can I come up?"

"Can't you just stay there and tell me?"

There was a brief pause, then, "It's important,

Cyn. Do you want me to stand down here shouting it so all your neighbors can hear?"

Cynthia hesitated a moment. "No, I guess not. Come on up." She pressed the button to release the inner door downstairs.

Then she grabbed her bathrobe and wrapped it tightly around her. Better not let Bobby see her in her nightgown—it might give him ideas.

There was a soft tap on the door, and she unlocked it. Pulling it open, she started to speak, but found her words cut off by a gloved hand slapped against her mouth. Startled, she lifted her eyes, and was horrified to find herself face to face with the man who had been following her.

He pushed her back into the room and slammed the door behind him. It was then that she saw the gun in his other hand.

"Don't scream. Don't even speak—or I'll kill you," he said, pointing the muzzle of the gun at her face. The words were delivered in a kind of whispery growl, and it struck Cynthia that there was something very odd about it—phony even. Why should he bother to disguise his voice?

He shoved her back to the studio couch—which she had just made up into her bed—and she fell onto it. Was this it, Cynthia wondered. Was this what he had come for—to rape her?

He stood over her, the gun at hip-level now, an obscene black phallus. His eyes were shaded by the tinted glasses, but Cynthia could still see the steely glint in them. Her blood congealed at the unbridled hatred she read there. It wasn't fair, she wanted to shout at him. *She* had never done anything to him. Why should she have to pay now for something someone else had done to make him despise women so?

"Don't move," he barked. "Stay just like that."

Cynthia nodded her head mutely, waiting for his assault.

But instead he backed away from her, slowly swiveling his head to look around the room. With the gun still pointed at her, he took several steps backward and then walked sideways over to her dresser.

Methodically, he began to ransack the dresser, tossing her sweaters into disorderly heaps on the floor as he burrowed in the drawers. He kept his body half-turned toward her, flicking his eyes back to her every few seconds—as if to reaffirm his complete control.

Cynthia watched him as he worked, all the while saying a silent prayer that he was only there to rob her, not rape her. Robbery she could deal with; there wasn't much to steal. She had no jewelry to speak of, and only twenty or thirty dollars in her purse.

Maybe she should tell him about the money, if that was what he wanted. But somehow she sensed that *he* must find it, that he must maintain his mastery over her, and that any words from her—no matter how helpful—would only enrage him. Cold terror seemed to have made her mind clearer, even though she was quaking from head to foot. It was as if her body had deserted her in her hour of need, and now her brain was taking over—comforting her with its lucidity of thought.

He turned his attention briefly to her closet, but after picking through the meager wardrobe she had brought to New York, he turned away, looking disgruntled.

Her purse and model's portfolio were sitting on top of the wooden kitchen table, and Cynthia felt almost relieved when he walked over to it. Maybe after he'd gotten her money, he'd go.

His body blocked her view so she couldn't see what he was doing when he rifled through her purse, but she assumed he had found the bills in her wallet and taken them. Then she heard him unzip the portolio and flip through it, the plastic sheets softly slapping against each other.

There was a single drawer under the table, where she kept her bills and important papers, and he pulled it open. Its contents seemed to interest him more than anything else in the apartment, and he pored carefully over them. Because there was nothing of value in the drawer, Cynthia was surprised to see him stuff some of the papers in his pockets.

Suddenly the harsh jangling of the phone split the air. The man turned to glare at Cynthia as if it were *her* fault, that she had somehow willed the phone to ring.

No one but Bobby would be calling her at this hour, Cynthia was sure. He knew she was there. If she didn't answer he might figure something was wrong and come over. It was a slim hope. She clung to it.

On the second ring the intruder waved the gun

at her face. "Answer it," he said. "And get rid of whoever it is—*fast*."

Heart sinking, Cynthia raised herself off the couch. Her legs nearly crumpled beneath her as she got to her feet, but she managed to make the few steps to the table. The man was by her side as it rang again and she picked up the receiver. He put his gloved hand over hers and turned the receiver so that he could hear the caller. With the other hand he shoved the gun in her ribs. Then he signaled her to speak.

"Hello?" Cynthia said, barely able to get her voice to work.

"Hi, it's Bobby. Just double-checking—you all right?"

Cynthia frantically tried to think of some way she could let Bobby know that she was in danger, something she could say that only *he* would know so he'd understand she needed help. But, God help her, she couldn't think of a thing.

"Oh, Bobby," she said hesitantly. "I-I was asleep. You woke me up."

Cynthia glanced at the man to see if he approved. His face was scant inches from her own, and this was the first chance she had had to observe him at such close quarters. He did not seem to be paying much attention to her; he was too intent on listening to Bobby apologizing to her for disturbing her sleep.

Cynthia surreptitiously studied his face: the even, boyish features, the large, light-colored eyes framed by the glasses, the reddish-brown eyebrows, mustache and sideburns, and the pale, downy skin.

Wait, that wasn't right. She stared at the skin on his chin and jawline, looking for signs of whisker growth. But there were none. Yet, how could he have such a thick mustache and sideburns? At this proximity—even if he had shaved closely—she should still be able to see the whiskers under the skin. But his cheeks were smooth, like a baby's. *Like a woman's,* Cynthia suddenly realized. Her mind whirled wildly. Could that explain the disguised voice, the hands that even now were gloved, the tinted glasses and hat pulled down low on the face? A woman trying to pass as a man would do all those things. Yes, that *had* to be it!

The gun was pressing against her ribs, and Cynthia heard Bobby repeating her name. "What?" she said. She hadn't heard a word he'd said.

"What happened? Did you nod off?" Bobby asked. "I was talking to you, and you didn't answer me. Are you all right?"

No, there's some nut here dressed up like a man and she's got a gun, Cynthia wanted to scream at him. Instead she said calmly, "Yes, I'm fine. Just sleepy."

Cynthia knew now that Bobby was not going to save her. No, she was going to have to do that herself. Her fright had given way to anger, a slow rage mounting in her brain, building to a sense of recklessness. A *woman* had done this to her, and she wasn't nearly as afraid of another woman—only the gun. Who this woman was and why she was doing this were questions that would have to remain unanswered for the time being. Now, if there were just some way she could get that gun.

"Well, I'm sorry I bothered you," Bobby said testily. "I was only looking out for your welfare."

"I appreciate it," Cynthia said, her mind only half on the conversation. "I'm just tired, that's all." *Surprise*, that's how she would do it. The woman would not be expecting her to fight back. She wasn't much bigger than Cynthia—disallowing the bulk of the ski parka—and they were probably fairly evenly matched in physical strength. If she took the initiative, she had a good chance of grabbing the gun before the other woman could even realize what was happening.

"Okay, I'll let you go back to bed now," Bobby said. "Talk to you in the morning."

"What? Oh, sure," Cynthia said uncertainly, stalling for a little more time while she completed her plan. "That's right. I remember. We made plans for tomorrow morning." She decided to go for the gun when she hung up the phone. He—*she*—would probably relax a little, relieved that Cynthia had gotten her caller off the phone without letting on that anything was wrong. Then Cynthia would strike. But she'd have to do it fast—while the gun was still within her reach.

"Jesus, Cyn," Bobby said, laughing. "You really are out of it. Go back to sleep. I'll see you tomorrow."

"Good night," Cynthia said, steeling herself for the attack she was about to make. As if from far away she heard Bobby say good night and hang up, and then the woman removed her hand from the receiver and started to back away. Her hand free now, Cynthia took the receiver and swung savagely with it—hitting the woman on the shoulder. The phone fell off the table, its chimes jangling harshly. With her other hand Cynthia snatched at the gun, trying to wrench it out of the woman's grasp. Reeling more from shock than from the blow, the woman staggered backward, and Cynthia went with her, her fingers clawing and clutching at the gloved hand on the gun.

They struggled fiercely, bound together in violent *pas de deux*. Tottering back and forth, their legs kicked clumsily at each other, while both pairs of hands were scrambling for the lethal hunk of metal between them. They crashed into a chair, and both nearly fell, but somehow they whirled and righted themselves, and continued their convulsive, desperate dance.

The only sound was of their rasping, irregular breathing, until Cynthia tried to scream for help. All that came out was a pitiful squawk. She wondered how long they could go on like this. The effort she was exerting was tremendous, and the other woman did not seem to be much stronger than she, so neither of them was prevailing. Maybe, her mind raced, if they made enough noise it would rouse some of the other tenants. Perhaps they'd come to the door to see what was wrong, even call the police.

She tried twisting to one side, pulling the other woman with her, heading for a nearby table. But the woman seemed to sense what Cynthia was after, and she pulled just as hard in the opposite direction. Their bodies were angled away from each other. Just then, the woman gave a violent jerk with her hands—as if to break free of Cynthia's tenacious grip. Suddenly the room was filled with a sound like muffled thunder, and Cynthia felt herself letting go, falling backward. She wondered how the woman had managed to give her such a vicious punch to the solar plexus—until she inhaled the acrid fumes in the air as she went down. It was only then she realized that she had been shot.

She lay on the floor, still feeling no pain—only numbness all over her body. The other woman's face floated above her, eyes glazed in fear, her mouth gaping as if to emit a silent scream.

Cynthia tried to speak, but she could not get her lips to follow her brain's directive. All the air seemed to have been sucked out of her lungs and she felt as though she was choking. She closed her eyes and prayed: *Dear God, please! I don't want to die!*

From a great distance she heard an anguished woman's voice cry out, *"No!"*

Cynthia opened her eyes again, but her sight was growing dim. Struggling to keep her vision in focus, the last thing she saw was a pair of long legs and booted feet. Then, the door slammed shut.

CHAPTER FIFTEEN

Andrea cracked open her eyes cautiously—afraid that she was still asleep, still locked in the nightmare that she had been obliged to play over and over again in her dreams last night: the gun in her hand exploding each time Andy's face popped up in front of her, just like ducks in a shooting gallery.

But, no, it was daylight; the shadowy night had gone. Yet the dream lingered on, punctuating her thoughts as she lay in bed staring dully at the ceiling. It had been so *vivid*—she could actually hear the sound of the gun going off. But she had lived with dreams like this for years. Why should this particular one bother her so?

Somehow, she knew the answer, but couldn't shape it into words; it was just a vague image of a woman's face, hollow-eyed and ghostly pale. Was it that image she had been shooting at—not Andy? Or was it the other way around?

Something had happened last night, she was sure of it. And yet she had no memory of it other than the dream. So why did she have this awful feeling that the dream had been real?

Throwing back the covers, she tried to shrug off the depressing aftereffects of the dream. Now it was back to her daytime nightmare—as usual, she was dressed as a man. When was this masquerade going to end, she wondered. When would she be able to call her body—and her mind—her own again?

Maybe the check from Paul would arrive today, and she could make an appointment with a psychiatrist. It was after eleven, the check might even be in the mailbox now—she should go and see.

She got up, tearing off the male attire and fake whiskers, walked over to her dresser to get some clean underwear, and her heart lurched. The gun was sitting right out there in the open on top of the dresser. Who had moved it? She knew *she* hadn't touched it. Then she saw some papers lying next to the gun. *Someone* had left these things purposely for her to find.

On the top was an official-looking printed document with an embossed seal. Gingerly, she picked it up and unfolded it. Her breath came in shallow, panting sighs as she read the legal phrases of a divorce decree granted to Cynthia Rossiter Wilson against Robert Allen Wilson, dated July 1977. Over a year and a half ago!

Andrea flung the paper down on the dresser.

She wanted to tear it into a thousand pieces or set it on fire—but what good would that do? The truth of it would still remain: Bobby had lied to her. He had never meant to marry her. It was all a sham, a cruel joke at her expense. All these months of telling her he loved her, that they'd be married just as soon as his divorce came through—all a *lie*.

Was there more? What other little surprises were in store for her? Underneath the document had been an envelope, and Andrea looked at it now. It was apparently a letter to Cynthia from Bobby, and it was postmarked December 27th. Andrea picked it up and took it over to the bed.

There were several folded sheets inside, all covered with Bobby's familiar scrawl. He began by telling Cynthia what a smart move she was making by coming to New York to be a model, then went on to describe all the arrangements he had made for her in the city. Andrea read them over with mild curiosity; most of this she had already heard from Bobby himself.

But then the tone of the letter changed abruptly, and Andrea felt herself growing ill, as she read, so stunned that she had to go back and reread the letter, just to make sure that her eyes had not deceived her. But the second reading only confirmed that she had not misconstrued a single word. The phrases began to burn themselves indelibly into her brain: "My life has been so empty without you and Jennifer . . . There will never be another woman for me but you . . . I love you with all my heart and soul and every fiber of my being . . . I can't sleep at night, thinking of you and how much I've lost . . . I pass other women in the street and they don't even exist for me . . . You'll see how much this terrible loneliness has changed me . . . My constant prayer is that you'll forgive me all my sins, and we can be together again—our little family."

On and on it went, all in the same vein.

So Bobby had prided himself on being such a wordsmith, Andrea thought bitterly. What a dreamer. But between the lines of those simple sentences with their mawkish, unimaginative language was one dirty little secret: that all the while he had been making love to her and proclaiming his devotion to her, he had been in love with his ex-wife and wanted her to take him back.

Andrea threw the letter on the floor. What trash! What filthy, disgusting trash—and how typical of Bobby it was. He had even written to Cynthia that he had been celibate since their divorce! No other woman can ever measure up to you in bed, he'd said.

There were tears stinging at her eyes, but Andrea refused to let them flow. Instead, she pounded her pillow in a blind fury. So Bobby had found her inadequate—both in and out of bed. God, how he must have laughed to himself over her pathetically passionate lovemaking! To her, their sexual embraces had been the most beautiful thing in the world, but to him they had only been casual rolls in the hay—and not very good ones at that.

A fiery rage burned within her. She could feel it blazing up from the pit of her stomach, consuming

her body, then her mind, with the scorching flame
of white-hot hatred. Bobby was unworthy. He had
defiled their perfect love, made a mockery of it—
and for that he could not go unpunished.

Suddenly Andrea gasped. An angry pain had
just shot through her chest, and already her mind
was beginning to grow cloudy. Then, through the
swirling gray mists, a memory came back to her, a
scene so sharp and clear that she could feel sunshine on her face, smell smoke from a dying camp-
fire, hear the voices of her friends. She struggled to
bring back the rest of it, and then it was there: a
4-H picnic she and Andy had gone to only days before he died. She had completely forgotten about
it—until now. All these years it had remained buried deep within her brain. Strange that it should
suddenly come back like this.

But it was as real to her now as the day it happened—all their friends gaily grouped on picnic
blankets, surrounded by baskets of food; the sizzle
of hamburgers and hot dogs cooked over an open
fire. After gorging themselves they had played a
wildly enthusiastic game of softball, and Andy had
hit the winning home run, which had made him
the hero of his team. Even though Andrea had
been on the opposite side, she had secretly gloated
over his athletic prowess. Then, hot and dusty
from the game, they had all gone swimming in a
nearby creek. Andrea had only stayed in the water
a short while before she got out to lie in the sun and
gossip with several of her girlfriends. She had paid
no attention to Andy, assuming that he was with
the rest of the boys, playing an impromptu game

of water polo. When the game ended and the boys were lying like slippery fish on the bank of the creek, she didn't see Andy among them. Still, she'd thought nothing of it. Only later, when it was time to go home, did she begin to ask Andy's friends if they had seen him. One of the boys gave her a wink and told her that Andy had gone off into the woods. As she set off to look for her brother she could hear the boys laughing behind her back, but put it down to their juvenile sense of humor. She called Andy's name a couple of times as she tramped through the underbrush. When there was no response she thought he might be hiding from her—waiting to jump out from behind a tree—so she began to creep noiselessly along, imitating the Indians who had once walked so silently through these very woods. Finally she spotted Andy, lying under a tree. But as she stole closer she could see he was not alone. There was a girl with him—Brenda Fisk, the local teenage sexpot. They were kissing and writhing together there on the ground, and their swimming suits were half off! Andrea had been so shocked that she nearly let out a cry. Instead, she had slipped behind a tree and cowered there, while she threw up most of her picnic lunch. Then she had run, crashing blindly through the forest. She had not gone back to the others, but had walked across the fields to the farm. Unable to stomach the sight of her brother's face, she had feigned a headache and gone to bed before he even returned home.

It was a painful and awful memory; no wonder

she had blocked it out. Even the doctors at the Clinic had never been able to drag it out of her.

But now she realized why the memory of the picnic had come back to her so clearly today: that was the one other time in her life when she had felt so . . . *betrayed.*

Bobby had done to her just what Andy had done all those years before. Only what Bobby had done was worse; he had deliberately lied to her. This wasn't just a boyish sexual escapade—it was an elaborate scheme, concocted to service his base, animal needs while he waited around for his ex-wife to take him back. Maybe Andrea hadn't been the only one. There had been plenty of nights—even while she was living with him—when Bobby had "worked late" or said he needed to be alone "to do some writing." Excuses, she realized now, more lies to allow him to sneak in a few extra women on the side.

Well, all that didn't matter much anymore, did it? The important thing was that she knew the truth. Armed with that, she was going to drive him to his knees, make him beg *her.*

She would have to plan her revenge carefully, time it just right. Maybe she'd lead him on a little, let him think everything was still the same between them—before she sprang it on him. He might even try and weasel out of it, but she would have proof, the divorce decree. She could even show it to him—no, then he would wonder where she got it, and that was a question she couldn't even answer herself.

No, it would be better to simply tell him that

she knew. Let him guess the source—he might even think it was Cynthia, and that would certainly throw him for a loop.

The sudden, harsh ring of the phone interrupted Andrea's thoughts and brought her back to reality. She stared suspiciously at it as it rang again. It could only be Bobby, and she braced herself to speak to him.

But it wasn't Bobby, it was Sam. "Hi," he said. "I've been thinkin' a lot about you, so I decided to call you up and see how you are. How's it goin'?"

"Great, Sam." She was trying to sound cheerful and carefree. "Gee, it's really good to hear from you. How are things at the Center Stage?"

"Same as ever. Dull—you know the routine."

"Yeah, I sure do. And I don't miss it a bit."

"What you been doin' with yourself?"

"Oh—things. Nothing special."

"How's the boyfriend? Still got the same one?"

"Yeah, sure. Why wouldn't I?"

"No reason. I just thought a pretty girl like you might get tired of hangin' around the same guy all the time."

"Well, I haven't—not yet."

He had caught the hesitation in her voice.

"Does that mean you're thinkin' about it?"

Andrea hesitated. Sam had once been a good friend to her. Even though she would hate to admit to him that he had been right about Bobby all along, it would be good to be able to talk to somebody about it. But she didn't want to tell Sam the whole story—at least not now. "I don't know, Sam," she said. "It's just that things haven't worked out exactly like I thought they would. Maybe I'll come over to the Center Stage some night and tell you all about it."

"Sure, kid. You do that. I'm a great listener, you know."

"Aren't all bartenders?"

"Yeah, but some of us are better than others. Me, I listen good, but sometimes I open my big mouth too much. People don't always like that—they don't want to be told what to do with their lives."

Andrea smiled wistfully to herself. "I guess they'd rather make their own mistakes," she said.

"Yeah. Well, I always say you learn more from the things that go wrong than the things that go right."

"I never thought about it that way—but I suppose that's true."

"Sure it is—but only if you figure out what went wrong so it doesn't happen again the next time."

"Is that how you got to be so wise, Sam?"

He laughed. "Yeah. Believe me, I made a lot of mistakes. And I'm still makin' 'em—all the time."

Andrea sighed. "I guess that's part of life."

Sam laughed again. "Listen, I didn't call you up to get into any heavy philosophy discussion. But like I said, I been thinkin' a lot about you lately—"

"Any special reason?"

"Yeah, it's a funny thing. This guy came into the bar last night, and he looked enough like you to be your twin brother—"

"My *what*?"

"Your twin," Sam said, sounding clearly puzzled by Andrea's reaction. "Hey, what's the matter? Did I say something wrong?"

Why should she hide the truth from Sam? "Well, yes," Andrea said, "but you couldn't have known. You see, I *did* have a twin brother—but he's dead."

"Oh, Jesus, kid. I'm sorry."

"It's all right, Sam. I never talk about him, that's all. Anyway, you say this guy looked just like me?"

"Yeah."

"Describe him."

"Well, he was actually kind of weird lookin'. I mean, there was nothing physically wrong with him, but he had these dark glasses on and he kept them on in the bar and he didn't even take his gloves off when he was drinkin' his beer."

Andrea's skin began to crawl. "Was there anything else?"

"Nah, not really. I tried talkin' to him, but it was like talkin' to a wart. He musta been some kinda junkie."

"But what did he *look* like?"

"Oh, you know, like a million other guys. His hair was kinda reddish—like yours—and he had a mustache. He was wearin' this cowboy hat with the brim dipped down real low in front—like he was tryin' to hide his face—and I think he had on this ski parka. Hey, do you think you know this guy?"

"No," Andrea said quickly. "I was just curious. You know how it is—people are always telling you they know somebody who looks just like you, and you always wonder if you've got a double some-where in this world."

"Yeah. Listen, if this guy ever comes in again, maybe I'll call you up so you can come over and get a good look at him."

"Sure. That ought to be good for a laugh," An-drea said. *But it'll never happen, because that "guy" is me.* "Uh, Sam, I'm sorry but I can't talk anymore," she said, making her voice sound rushed. "I've really got to run. But I'll come over to the Center Stage some night and we can have a good talk then—like old times."

"Great, kid. Soon?"

"Very soon, Sam. I promise."

"Okay. See you then."

"Right," Andrea said. " 'Bye." She hung up the phone, her mind a jumble of thoughts.

It couldn't be coincidence that someone who looked just like she did in her male disguise had walked into the Center Stage last night—no, that was too much to hope for. So, obviously *she* had done it in her blackout. How many other places had she been—and more important—what had she done there?

CHAPTER SIXTEEN

The call came from Bobby at six o'clock. Andrea let the phone ring four times before she picked it up.

"God, where were you?" Bobby asked. "I was afraid you weren't home." His voice was slurred.

"I was busy. What's the matter, are you drunk?"

"Yeah, I'm drunk—and I wish I were drunker."

"Why? Has anything happened?"

"Has anything happened!" Bobby repeated incredulously. "You mean you don't know? Haven't you seen the papers?"

"No. I've been in the apartment all day—I've had a lot of things to think over. What happened?"

"I don't want to tell you over the phone. Can you come over? *Please.* I need to talk to somebody."

And I'm convenient, Andrea thought to herself.

"Okay," she said reluctantly. "I'll be over in a little while."

"Hurry, will you? Take a cab. I'll pay for it."

"Okay, okay. I'm on my way." Andrea slammed down the phone in annoyance. What the hell could have happened to Bobby to make him so upset? Well, he'd have plenty more to be upset about before this evening was over. She'd see to that.

Bobby was sprawled on the couch when Andrea let herself into his apartment, a bottle of Jack Daniel's in his outstretched hand. "Have a drink," he said, offering her the bottle.

"No, thanks," Andrea said, taking off her coat. "You owe me some money."

"Oh, yeah—for the cab." Bobby reached down and pulled the wallet Andrea had given him for Christmas out of his pocket. He tossed it over to her. "Take out whatever you want," he said. "Hell, take it all. I don't give a shit."

Andrea gave him an exasperated look, drew some singles out of the wallet and put it down on the desk. Then she sat down, crossed her legs, and folded her arms in front of her chest. "Okay," she said. "You wanted somebody to talk to. I'm here—so talk."

Bobby took a large swig from the bottle. "Look in the paper." He waved toward a pile of newspapers on the floor. "It's all there."

Andrea watched him as he tipped the bottle to his mouth again. Then she reached over and picked up that afternoon's *Post*. The front page was all international news, so she opened it up and skimmed the headlines for the stories on pages two and three. "Model Slain on West Side" caught her attention immediately. She began to read: "The body of model Cynthia Wilson, 26, was discovered in her West Side apartment this morning by her estranged husband, Robert A. Wilson . . ."

Andrea stopped reading, slowly lowered the paper, and stared at Bobby. "I don't know what to say," she murmured. "It must have been a terrible shock for you."

Bobby flung a heavy hand over the back of the couch and pulled himself up into a sitting position. "I still can't believe it," he said, the words coming out disjointed and listless. "I just saw her last night—she was fine then, full of life."

Andrea frowned. She wondered what had gone on between them last night.

"I've got to talk about it," Bobby said wearily. "I spent practically the whole day with the police, just going over and over everything until I couldn't stand it anymore."

"Then why do you want to talk to me? Didn't you talk enough to the police?"

He squinted at her. "That's not the same. With them it's just questions, questions—I know they've got to ask them, but I wasn't in very good shape to answer them."

"All right, talk. Tell me everything—right from the beginning."

Bobby started to lift the bottle to his lips, then seemed to think better of it and put it down on the floor. "Oh, God," he moaned. "If I'd only known."

Andrea felt a stab of pity for him. He looked so pathetic, so lost—nothing at all like the monster she had thought he was this afternoon. "How did you happen to find her?" she asked.

Bobby looked down at his hands lying in his lap as if there were a script there from which he was reading. His voice was dispassionate. He had already been through the story several times with the police; all emotion had been drained from it, and now, it came out as if by rote. "I knew something was wrong when she didn't call this morning, so I called her. The line was busy, and I waited a while and called back. I kept doing that every few minutes, and then I got the operator to check if the line was off the hook. She said it was, but I knew Cynthia had a ten-thirty appointment this morning and it was already after ten. I couldn't imagine that she would be sitting yakking on the phone and forget about her appointment— that just wasn't like Cynthia. So I hopped in a cab and went down to her building. Somebody else was coming out and I slipped inside and went upstairs and pounded on her door for maybe five minutes. When she didn't answer I got worried, so I went to look for the super. It took me a while to track him down, and it took me even longer to persuade him to open up her door. When he did, we both saw her right away. She was lying in the middle of the floor, and her eyes were open, looking right at us. But she'd been dead for hours."

"How was she killed?"

"She was shot—in the stomach," Bobby answered. Then with more energy he said, "The bastard shot her and just left her there to die."

"You mean they found whoever did it?"

"No, but *I* know who it was. The police aren't so sure, but if I have to, I'll get him myself. I don't know his name, but I know where to find him."

"I don't understand. How do you know who did it?"

"Because I *saw* him, that's why! He'd been following her around for days. And I saw him last night. He was following her on the street, and I chased him away. But then I saw him again when I left her building later. He was hanging around across the street—just waiting for me to leave, I guess."

A cold hand seemed to run its fingers down the length of Andrea's spine. No, it couldn't be true. She had only followed Cynthia once dressed as a man—*but she didn't know that for certain, did she? Not after what Sam had told her.*

"Wh-what makes you so sure it was this man who killed Cynthia?" Andrea said, hardly daring to ask the question.

"Because she was scared of him—she must have sensed he meant to hurt her. Me, I just thought he was some harmless pervert—and I practically laughed it off. Don't you remember? She called me one time when you were here. That's when she first told me about him. I thought she was imagining things, seeing bogeymen behind every doorway."

"But he was very real," Andrea said—more to herself than to Bobby.

"Oh, yeah, and he murdered her!" Bobby snarled. "He shot her down like a dog and let her bleed to death."

"What do the police say?" Andrea asked, trying to get him off this particular subject.

"Oh, hell, what do they know? At first, I think they thought I did it—maybe they still do. You know, I'm the estranged husband, I was the last one to see her alive. Sure, I know how to shoot a gun, but I've never owned one in my life. Anyway, what reason would I have for killing Cynthia?"

"But they let you go. Doesn't that mean that they don't suspect you anymore?"

"Oh, they let me go all right. But you'd better believe they're going to do some checking up on me. They'll just be wasting their time when they could be out finding the real murderer. I gave them his complete description, even told them where I think he lives."

"How do you know that?"

"Because he lives right across the street from Cynthia, I'm sure of it. I saw him go into that building, and I'm convinced that's how he spotted Cynthia. He probably saw her in the street and just started following her around. What I can't figure out though, is how he ever got into her apartment. Cynthia would never have let him in, I know that."

"Then isn't it possible that it wasn't that man? Maybe it was a burglar." Yes, yes, that was it, Andrea told herself. A burglar did it.

"Oh, yeah, it's possible. The place *was* ransacked. But it's too damn much coincidence for me to swallow. Besides, the police say it looks like she fought with him—the phone was on the floor, knocked off the hook, and some of the furniture was turned over. Why would she fight with a burglar—especially if he had a gun? She would have just let him take whatever he wanted."

"Maybe he tried to—you know—rape her."

Bobby sighed. "Yeah. I thought about that. He probably tried to, and that's when they fought. But that makes me believe more than ever that it was the guy who followed her who did it."

"Why?"

"Because that's what he wanted from her in the first place! He probably sat up there in his apartment jerking off and slobbering over Cynthia every time he saw her in the street. Then he decided to go after the real thing."

"What did the police say when you told them about him?"

"I'm not sure if they believed me. You see, the problem is that no one but Cynthia and I ever knew that he existed—except you."

"*Me?*"

"Yeah. You could tell them you were here when she called me that time. You can at least corroborate my side of the conversation."

"But I—well—I really don't remember it all that well, Bobby. Anyway, they'd probably think you put me up to it."

"Yeah, you're right. But if the police don't find him, I will. And, believe me, this guy better be praying that the police find him first."

"But he's got a gun. He might shoot you, too."

"So? Listen, there are plenty of guns floating around this city. It shouldn't be all that hard for me to get my hands on one."

But it's going to be a lot harder for you to find a man who doesn't exist—who never existed, Andrea thought to herself. Out loud she said, "Stop it, Bobby. You're talking nonsense. This isn't the Old West, this is New York City. You can't just go out and shoot a man down in the street."

Bobby stood up, swaying slightly on his feet. "Oh, yeah? Just watch me. I'll do it. I'll find him and kill him."

Andrea was suddenly disgusted by this macho, ridiculous posturing. "You're drunk," she said, "And you don't know what you're saying."

"The hell I don't!" Bobby took several somewhat unsteady steps toward her. "But I know what your problem is, you don't like me talking about guns, do you?"

Andrea stared at him. There was an oddly menacing gleam in his eye.

"And I know why, too," Bobby said, coming even closer.

Andrea stood up. "Yes, I told you. Now can we please drop it?" She started to sidestep away from Bobby, heading for the couch.

But Bobby grabbed her by the arm and held her there. "Only you never told me the whole story," he said. "You told me that you were there, but you never said that you were the one who shot your brother."

Andrea's free hand instinctively flew to her chest, ready for the pain that came a second later.

"That's not true," she cried. "Who told you that?"

"Oh, I have it on the best authority," Bobby said. "You see, your friend Sam isn't the only one who's good at checking up on people. I'm not so bad at it myself."

Andrea's legs were quivering, but the pain had gone—and she knew she was not going to black out. "Let me go," she begged. "I've got to sit down."

Bobby released her arm. "Sure," he said. "It must be quite a shock to you—to realize that I know the truth."

Collapsing onto the couch, Andrea tried to console herself with the thought that Bobby must be bluffing. There was no way he could have found out. "You're lying," she said. "You don't know anything about it."

"Oh, don't I? Would you like to hear all the details? Let's see, your brother's name was Andrew, he was actually your twin brother, you shot him with a Walther PPK, and all this happened in August, 1968. Am I right so far?"

Andrea's whole body had gone limp. There was roaring in her head, and she was unable to move or speak, but her eyes panned the room like an unseeing camera.

Bobby watched her for a moment. "Don't you want to know how I found out?" he asked. "I'm kind of proud of my detective work—it was really ingenious, I thought."

Andrea said nothing. She just sat there, looking stupidly at him.

Perching himself on the edge of the desk, Bobby lit a cigarette. "You see, I was curious. You were so mysterious when I talked to you about it that I figured there had to be more to the story. I knew a shooting incident like that had probably made the papers, so I got on the WATS line and called our stringer in Milwaukee. He's always eager to do more work for us, so I knew I could get him to do a favor for me. He works on the paper there, so he has access to their morgue—you know, their files of old stories. I told him your name and the fact that this had probably happened a few years ago, and he said he'd get to work on it. Well, it didn't take him too long, and he called me back with the story they'd run in the Milwaukee paper. It was only a short item and a little skimpy on details so I asked him if there was any way he could get any more particulars, and he said he thought he could probably do that, too. That took a bit longer, but it seems he called up someone on your hometown weekly and they were only too happy to give him all the facts—including the ones they left out of the papers. It was a pretty big scandal there—wasn't it?— and smalltown people aren't likely to forget something like that. You must have been the major topic of conversation there for a long time." He puffed on his cigarette and looked at Andrea, who was sobbing vocally.

"But, of course," he went on, "you never knew anything about that, did you? After you flipped out, they whisked you right out of town to that cushy Clinic in Massachusetts. They said you were always a little weird—even before you shot your brother. But I don't believe that, I think that's just hindsight talking. Still, you sure did spend a long time in that Clinic—nearly eight years, wasn't it?"

"Shut up!" Andrea screamed at him. "Shut your filthy mouth!"

"But I haven't finished yet," Bobby said.

"I don't want to hear anymore!" Andrea shouted at him.

"Actually, I don't know why I'm telling you all this now," Bobby went on in a normal conversational tone. "I never really intended for you to find out that I knew—and that I've known for some time. I thought you might even tell me about it yourself someday." He put out his cigarette. "Maybe I told you tonight because I'm feeling guilty over Cynthia's death—you know, that I'm responsible for it in a way—and I know that you know what that feels like."

Andrea shuddered. "Oh, dear God," she said in a barely audible voice.

"Of course, it's not exactly the same kind of guilt," Bobby said. "After all, you broke the ancient taboo."

"What do you mean?" Andrea asked, her eyes narrowing in suspicion.

"Well, fratricide has been against the law ever since Cain slew Abel, you know. Now *there* was a real case of exaggerated sibling rivalry. I suppose it must be even worse between twins. Is that why you shot your brother?"

"You bastard!" Andrea shrieked. "It was an accident! Didn't your reporter friend tell you that?"

"Oh, sure. He said that everyone more or less assumed it was an accident—even though you couldn't tell them how it happened." Bobby paused and added almost slyly, "But you can tell me the truth. It wasn't really an accident, was it?"

Andrea leaped to her feet, out of control and trembling with rage. "You—you're an animal!" she cried, her ragged breath chopping off the words. "You're the—the vilest, m-most contemptible human being I've ever known! I can't stand the sight of you anymore!" She grabbed her coat and began walking toward the door.

Bobby seemed surprised to see that he had caused such a violent reaction. "Hey, Red. Don't leave me. I need you," he said, as if he expected that everything would be all right again between them if he just said the right words. He came after her and caught her by the arm as she opened the door. "I don't know what made me say that," he apologized. "I'm drunk and I'm grieving and it's made me a little crazy. I'm sorry if I hurt you."

Andrea stared at him, open-mouthed. "You're sick!" she said. "There's no way I'll ever forgive you for what you've done to me. You must be mad if you think I would. Now get your stinking hands off me." Her eyes were so icy and her voice so low and threatening that Bobby obeyed her instantly.

Andrea took a step out into the hall and turned to face him. "I hate you more than you could possibly know," she said, her lips pulled back from her teeth in a snarl of revulsion. "Don't you ever come near me again—or I swear I'll kill you!" Then she reached for the doorknob and slammed the door shut on Bobby's shocked expression.

As she stormed down the hall past Mrs. King's door Andrea thought she could see some movement behind the tiny peephole. Oh, no! Mrs. King must be there, her eye glued to the peephole, clucking to herself over the newlyweds' lovers' quarrel. As far as Andrea was concerned it was just one more humiliation to be added to all the others she had suffered that day. But it broke her spirit, and she began to cry again, weeping softly as she made her way out of Bobby's building into the comforting darkness of the night.

CHAPTER SEVENTEEN

There was no moon and the air was raw and heavy with the promise of snow, but Andrea was oblivious to the cold as she wandered along the streets. The thought of going back to her tomblike apartment filled her with dread, for she was completely alone now—perhaps more alone than she'd ever been in her life—and locked by herself in that tiny room she would be forced to come face to face with the full extent of her isolation from the rest of the world.

At least out here, on the street, she could maintain the semblance of normality. It was still early evening. There were plenty of people about and she was able to pass among them as if she were one of them.

Eventually her steps brought her near Lincoln Center, and she was drawn by its beacon of glowing crystal lights and air of elegant festivity. Once, years ago it seemed, Bobby had brought her here to a ballet—but only after she had needled him about it for days. Now she couldn't even remember what ballet they had seen.

She climbed a broad flight of terrazzo steps to the central plaza, crossed thê concentric circles of its paving to the fountain at its center, and sat down on the edge. She sat facing the Metropolitan Opera House, with its lofty arches and the seductive lushness of the Chagall murals on two flanking walls.

She gazed wistfully at the murals, thinking that any other night she would have been entranced by their frenzy of brilliant colors and floating, dreamlike images, but tonight they could only be a momentary diversion to her. And although her eyes continued to stare, she no longer saw them.

It was after curtain time and all the evening's performances had begun, but here and there figures traversed the plaza, occasionally glancing at Andrea, who remained unaware of them. She sat, elbows leaning on her knees, her fingers intertwined under her chin, looking for all the world like a worshipper at prayer—and in a way she was praying, praying for surcease from the anguish that the day had heaped upon her.

She had long since stifled her tears; there was no solace in them anymore. There was no solace anywhere—not after what Bobby had done to her tonight. She felt as if her flesh had been ripped apart, and dirty, prying fingers had reached in to pluck out her soul and squeeze out its secrets—all for the sheer amusement of it. Her agony had been

Bobby's plaything, and he had bandied it about like a football, tossing it just beyond her reach.

To think that he had known—*everything*—and for months kept it a secret from her. All the nights she had lain in his arms, tormenting herself with the thought that someday she must tell him the truth about herself—and all along he had *known*.

But even worse than that was the fact that he had actually accused her of *intentionally* killing Andy. No, that was too much. That was more than she could bear.

It was an evil, vicious thing to say, but then Bobby was an evil, vicious person. She had found that out today. All his lies had been exposed to her, but it was maddening to think that he didn't know she knew about them. She had intended to tell him tonight, but instead he had managed—so fiendishly—to turn the tables on her.

She had said she never wanted to see him again, but now she began to change her mind. Because she wanted to see his face when she told him that she knew about his divorce and his wretched love for his ex-wife. She longed to see him squirm, to realize—too late—that his deceit had been discovered and that there were no more lies between them. Yes, she wanted him to know everything—even that *she* had been the man following Cynthia around.

Of course, Bobby had been mistaken in his insistence that her disguised counterpart had been the one who killed Cynthia. She'd been home last night, asleep. And besides, she hadn't been anywhere near Cynthia since that one time she'd followed her.

But Bobby was a different matter.

She wasn't finished with him yet; there were still things left unsaid and undone between them. She couldn't rest until they were all accomplished. And there was a way to do it too—a way that would shock him and hurt him as much as she had been shocked and hurt that night.

She continued to sit, planning her vengeance until she had all the details worked out in her mind. Then, when she was satisfied, she got up and walked at a leisurely pace to her apartment, savoring the sweetness of the revenge she was about to take on Bobby.

Slowly, she walked back to her room. It was going to be dangerous, more dangerous than anything she had ever done.

But she had to chance it.

Bobby was lying on the couch, exactly as she had seen him earlier in the evening—only this time he was passed out in a drunken stupor. The bottle of Jack Daniel's was on the floor beside him, empty.

She had kept her hand on the gun in her pocket as she opened the door, and now she took it out. She was no longer afraid of it—in fact, she felt oddly comforted having it in her hand.

She moved noiselessly across the room until she was standing over him. Bobby was snoring in deep, sonorous breaths, and his mouth was open. Andrea thought how easy it would be to stick the muzzle of the gun in that gaping, piggish hole and pull the trigger, but instead she nudged him in the midriff with the gun. He groaned and tried to roll over, but she held him back and poked harder.

"Go 'way," Bobby said, his eyes still tightly shut.

Andrea poked him again. This time his eyelids parted lazily, and Andrea thrust the barrel of the gun on a level with them, only inches from his face. As Bobby's eyes focused on it they widened. All he could see was that ominous black-metal eye staring back at him. Then he looked past the gun, up the length of the arm, to the face. "Oh, Jesus!" he blurted out. *It was him—the guy who killed Cynthia!*

Andrea hid her smirk under the mustache. The look of terror and surprise on Bobby's face was worth the risk she had taken in coming here.

She stepped back, casually drew up a chair, and sat down, with the gun resting on her thigh, still pointed at Bobby.

Cautiously, he pulled himself up into a sitting position. "Wha—how'd you get in here?" Bobby asked in a voice thick with alcohol and sleep.

Andrea didn't say a word. She sat staring at him for a long minute, then, ever so slowly, she reached up with her free hand and took off the hat, then the dark glasses and put them on the desk behind her—all the while never taking her eyes from Bobby's face. A flicker of curiosity appeared there and was gone, followed by a strange mixture of horror and fascination. Andrea could see the truth was beginning to dawn on him. When she took off her gloves—shifting the gun gingerly from hand to hand—and then, with a sweeping, dramatic gesture, pulled off the mustache, Bobby's face froze into a mask of disbelief. "No!" he said, his eyes transfixed and bulging. "No! *No!*"

"Yes, Bobby," Andrea said, smiling coldly. "It's me. Andrea."

He dropped his face into his hands, his head shaking wildly back and forth. "No!" he said in a choked voice. "It's impossible!"

"But it's true," Andrea said.

Bobby pulled his hands away from his face. "Then you—you killed Cynthia!"

Andrea narrowed her eyes at him. "No, you got that wrong, too. I was home last night—it had to have been a burglar."

"But I saw you!"

"No, you didn't. Maybe you *thought* you saw me, but I told you—it wasn't me. It must have been somebody else who killed her."

Bobby sat digesting this for a moment. It was obvious he wasn't satisfied, but he wasn't about to argue with Andrea as long as the gun was in her hand. "Why?" he asked. "Why did you follow her?"

Andrea shrugged. "It's hard to say. In the beginning I just wanted to get a look at her and see what she wanted with you. After a while I did it for the hell of it—it was exciting."

"How—how long did you do it?"

"Oh, for a lot longer than Cynthia was aware of. I disguised myself as women at first, and she never even noticed me. But when I cut my hair, you told me I looked like a man so I hit on the idea of dressing up like a man—it was funny, she spotted me right away."

"Then you never meant to—to hurt her?"

"No, I just wanted to scare her. I thought I might get her to leave town."

Bobby's gaze wavered. "She was thinking of doing that—she was really terrified of you."

Andrea laughed. "If she'd only known."

"I still can't believe it was you." Bobby was shaking his head in disbelief. "I never *dreamed* you were capable of doing something so—so awful."

"Oh, but I'm only an amateur compared to you, Bobby," Andrea said with a sly grin.

Bobby looked blank. "Me? I've never done anything like that in my life."

Andrea cocked an eyebrow at him. "Oh no? You've never lied—pretended to be something you weren't?"

"I—no. Not to you ever." Bobby's eyes dropped to the gun. "Why don't you put that thing away?" he asked. "It makes me nervous."

Andrea waved the gun nonchalantly at him. "No, I think I'll keep it a while longer."

Bobby sighed. "Suit yourself. But can I at least have a cigarette?"

"Be my guest."

Bobby reached over and picked up his pack from a nearby table. He pulled out a cigarette and lit it. Andrea saw that his hands were shaking.

"I'm going to ask you again," she said. "Because I don't think you understood before that, as of tonight, there aren't going to be any more secrets between us. So be very careful how you answer this question: Have you ever lied to me?"

Bobby puffed on his cigarette, and behind the cloud of smoke his eyes regarded her anxiously. "You're toying with me," he said. "Why don't you just come out and say what you're driving at?"

"Toying with you," Andrea repeated maliciously. "I like that expression—I think it's a pretty good description of what you've been doing to me for the last six months."

Bobby remained silent, but a muscle twitched in his cheek.

"Still, I must say you were very good at it," Andrea went on. "I may have suspected something was wrong, but I never even guessed at the truth."

Bobby flicked a nonexistent ash from his cigarette into the ashtray. "I wish you'd come out with it," he muttered. "Stop torturing me."

Andrea gave him a long, steady gaze before she said in a voice almost bereft of emotion, "You're divorced, Bobby. You've been divorced for more than a year and a half. You never intended to marry me."

Bobby grimaced. "That's a lie! Who told you that?"

"Oh, I have my sources," Andrea said airily. "This one happens to be unimpeachable."

Suddenly Bobby's face screwed up into an expression of pain. "Not Cynthia?"

"No, not Cynthia. I never met her, remember? I don't think she even knew who I was—unless *you* told her."

Bobby shook his head.

"I didn't think so," Andrea said with a smug smile. "Because I also happen to know you were still in love with her. You were even hoping that her coming to New York would give you a chance to get back with her."

"Wha— How do you know that?" Bobby sputtered, nearly choking on the smoke from his cigarette.

"What's the matter? Did you think that you and Cynthia were the only people who knew about that?" Andrea said scornfully. Then she added, "Anyway, it's not important *how* I know, just that I *do* know. I want to hear your side of the story, Bobby—so why don't you make a clean breast of it?"

Bobby's eyes went to the gun. "You want to know the truth? No more lies?"

Andrea gave him an emphatic nod.

Bobby put out his cigarette, started to speak, then closed his mouth and rubbed a hand across his forehead, as if to relieve some tension there. "I didn't mean to hurt you, Red—honest," he said, his voice just above a whisper. "But I—I needed you, and I was afraid if you knew about the divorce and how I felt about Cynthia you wouldn't stay with me."

Andrea remained implacable. "So why did you ever ask me to marry you?"

The muscles in Bobby's face went slack. "I don't know. I really *wanted* to, I guess. You were so sweet to me, you made me feel like a man—like I was worth something, and I just couldn't stand being alone anymore. Don't you see? I didn't plan anything. I just knew that you wanted to get married—so I asked you. I thought it would make you happy. I didn't think about the consequences. I didn't think about *anything*."

"But right from the very beginning you told me a lie—you said you were just separated from Cynthia, not divorced."

"I know. I tell everyone that. It makes me feel better. You see, I never wanted the divorce in the first place. If I pretended it didn't exist, it made it easier to live with."

"You're incredible," Andrea said. "I'll bet you even told the police you were still married to Cynthia—the paper called you her 'estranged husband.'"

Bobby winced. "That was dumb, I know. But it just kind of slipped out."

"And what about all those things you said about her—about finding her in bed with another man? Was that a lie, too?"

"Yeah." Bobby looked away. "I thought it made me more sympathetic. You know—women would feel sorry for me and try to make it up to me for what another woman had done."

"Oh, that's good, Bobby. Real good. *I* certainly fell for it—I bet lots of other women did, too. Am I right?"

"A few."

"What's the matter? Didn't you have any confidence in your sex appeal?"

Two deep vertical lines appeared between Bobby's eyebrows. "I guess not. I've always been a little unsure of myself when it comes to women."

"You certainly hide it well."

"Yeah, sure. If you do it often enough it's just like second nature after a while."

"I guess I know a little bit about that myself," Andrea said bitterly. "I lived a lie for long enough."

Bobby's eyes grew watchful, probing. "I'd say you had a pretty good reason though." His voice was gentle, even sympathetic. "What happened to you isn't the kind of thing you want to broadcast to the world. It must have been hard on you." He paused for a second then asked: "Were you ever going to tell me about it?"

Andrea dropped her own eyes to her lap. She opened her mouth to speak, then realized she had let Bobby get to her for a moment. It wouldn't happen again. "Oh, I wanted to," she said, putting a cutting edge on her words. "Sometimes I worried myself sick about it—thinking it was wrong to hold something back on you. Ironic, isn't it?"

"I wish you'd told me. Then I wouldn't have had to do my detective work."

Andrea shot a glance at him. "But you *enjoyed* that. Didn't you? It was a real challenge to your ingenuity."

Bobby's eyes slid away from hers. "I'm not proud of that," he said.

"My, my. Singing a different tune now, aren't we? I had the definite impression earlier that you *were* proud of it."

Bobby looked at her sharply and then his eyes fell to the gun. "That was the booze talking," he mumbled.

"And am I supposed to believe you now?" Andrea said, pointing with the gun to the empty bottle on the floor.

Bobby's lower lip jutted out. "I'm more sober now than I was then."

"No, I just think you're more scared." Andrea leaned back in her chair and smiled cruelly. "I didn't have a gun then."

Bobby seemed to shrink visibly, then he caught himself and straightened up. "Yeah, where did you get that thing?" he asked in a voice that tried to imply that the gun was no threat to him. "I thought you were scared to death of them."

"Are you trying to ask me what I plan to do with it?"

"No, well—uh, why don't you just put it down? And take off the rest of that ridiculous disguise— then we can talk some more."

"I like things just the way they are."

"Okay." Bobby started to reach for his pack of cigarettes again, then hesitated. "Is it all right with you if I have another cigarette?" he asked.

"Sure."

Bobby picked up the pack, fumbled a cigarette out of it, and had to use two matches to light it.

Andrea watched him complacently. He was behaving exactly the way she thought he would. He was nervous, very nervous, and he kept trying to reestablish the old rapport between them, thinking that he could somehow sweet-talk her into giving up the gun. It wouldn't work.

She threw her free arm over the back of the chair, letting Bobby think she was beginning to relax when she was really getting ready to deliver the *coup de grâce*. She let several minutes go by before she gave him a cunning, theatrical smile. "Tonight is the night when all secrets are revealed, so there's something else about me I want you to know," Andrea said, her eyes boring into Bobby's. "It's a secret that even your sneaky reporter friend would have had a hard time finding out."

Bobby's dark brown eyes turned somber under her gaze. He said nothing.

"You see," Andrea continued, "nobody knows about it, except me." She paused, then added: "Even the doctors at the Clinic never guessed at it. It was *our* secret—mine and Andy's—and I never wanted to share it with anyone else."

"Then why are you going to tell me?" Bobby asked, frowning.

"Because you accused me of shooting Andy on purpose!" Andrea shouted at him, letting her anger get the better of her.

"No! No, I never really thought that," Bobby protested. "I didn't know what I was saying—"

Andrea held up her hand to silence him. "It doesn't matter," she said. She felt calmer now; she actually felt good. Bobby was finally going to learn the truth.

"But I didn't mean—"

"I don't care," Andrea cut him off. "Because what I'm going to tell you will prove to you that my shooting Andy was an accident."

Bobby's face was guarded, as if he weren't certain he wanted to hear what was coming next.

Andrea smiled. It was a sad smile—full of remembrance. "I loved Andy," she said softly. Her eyes drifted away, then came back to Bobby's. "Yes, I loved him. He was my brother, my twin brother. But he was even more than that to me—he was my lover."

Bobby blinked at her. Andrea could see he was struggling to keep astonishment off his face.

She laughed. "What's wrong? Have I shocked you? Is incest too heavy for you to handle?"

"N-no," Bobby said, shaking his head a little too vigorously. He took several quick drags on his cigarette and put it out. "You were just kids—probably curious about sex. I'm sure it happens more than people think."

"It wasn't like that between us!" Andrea burst out. "You make it sound like it was all just a part of growing up, but it *wasn't*—not with Andy and me. We *belonged* together. We were—we were like two halves of the same self. It was perfect—it was the most perfect love that ever existed."

Bobby's eyes crisscrossed Andrea's face as if they didn't know where to settle.

"He was the only one I had sex with," Andrea said. Then she added sourly, "Until you. And you know why I picked you?"

"No, why?"

"Because you reminded me of him." Andrea pointed with the gun at Bobby's left hand. "Your birthmark—it's just like Andy's. I thought it was a sign. I kidded myself into thinking that somehow made it all right."

Bobby brightened perceptibly. "But it *was* all right. We loved each other."

Andrea gave him a withering stare. "Love? What do you know about love? Your idea of love is getting as much as you can out of somebody without giving anything in return."

Bobby looked hurt. "That's not fair, Red. I really did love you—in fact, I still do."

"And what about Cynthia?" Andrea sneered. "Where did she fit into your little scheme of things?"

"Well, of course, I still had some feelings for her," Bobby said defensively. "After all, she was the mother of my child."

The muscles around Andrea's mouth tightened. "You're lying again, Bobby," she said. "Don't kid yourself that I don't know just exactly how you felt about Cynthia. You were in love with her and you were hoping to get back together with her."

Bobby considered this for a moment. "Okay, I loved her," he admitted finally. "But I loved you, too. She"—his voice cracked ever so slightly—"she's gone now, but you and I are still here."

A twisted smile hovered about Andrea's lips. "Does that mean you want to get married now?"

"Uh, sure," Bobby said quickly. "If that's what *you* want."

"When? Right away?"

"Well, I think we ought to wait a little while—at least a decent interval, you know. I'll—I'll have to take Cynthia's body back to North Carolina. Then I'd like to spend some time with Jennifer alone—before I bring her back up here."

"Of course."

"You'll like Jennifer. She's a very sweet little

girl. She's only three and a half now, so she probably won't even remember Cynthia when she grows
up."

"What a shame."

If Bobby had noticed the caustic tone in Andrea's response, he gave no sign. Instead, he went
on, his voice high and strained. "Of course, we
won't be able to live here—it'll be too small for the
three of us. We'll have to get a bigger apartment—
or maybe we could even afford a house in the suburbs."

"Just what I've always wanted."

"You'd be happy there, I know. It'd be a lot
more like what you grew up with—you know, trees
and grass and all that."

"Sounds great."

"And I wouldn't mind the commuting too
much—I could get a lot of work done on the train."

"Terrific."

"Well," Bobby said, forcing a laugh. "That's all
settled then. As soon as I get back from North Carolina we'll do it."

Silence. Then: "Maybe I should come to North
Carolina with you—to give you moral support."

Bobby looked at Andrea and swallowed hard.
"Sure. You could do that," he said. "But it's not
necessary. And it might be, ah—well, you know,
awkward." Then he added hastily, "Not for me—
for Cynthia's family, I mean."

"I see," Andrea said smoothly. Then she leaned
forward and tapped the butt of the gun against her
thigh. "I think I get the picture, Bobby—the *whole*
picture."

Bobby's eyebrows came together. "I don't understand."

"Maybe you don't, but *I* do, Bobby. You were hoping to split, weren't you? You'd go down to North Carolina, and I'd never see you again."

"No, I swear—" Bobby held out his hands, palms up. "I wouldn't do that to you. I-I *love* you, we're going to get married—"

Andrea laughed harshly. "I know. You're *dying* to marry me."

Bobby shifted his eyes from her face to the gun, then back again. "Well, if you don't want to get married, that's all right, too."

"So now you don't want to get married?"

"No, no. I do."

"Why?"

"That's a funny question, Red. Because I love you."

"As much as you loved Cynthia?"

"Well, of course."

"More?"

"I think so," Bobby said, his face the very image of sincerity. "As a matter of fact, you're probably the only woman I've ever really loved."

"I'm glad to hear you say that, Bobby. I really am." Andrea got to her feet in one swift movement. "It makes what I have to do easier."

Bobby's whole body stiffened. His hands went down to his sides, pressing against the cushions of the couch, ready to propel him forward. "Wha . . . what are you going to do?" he asked.

Andrea observed the position of his hands and stepped back—out of his range if he should try to rush her. With a slow, deliberate motion that she made certain he didn't miss, she put her thumb on the hammer of the revolver and pulled it back. The gun was cocked now, ready to go off with the slightest pressure of her finger on the trigger. "Don't be a fool, Bobby," she said. "You could never move as fast as I can shoot."

His eyes on the muzzle of the gun, Bobby let his hands go limp. "You're not going to—use that thing, are you?"

Andrea said nothing. She picked up the fake mustache and pressed it tight against her upper lip. Then she slipped the tinted glasses and hat back on.

Bobby's face had gone white. "You're going to kill me!" he said, the words seeming to escape from his mouth, almost unbidden.

"Not me," Andrea said in a mocking, insinuating voice. "A stranger. The man who followed Cynthia."

"But you can't!" Bobby cried. He was desperate now, pleading for his life.

"Oh, but I can," Andrea said. "It's very simple. All I have to do is pull the trigger—and at this distance I can hardly miss. Besides, I've done it before, remember?"

"Yes, but that was an accident," Bobby said, talking very fast, as if he could somehow stall her off. "You didn't mean to kill your brother. But this—this is cold-blooded murder."

"You don't think I'm capable of that?"

"No! You could never kill anyone deliberately. You're too good, too kind. You just haven't got it in you to even hurt anyone. That's—that's one of the reasons I fell in love with you."

"You're right, Bobby. I couldn't do this to anyone else—only you."

"But *why?*"

Andrea spoke in a voice echoing with the fervor of righteousness. "Because you're evil, Bobby—and evil has to be eliminated."

Bobby drew in a sharp, rasping breath as he watched Andrea plant her feet in a wide-apart stance. Then, with both hands on the gun, she straightened her arms and raised them to the classic target-shooting position—the one that Andy had taught her.

As Bobby stared at her, his face took on a pinched, angular quality. "No! Please! Don't!" he begged. "You—you'll never get away with it!"

Andrea bent her arms, pulling the gun back. "I wouldn't worry about that, if I were you," she said. "But chances are, I won't get caught. Even if anybody should see me, they'll think I'm a man. And after tonight that man won't exist because I'm going to destroy the disguise." Then she stiffened her arms again, squeezed shut her left eye and sighted down the barrel—aiming point blank at Bobby's chest. She inhaled sharply and held the breath, ready to fire.

Bobby put his hands out in front of him and leaned forward, as if he were about to get up. "Oh God, no! Don't do—"

Crack! The gun exploded, cutting off the rest of his words. Blood spurted out of the front of his shirt and his body collapsed, like a marionette when the puppeteer releases the strings. His head lolled grotesquely on one shoulder and his mouth fell open, with a string of saliva dribbling from one corner. His eyes went dull and fixed, and there was a bright red flood down his chest, coming from a hole just left of his breastbone. The bullet had hit directly on his heart.

Slowly, Andrea lowered the gun. She was amazed at the accuracy of the shot, for she'd been worried that she might have to use more than one bullet to kill him. But now the deed was done, and there was no time to waste. She had to get out of his apartment as quickly as she could—before any of the neighbors could come out to investigate the sound of the shot.

But as she turned toward the door, she realized she was feeling strangely lightheaded and there was a heavy, oppressing ache in her chest. Fighting these sensations, she reached for the door, the gun still in her hand.

Mrs. King sat bolt upright in bed. What was that noise? It sounded like a car backfiring, but she was sure that it had come from across the hall— Andrea's apartment.

She turned on the light and reached for her bathrobe and slippers. Padding softly across the floor to the front door, she opened the peephole. Nobody in the hall. But there had been that awful argument earlier, sounds of shouting she had tried not to hear, and now, the awful noise, like an explosion—or a shot. Should she go over there, see if anything was wrong?

She cracked open the door, stuck her head out and peered up and down the length of the hall. Not a soul in sight. Was she the only one who had heard it?

Cautiously, she stepped out into the hall and crossed it. She was about to raise her hand to ring Andrea's bell, when the door swung silently open. Mrs. King gasped. A strange-looking young man was standing in the doorway and he had a gun in his hand. It was pointed at her.

Instinctively, Mrs. King began to back up. "Don't shoot," she whimpered. "Please, don't shoot me. I'm an old woman."

The young man took a menacing step toward her and let the door close in back of him with a dull click. Mrs. King had the impression he was hiding something in the apartment behind him, something he did not want her to see.

"Oh, my God," she said without thinking. "Have you hurt Andrea?"

A question flickered in the young man's eyes and his brow furrowed, as if he were trying to remember something. Then his eyes went opaque again and he started to raise the gun.

Dear God, he's going to kill me, Mrs. King thought, panic-stricken. *All because I was here, because I happened to see his face.* "Young man," she said, her voice thin and cracking with fear, "I won't tell the police—I won't say a word to them."

The hand with the gun in it faltered. Then—did she imagine it?—his face began to soften, to take on more feminine lines. Mrs. King gaped at him. That face was suddenly so familiar. Why hadn't she seen it before? This was no man, it was a woman—it was *Andrea!*

Mrs. King let out a feeble cry and lay a hand protectively on her chest. Her heart had been pounding before; now she was sure it was going to burst. "Oh, Andrea, Andrea," she moaned. "What are you doing? What have you done?"

Andrea stared back at Mrs. King as if she were seeing her for the first time. She lowered the barrel of the revolver until it was pointing at the carpet. Then her face screwed up into an expression of such anguish that Mrs. King thought she must be wounded. "Andrea! Are you all right?" she asked.

Andrea didn't answer. Her eyes had a wild look to them as they darted from Mrs. King's face to the gun in her own hand. Then she began to move sideways, toward the door to the staircase.

"Please, Andrea. Let me help you," Mrs. King begged. "Don't go, *please.* I want to help you— whatever it is, we can work it out."

Andrea jerked her head sadly from side to side. Her mouth opened and she seemed to be trying to speak, but no sound came out. Then she pitched herself toward the exit door, and Mrs. King heard her footsteps echoing down the stairwell. She stood there in the hall until they died away.

Suddenly feeling very old and very tried, she pushed open the door to her apartment. What should she do now? What *could* she do now?

"I can't call the police on that poor girl," she said aloud. "They wouldn't understand."

Not that she understood either. But still, *she*

wouldn't be the one to bring down the police on Andrea—no matter what she had done. Anyway, the child looked as if she were already suffering enough.

It was going to be a long night—a very long night. There would be no more sleep for her now. She went into the kitchen to make herself a pot of tea.

Trembling, Andrea pocketed the gun when she reached the foyer of Bobby's building. Her head was spinning with pain and confusion. What had just happened upstairs? Where had Mrs. King come from?

She remembered putting her hand on the doorknob in Bobby's apartment. Then everything went blank—until she found herself face to face with Mrs. King, aiming the gun at her. Had she almost shot Mrs. King, too?

Andrea shuddered. Killing Bobby was one thing, but killing that harmless old woman would be monstrous. Thank God she had come to in time.

But now she had to get out of here. The police might be on their way.

She crossed the foyer and stealthily opened the doors. The street was quiet, but not empty. She could see two men walking down the block away from her.

She strode rapidly in the opposite direction and, when she reached the corner, hailed a passing cab. The driver squinted at her in the rearview mirror as she collapsed into the back seat. "Somethin' wrong with you, mister?" he asked warily.

Andrea shook her head. "Just a little heartburn," she managed to say as she clutched at her chest.

The next thing she knew she was stumbling out of the cab onto the sidewalk in front of her building. Weak with pain, she staggered up the stairs. By the time she reached her own apartment the pain had grown to a nearly suffocating intensity. She fell into the room and pulled herself across the floor up onto the bed. Then she lay there writhing, hoping death would come to end her agony. But it wasn't death that came—not then.

CHAPTER EIGHTEEN

Sam stole another glance at the clock over the bar. It was nearly midnight. *Where the hell was Andrea?* He had been calling her since shortly past six, at least once an hour, but there had been no answer. He had even thought about looking up Bobby's number in the phone book and trying her there, but had decided that wouldn't be too cool. Not after what he had seen on the television news earlier this evening—that was why he was calling Andrea in the first place.

He had read the item in the late afternoon paper but hadn't picked up on the name until he saw the TV news film. The TV was mounted above the bar and he always kept his eye half on it whenever the news was on. A lot of customers liked to watch the news, and he had made it a habit to turn the set on each night at six o'clock. So he happened to be looking at it when the anchorman reported on a murder that had occurred just a few blocks uptown. Then the film came on, and there was a shot of the exterior of the building where the victim lived. The voice of the unseen reporter was saying that the police were taking in the victim's husband for questioning, when the camera zeroed in on the husband's face as he was getting into a police car. It was only a fleeting image, but Sam had recognized the man immediately. And then he heard the name to go with the face, and there was no mistaking it—that was Andrea's Bobby.

Sam had listened to the rest of the details the TV reporter gave, and then he had gone back and reread the newspaper story. He wasn't at all surprised to learn that Bobby was married—separated from his wife, according to the news accounts—that was just what he expected from a guy like that. But, shit, his wife had been murdered, and that was a tough break for anybody—even a creep like Bobby. Unless maybe he did it, but Sam couldn't imagine Bobby having the guts to kill anyone.

Sam wondered about Andrea. She must know by now—although obviously she hadn't when he'd talked to her earlier that afternoon. She would be really upset, he was sure of that. She might even need a shoulder to cry on—or at least a friendly ear to listen to her troubles. And so he had called her— and kept on calling her, determined to get through.

On the stroke of midnight he went to the phone and dialed her number again. He let it ring six, seven, then eight times and was on the verge of hanging up when someone picked it up at the other end, slammed the phone back on the receiver, and then took it off the hook again. Sam was certain he must have a wrong number and was about to hang up and try again, when he heard Andrea's voice asking, "Who was that?" She was not speaking into the phone, but sounded as if she could only be a few feet away from it.

"I dunno," a man's voice responded. "I hung up on him. But whoever it was won't be calling back. I took the phone off the hook."

Sam realized that he was still able to hear what was going on at the other end because *he* had placed the call and therefore the connection had not been broken. He also knew that by all rights he ought to hang up rather than listen in on Andrea and the man she had with her. The man was not Bobby, Sam was positive of that—the accent wasn't right—and he had to admit he was unabashedly curious about who he might be. The man's accent was very much like Andrea's—broad, flat, and definitely Midwestern—and his voice seemed harsh, as if he were vaguely angry, and that bothered Sam.

Then Andrea spoke again. "It was probably Sam. I don't know who else would be calling now."

Sam was alerted at the mention of his own name. Well, maybe he'd stay on the line just a little while longer.

"Oh, yeah," the man said. "Your bartender friend."

"How do you know about him?" Andrea asked.

"I've seen him," the man responded. "I went to the bar and checked him out."

"When?" Andrea asked, her voice suddenly sharp.

"Last night," was the man's answer.

Could this be the strange guy who'd reminded him of Andrea, Sam wondered.

"You went to the Center Stage last night?" Andrea asked. Her voice sounded queer, like she was scared of something.

"Yeah," the man said. "Just for a few minutes."

"Did you go anywhere else?" Andrea asked. Now she definitely sounded frightened.

A couple of seconds passed. Then the man spoke slowly. "You know I did. It wasn't a dream you had last night—it really happened."

"No!" Andrea cried out. "You mean *you* killed her?"

Sam sucked in his breath. My God! Andrea was in her apartment with a murderer! What should he do—call the police? But how quickly would they come? He could get to her place almost as fast as they could, maybe he should run over there himself. He was trying to decide what to do when the man spoke again. What he said made Sam's blood run cold.

"It was an accident, I *swear*," the man said. "She was fighting me, and the gun just went off. I didn't mean to do it—not like the way you killed Bobby."

What was he saying? That Andrea had murdered Bobby? Sam clung to the telephone receiver like a man frozen to the steering wheel of a car gone out of control. There must be some mistake; maybe he hadn't heard right. But if she *had* killed Bobby, Andrea must have had plenty of provocation. Maybe she had done it in self-defense. But whatever the cause, there could be no question of calling the police now—not if that would put her in jeopardy. No, he must stay on the line, find out as much as he could if he was going to help her.

From a few feet behind him, Sam suddenly heard the jingle of coins. He whirled to see a man standing over the jukebox, about to drop some change in the slot. *Oh God, no! He'd never be able to hear over the music!* Sam quickly slipped his hand over the mouthpiece and held the phone at arm's length. "Hey, buddy!" he said, getting the man's attention. "Don't waste your money. It's not working."

The man's hand hesitated over the slot.

"Didn't you hear me?" Sam barked. "It's out of order!"

The man scowled at him, stuffed the coins back in his pocket, and walked away.

Sam let out a sigh and put the receiver back to his ear.

"I don't want to talk about Bobby," Andrea was saying. "You seem to know all about that, anyway." Then in a stronger voice she added, "But I want you to tell me why you went to her apartment in the first place."

"Well, it was *your* idea," the man said. "I only carried it out. You wanted to scare her good, but you would never have been able to do that. *I* could, and besides, I had the gun. Hell, I never intended to hurt her. I couldn't believe it when she tried to get the gun away from me. She shouldn't have done that—I would have just taken what I wanted and left her alone."

Andrea said something that Sam couldn't catch, and then she asked: "What did you take?"

"C'mon Andy. You know that. I was just going to take her money as a blind," he went on. "So she'd think it was a real robbery. But then I found the divorce decree and that letter in a drawer—and I thought you'd be real interested in those."

"So *that's* where they came from," Andrea said in a startled voice.

"Yeah," the man said. "You didn't even think about that, did you? You were so blown away by what they said you never even bothered to wonder where they came from."

"Well, there'd been so many mysterious items that just seemed to appear overnight," Andrea said. "I thought I was going crazy again, but it was *you* who put them all there, wasn't it?"

"Sure," the man said. "I wanted you to know that something was going on, but I didn't want you to know what it was until I was ready to show myself to you."

Sam was becoming puzzled by the distinctly curious twist the conversation had taken. *What in the hell were they talking about?*

"You seem to know everything about me," Andrea said. "Even my thoughts. So why didn't I know about you?"

"Because I didn't want you to," the man said.

Andrea sighed. "I still don't understand. Where

did you come from? Where have you been all these years?"

"Oh, I've been with you all along," the man said. "Just biding my time, waiting for the right moment to come out."

"Why did you pick now?" Andrea asked.

"Because you gave me the opportunity," the man said. "When you got all the men's stuff to follow her around, *I* used it at night. That way I was free to come and go as I pleased."

"To do what?" Andrea asked.

"Whatever I felt like doing," the man said. "I went to all the places you'd never go, hung around with people you wouldn't like, and I even got drunk a few times and smoked some dope—things you'd never *dream* of doing."

"And you used my money for this?" Andrea said.

"Naturally," the man responded. "What'd you want me to do? Go out and steal it?"

"No," Andrea said. "But you spent so *much* I was getting frantic. You know I had to break down and call Mother."

"I know," the man said. "I felt sorry for you when you had to do that. But what did you expect from her? You know how she feels about you."

"She *hates* me," Andrea said vehemently. "And I hate *her*. She always loved you better than me—always."

The man made a kind of snorting sound. "But Dad made up for that," he said. "You were always his little darling—who could never do any wrong."

"I miss him so much," Andrea said. "He's dead, you know."

"I know," the man said. "I was there at the funeral."

"Where were—" Andrea started to ask, and then she interjected: "Oh, I remember! When I blacked out."

"Yeah," the man said. "It was me. It was always me. All those blackouts—*I* did that. It was my way of asserting myself. I gave you those pains in the chest, too—so you'd remember me."

"Why was the one tonight so bad?" Andrea asked. "It was the worst one I'd ever had."

"Don't worry, there won't be any more," the man said. "I did that so you'd be ready for me—so you wouldn't fight me any longer."

"I see," Andrea said thoughtfully.

There was silence for a minute, and Sam wished he could see what they were doing. From what he had just heard he had figured out that the man with Andrea must be another brother, and he had only recently come back from wherever he'd been. Yet Sam still hadn't been able to pick up the gist of their conversation—whatever they were talking about was too crazy for him to comprehend.

Suddenly a chilling thought struck him: he'd been on the phone a long time, at any second the operator could cut in, betraying his presence with that recorded message demanding more money. *Sweet Jesus, what would that guy do to Andrea if he thought someone was listening in?* Sam dug deep into his pocket and fished out several coins. A quarter, that ought to buy him quite a bit more time. He slipped the coin in the slot and held his breath as it dropped with what seemed to be an unnaturally loud clang. *Oh God, please don't let them hear it, too.*

"Where did you get the gun?" Andrea asked suddenly.

Sam heaved a sigh of relief. It was all right. They hadn't heard.

"On the street," the man replied. "I just had to ask around until I found the right people. I had to pay top dollar for it, but it's a beauty—real clean. A .38 Smith & Wesson—the kind detectives carry—and it's real accurate at close range. You saw what it did to Bobby."

"I didn't expect it to be that easy," Andrea said so softly that Sam could barely hear.

"But you remembered everything I taught you," the man said in a voice with a strong note of irony in it. "You weren't too good at shooting targets, but you're real deadly when it comes to people."

It sounded like Andrea gasped. Then she said in a high-pitched voice, "He deserved to die."

So it was true, Sam realized. Andrea had admitted that she killed Bobby. It must have just happened. Tonight. The poor kid probably hadn't known what she was doing.

"I won't argue with you there," the man said. "I never liked him. I *hated* it every time you went to bed with him. And he hit you—that made me angry. I wanted to beat him up myself when he did that to you."

Sam felt outraged. *That bastard Bobby had hit her!* No wonder Andrea had done what she'd done. She must have been trying to defend herself from another beating.

"He lied to me," Andrea said in a jerky, breathless voice. "He lied to me about his divorce, and he made me think he hated Cynthia when he was really in love with her. And he knew about you—all along."

"He was an asshole," the man said. "I was glad to see you pop him." Then he paused for several seconds before he added solemnly, "But he was right about one thing, you know."

Andrea seemed to hesitate. "No. What?" she asked.

There was a deathly stillness on the other end of the line, and then the man spoke in a strange, taut voice. "You did it on purpose."

"*Andy!*" Andrea cried. "What are you saying?" The words were more wailed than spoken.

"The truth," the man said. "The truth that you've hidden from yourself all these years."

"Oh God, Andy," Andrea moaned. It sounded as though she might be sobbing. "Please don't say that. You know it isn't true. I loved you—I would never have done anything like that to you on purpose."

"You *think* you wouldn't have," the man said, and his voice seemed choked, too. "But you don't know, because you can't remember. And the reason you can't remember is that you don't want to!"

"No, no! I *do* remember!" Andrea said, sounding so desperate she was nearly shouting. "The gun just went off! It was an accident!"

"That's what you *told* yourself!" the man said,

his voice as intense as Andrea's. "That's what the *doctors* told you! But the truth is you really don't *know* that—do you?"

Sam could hear the sounds of Andrea whimpering. Jesus Christ, why didn't this guy just leave her alone? Couldn't he see she was in no shape to deal with his asinine accusations?

"It's all a blank to you," the man went on, a little softer now. "Your mind just blotted it out. And you've been lying to yourself about it ever since."

Sam noticed that Andrea had stopped whimpering when the man was speaking, as if she were listening raptly to him. Sam wanted to shout at her not to pay any attention to him, that he'd be right there; that it would be all right—but he didn't dare.

"Please don't do this, Andy," Andrea said in a small, pathetic voice. "I won't be able to live with myself if—if what you say is true."

"It's true, all right," the man said. "And that's why I came—so you'd admit it. If you do that, we can be together again."

"Really?" Andrea said, sounding suddenly hopeful. "We can be together—like before?"

"Yes, like before," the man said. "There won't be anyone between us—ever again."

"What about Brenda Fisk?" Andrea asked petulantly. "*She* came between us."

"Oh, Christ," the man said. "Brenda was nothing to me—not worth killing over, anyway."

Sam was confused. Who were they talking about, not Bobby or his poor wife, he was sure.

"You—you think that's why I did it?" Andrea said in a strained voice.

"You *told* me that," the man said. "*I* haven't forgotten and deep inside you you haven't either. Remember?"

"No!" Andrea shouted out.

"Yes, you do," the man said. "I'm going to *make* you remember. I'm going to tell it to you exactly the way it happened. It was a long time ago, but it's as fresh in my mind as if it was just yesterday."

"I don't want to hear," Andrea said, her voice muffled.

"Well, you're *going* to," the man said roughly. "And there's nothing you can do about it." Then he cleared his throat before he spoke again in a calmer tone. "You acted real cold to me for a couple of days after the 4-H picnic, and then all of a sudden you started buttering me up, teasing me to take you out target practicing. I thought it was kind of odd, but I decided to go along with you. Then when we got out in the field you seemed nervous, but I put that down to your not knowing much about guns and being a little afraid of them. And when you missed a shot I laughed at you, and you got mad and turned around and told me to stop laughing. Only when you turned around you had the gun pointed right at me. I started to tell you to lower it, but you got this real funny look on your face, and then you told me that you had seen me with Brenda at the picnic and how disgusted you were. I tried to explain it to you—that I was just messing around with her—but you wouldn't listen. You said I had *betrayed* you and I wasn't worthy of you anymore and some other crazy stuff, and then you just—pulled the trigger. That's the way it happened—it was no accident."

Sam's hand on the receiver was slippery with sweat. He wanted to scream at her: *Tell your fucking brother he's lying, Andrea! Tell him to shut up and leave you alone!* But he said nothing.

Andrea was sobbing loudly and blubbering something that Sam couldn't understand. Then he heard her say in a strangled voice, "Yes, yes, it's *true*. I remember now—that's what I did. I wanted to hurt you, the way you'd hurt me. I thought I wanted you dead, but then it was too late—and I wanted to die myself."

For several minutes there was no sound but Andrea's weeping, and when that quieted down there was silence.

Finally, there was a rustling noise, and then the man spoke. "I bought this for you," he said almost tenderly. "So we can be together again."

Several seconds passed before Andrea spoke. "I-I understand," she said in a voice that was subdued and yet somehow serene. "It's what I want, too. I've known all along that this was the way it had to be. Will—will you be there—waiting for me?"

"Yes," the man said. "I promise."

"Then *you* do it," Andrea said. "That way we'll be even."

"Now?" the man asked. "Are you ready?"

It sounded like Andrea took a deep breath. "Yes, Andy," she said. "Do it now." Then she added quickly, "Andy?"

"What?" the man responded.

"I love you," Andrea sighed.

"I love you too, Andy," the man said in a voice so sad that Sam thought he must be crying. Then there was a deafening *pop!*—like the sound of a firecracker going off. Stunned, Sam jerked the receiver away from his ear, but it still took a while before the ringing in his head stopped and he could hear again. And then what he heard sent paroxysms of shivers up and down the length of his spine. Stillness, absolute stillness on the other end of the line.

Without thinking, he shouted into the receiver, "Andrea!" Did he imagine it or was that a moan? "Andrea! Are you all right?" Nothing. *Oh shit!* That had been a stupid thing to do. If the guy had shot Andrea and was still in the apartment he would have been warned that somebody had been listening in on the phone—he was probably halfway down the stairs by now.

Sam banged the phone onto the hook and grabbed his jacket from the nearby rack. Then, trying his damnedest to be discreet about it so as not to excite the restaurant's patrons, he motioned to the waitress who was watching the bar for him. As calmly as he could he told her he had to go out, and she was to give him a few minutes and then she should call the police and have them send an ambulance and a patrol car to the scene of a possible shooting. He was in such a rush she had to remind him to give her the address.

Then, forcing himself to take easy strides, he walked the length of the bar to the door, nodding good night to the customers who turned to stare at

him. When his feet touched the sidewalk outside
he broke into a run, impelled forward by the
knowledge that Andrea's life might be hanging in
the balance. That she might already be dead was
unthinkable. Saving her life was the only thing
that mattered right now; later he would worry
about saving her skin. If she was not unconscious
he could caution her against saying anything to the
police about Bobby. He supposed he would have
to tell the police most of what he had heard in her
conversation with her brother, but he would leave
out the part about Bobby—at least until he had
heard Andrea's side of the story.

It was only three blocks to Andrea's apartment,
and he raced over them. It wasn't until he was
halfway there that he noticed it was snowing. He
was suddenly grateful he'd worn his hiking boots
that day, otherwise he would have surely slipped as
he pounded along the slippery pavement.

Wheezing and gasping for air, he finally made it
to Andrea's building and fell against the outer
door. It opened from the sheer weight of his body,
and he stumbled into the tiny entryway. He
jabbed furiously at the intercom button. When
there was no response, he began pushing the buttons of the other tenants. At last, someone gave an
answering buzz which released the inner door, and
he bounded through it. Then he attacked the
stairs two at a time, ignoring the protesting thud
of his heart. From the stairwell above him, a man's
voice shouted out, demanding to know who was
there, but Sam paid no attention to it.

On the landing outside Andrea's door he caught

his breath and then, summoning all the strength left in his body, kicked at the door with his foot—flat against the lock. He heard wood splitting and the door gave slightly. He kicked again. With a loud bang, the door flew back and slammed against the wall behind it.

Sam leaned against the doorjamb and peered into the apartment. Someone was lying on the bed. and as Sam stepped into the room he recognized the man who had come into the bar the night before. Dead. Even at a glance, it was clear he was dead.

Dear God, where was Andrea?

She was not in the room, but Sam checked out the bathroom, the minuscule kitchen, even the closet before he let himself breathe a sigh of relief. If she had managed to run away, she must be all right. She was probably outside somewhere now, shivering in the snow, afraid to go back to her apartment. Maybe he could find her before the police did.

But first he'd have to see to the man on the bed. There was no question he was dead. The front of his parka was open, and his chest was covered with so much blood Sam couldn't even tell what he was wearing underneath. There was a gun in his right hand and it was resting on the bloody mass. The brim at the back of his hat was crushed under his head, pushing the front of the hat down so low it nearly covered the glasses over his half-shut eyes. In this light his face looked even younger than Sam remembered.

The two of them must have fought over the gun,

Sam figured. Of course, he hadn't *heard* any struggle over the phone. Maybe Andrea had just grabbed the man's hand and turned the gun against him as he fired.

Whatever, at least she was alive. And safe—for the time being. The police would be here soon, and he'd have to explain about overhearing everything on the phone. That would probably be a new one on them. The phone was on a table at the head of the bed, still off the hook. They had probably been sitting on the bed—that explained why he had heard them so distinctly.

Sam walked closer to the bed and looked at the dead man's face again. It actually seemed peaceful, not at all like someone who had died a violent death. And more than ever now, the man looked like Andrea—which wasn't surprising; he *was* her brother.

As he stared at him, Sam could see how the dim light of the bar hadn't done justice to the similarities between their faces. In this bright light he realized that—except for the mustache—their faces were almost exactly the same. But the mustache looked out of place, it was so thick it might even be phony—like stage makeup. He bent down, and his expert actor's eye could see it—yes, a bit of adhesive on the smooth skin alongside the red bristles.

As Sam straightened up, his mind went spinning crazily. *Smooth skin . . . face like Andrea's . . . like Andrea's . . . smooth . . . face . . . skin . . . Andrea's . . .* He let the words revolve in his head, but he recoiled from letting them fuse into a thought.

He wanted to turn around and run out of the apartment, yet his feet wouldn't move. *Run. Can't. Can't leave—not until* . . . He knew he shouldn't touch the body, but he had to see, he had to make sure. With a faltering hand he reached out and tugged at the mustache. It came away in his fingers.

It was a reflex: he shut his eyes, wishing he'd never have to open them again. He didn't understand—he didn't *want* to understand. It was too terrible, too confusing. . . .

Then from far away he heard the sound of sirens, then, moments later, several pairs of feet pounding up the stairs. The police. In seconds they would be here, asking endless questions, prying and poking at the body, destroying the privacy of the dead.

He would look one more time. To say good-bye. His eyes swept across that placid face. Andrea, it was his sweet Andrea—so quiet, so pale—with her lips curved upward into that familiar, gentle smile of hers.

Maybe she was happy now.

Bonfire

by
Charles Dennis

Alan Farrel was a runaway at age 12, an ex-con at 15, a drifter, a boxer and a man no woman could refuse. Tough, charismatic, he rose from the teeming slums of New York to Hollywood's starry heights. His life was the dream-stuff movies are made of and his Polly was the only woman who lived life as lustfully as he. She loved him and had the power to destroy him!

A Dell Book $2.25

Mortal Friends

JAMES CARROLL

A NATION-WIDE HARDCOVER BESTSELLER— NOW IN PAPERBACK!

A rich tale of love, class and ethnic struggle that moves from the blood-stained Irish Rebellion in the 1920's to the tumultuous Boston of Mayor Curley and the Kennedys. It is the story of Colman Brady, an Irish immigrant who rises to political power in Boston's heyday

James Carroll expertly blends fiction with fact, mingling imaginary characters and the celebrities and scoundrels of the era with seamless ease.

A Dell Book $2.75

THE DARK HORSEMAN

Marianne Harvey

Beautiful Donna Penroze had sworn to her dying father that she would save her sole legacy, the crumbling tin mines and the ancient, desolate estate *Trencobban*. But the mines were failing, and Donna had no one to turn to. No one except the mysterious Nicholas Trevarvas—rich, arrogant, commanding. Donna would do anything but surrender her pride, anything but admit her irresistible longing for *The Dark Horseman*.

A Dell Book $2.50

Dell Bestsellers

- ☐ **CRY FOR THE STRANGERS** by John Saul $2.50 (11869-7)
- ☐ **WHISTLE** by James Jones $2.75 (19262-5)
- ☐ **A STRANGER IS WATCHING** by Mary
  Higgins Clark $2.50 (18125-9)
- ☐ **MORTAL FRIENDS** by James Carroll $2.75 (15789-7)
- ☐ **CLAUDE: THE ROUNDTREE WOMEN
  BOOK II** by Margaret Lewerth $2.50 (11255-9)
- ☐ **GREEN ICE** by Gerald A. Browne $2.50 (13224-X)
- ☐ **BEYOND THE POSEIDON ADVENTURE**
  by Paul Gallico $2.50 (10497-1)
- ☐ **COME FAITH, COME FIRE**
  by Vanessa Royall $2.50 (12173-6)
- ☐ **THE TAMING** by Aleen Malcolm $2.50 (18510-6)
- ☐ **AFTER THE WIND** by Eileen Lottman $2.50 (18138-0)
- ☐ **THE ROUNDTREE WOMEN: BOOK I**
  by Margaret Lewerth $2.50 (17594-1)
- ☐ **DREAMSNAKE** by Vonda N McIntyre $2.25 (11729-1)
- ☐ **THE MEMORY OF EVA RYKER**
  by Donald A Stanwood $2.50 (15550-9)
- ☐ **BLIZZARD** by George Stone $2.25 (11080-7)
- ☐ **THE BLACK MARBLE** by Joseph
  Wambaugh $2.50 (10647-8)
- ☐ **MY MOTHER/MY SELF** by Nancy Friday $2.50 (15663-7)
- ☐ **SEASON OF PASSION** by Danielle Steel $2.50 (17703-0)
- ☐ **THE DARK HORSEMAN** by Marianne
  Harvey $2.50 (11758-5)
- ☐ **BONFIRE** by Charles Dennis $2.25 (10659-1)

At your local bookstore or use this handy coupon for ordering:

Dell **DELL BOOKS**
P.O. BOX 1000, PINEBROOK, N.J. 07058

Please send me the books I have checked above. I am enclosing $_____
(please add 35¢ per copy to cover postage and handling). Send check or money
order—no cash or C.O.D.'s. Please allow up to 8 weeks for shipment.

Mr/Mrs/Miss_____

Address_____

City_____ State/Zip_____

Claude— The Roundtree Women

BOOK II
OF THIS SPELLBINDING
4-PART SERIES

by Margaret Lewerth

A RADIANT NOVEL OF YOUNG PASSION!
Swept away by the lure of the stage, Claude was an exquisite runaway seeking glamour and fame. From a small New England town to the sophisticated and ruthless film circles of Paris and Rome, she fled the safe but imprisoning bonds of childhood and discovered the thrilling, unexpected gift of love.

A Dell Book $2.50 (11255-9)

Come Faith, Come Fire

Vanessa Royall

Proud as her aristocratic upbringing, bold as the ancient gypsy blood that ran in her veins, the beautiful golden-haired Maria saw her family burned at the stake and watched her young love, forced into the priesthood. Desperate and bound by a forbidden love, Maria defies the Grand Inquisitor himself and flees across Spain to a burning love that was destined to be free!

A Dell Book $2.50   (12173-6)

At your local bookstore or use this handy coupon for ordering:

THE TAMING

Aleen Malcolm

Cameron—daring, impetuous girl/woman who has never known a life beyond the windswept wilds of the Scottish countryside.

Alex Sinclair—high-born and quick-tempered, finds more than passion in the heart of his headstrong ward Cameron.

Torn between her passion for freedom and her long-denied love for Alex, Cameron is thrust into the dazzling social whirl of 18th century Edinburgh and comes to know the fulfillment of deep and dauntless love.

A Dell Book $2.50